OFFICE HOURS

KATRINA JACKSON

ONE

SEPTEMBER

Deja Evans glanced from the watch on her wrist to the line ahead of her to her phone and back, impatience oozing from every pore. She was in a rush. She was always in a rush when she was on campus, which meant that, of course, the campus coffee shop Go Brews! had a line out the door. And as always happened, that line was moving at the speed of glacial thaw one hundred and fifty years ago.

She'd just taught her last class of the day, "Introduction to World Cultures", her largest class of the semester, and her worst in terms of student participation. For a torturous fifty-five minutes, 105 students sat in their seats with blank, bored, or quizzical looks on their faces while she lectured. The only signs of life were when she changed the slide on her PowerPoint, and they wrote down what she'd typed but nothing she said. The more innovative students up front, however, couldn't even give her that. She changed slides, and they rotated their cell phones for a picture and then promptly turned to stare out of the window.

It was a demoralizing way to spend almost an hour three days a week. All of the jokes Deja told to try and lighten the mood and engage them in discussion bombed spectacularly, she always seemed to be half a lecture behind the syllabus, and she was already on the lookout for as many extra credit opportunities as possible because close to a third of the class had failed the midterm. She hated "Intro" most of all, and she just wanted to go home, lick her wounds, and slip into her baggiest sweatpants like she usually did on Mondays and Wednesdays.

Deja loved schedules, and she wanted to keep up with her regular sad evening routine of puttering around her apartment, thinking intensely about working on one of the many articles she'd half-written and then giving up to pour a glass of wine and watch an hour (or more) of reality television instead. Then she'd cap it all off by convincing herself that a gluten-free frozen pizza was a healthy dinner before falling asleep tired and sad.

Unfortunately, the monthly Faculty Senate meeting was preempting her regularly scheduled pitiful plans. She wasn't exactly sure how she'd gotten roped into being on this committee, but it was almost certainly a byproduct of her advisors' advice before she went on the job market. It was rare these days to get a tenure-track position on the first try, but Deja had, and she knew how lucky she was. She also knew that a terrifying amount of her job security depended on making sure that her colleagues liked her. She loaded up on service assignments and the large intro courses no one else liked to teach and ran herself ragged trying to prove herself as a "good colleague," even though she wasn't entirely certain what that meant; especially not what it meant for her senior colleagues to be "good colleagues" to her. But still, she went to nearly every departmental event, listened intently during faculty meetings and contributed thoughtfully — but always deferentially — because she wanted them to like her and feel certain that she didn't plan to challenge departmental hierarchy.

And what had all that good behavior gotten her? After two years, she'd gained all her colleagues' vaguely condescending respect and developed regular bouts of stress-induced insomnia. She had perpetually dry, itchy eyes and a worried optometrist, but not a single new publication on her curriculum vitae. But the cherry on top of all that wasted time was that Deja's third-year review was looming. At the beginning of the next academic year, she'd have to submit her portfolio for review, and anything less than glowing reports from her department might jeopardize her chances of getting an affirmative tenure vote at the end of her seven-year probationary period.

She understood it in concept, but she'd only just now come to appreciate that the tenure track was akin to a rain cloud hanging over her head for nearly a decade, and it was currently spitting down on her like a torrent. No matter what she did, what she hadn't done and couldn't do mattered so much more.

"Next."

Deja's mind had started to drift away into the familiar and very personal bubble of self-pity where she lived, more often than not, and she didn't hear when the cashier called out the first time. When they yelled for the next customer again, Deja started and smiled awkwardly at the cashier, who smiled back even though it didn't reach his eyes.

She ordered her latte with an extra shot and then moved quickly toward the pick-up counter. The line was almost spilling out into the student union lobby. Deja pressed herself against a wall, doing her best not to contribute to the obvious fire hazard. She fantasized about sitting on her couch and eating a frozen pizza — even her fantasies were pathetic — and hoped above all else that none of her students noticed her.

"Doc," someone called from across the cafeteria, cutting into Deja's distracted thoughts.

Deja recognized that voice, and she wasn't surprised that the person it belonged to had been able to spot her all the way across the lobby or that he'd yelled so loudly. She pretended not to hear the voice and stared at the kids behind the pick-up counter, willing whoever was making her drink to make it faster.

"Doc," the voice called again, closer this time.

Deja was considering abandoning her coffee and rushing to her office to grab a free cup there — even though the coffee in her building was terrible — when something brushed her left forearm. She jumped and turned toward that touch, and her mouth fell open.

She knew it was him with barely a glimpse of his suited chest.

Dr. Alejandro Mendoza.

As far as Deja was concerned, Dr. Mendoza was the best-dressed faculty member on campus. She always marveled at how put-together he looked no matter the time of day or season, or even when he was walking across campus between classes. He looked like a dapper runway model instead of a History professor at a mid-tier university in the Midwest.

Deja's eyes traveled up his body, appreciating his tweed earth-toned vest over his denim button-up shirt and dark blue tie. She gulped as his Adam's apple bobbed, and his mouth seemed to curve into a smile. Her eyes skimmed over his nose, and then she met his eyes and found him staring at her with a playful smile on his face.

In Deja's mind, the entire world slowed to a snail's pace as she catalogued every millisecond of this moment like she'd done so many times before. It was kind of sad, but Deja thought it was possible that staring at Alejandro was the only time her brain stopped running stress laps. She let herself just enjoy how gorgeous he was and how warm she felt when he sometimes looked at her this way; as if the two of them were sharing...something, even though they were really just ships passing in the sea.

Time sped up as Dr. Mendoza and Dr. Sheila Meyer, chair of the Department of History, stepped into the coffee shop line. Dr. Meyer was speaking excitedly to Alejandro, and if she noticed that he didn't seem to be paying close attention, it didn't stop her. Just like the fact that it was untoward to stare didn't stop Deja from doing just that. She angled her head so that she could watch him out of the corner of her eye, hoping she wasn't being as obvious as she felt.

"Doc, there you are," the voice said from right next to Deja.

When Deja turned, she came face-to-chest with her favorite but neediest advisee, Jerome Miles.

"I was calling your name, Doc."

She sighed. "My name's not 'Doc,' Jerome. You know this," she said for the hundredth time since she'd been assigned as his academic advisor.

"Deja," another voice called from the pick-up counter. This student, though, said her name like "dee-jay" instead of "day-juh." She sighed again.

"What's up, Jerome?" she asked over her shoulder as she grabbed her coffee from the pick-up counter.

He followed her and snatched a few napkins from the dispenser and handed them to her. She didn't need napkins, but she accepted and slipped them into her shoulder bag, nonetheless.

"I need some help," Jerome said.

Deja steered him to the small counter with sugar and

creamer. "Help with what?" she asked and tore open a sugar packet. She dumped it into her drink but then remembered that the Faculty Senate meeting was two and a half hours and ripped open another.

"Okay," Jerome started, "so my Stats professor, Dr. Rincorn, is trying to get me to switch my major, but I really like Sociology, and I like you." He paused to give her his best grin, a move she'd come to expect when he asked her for any kind of advice — which classes to take, which professors were best, her thoughts on his research projects, and morning versus evening courses. Deja assumed that he'd learned as a kid that the right smile could get him nearly anything he wanted because they accentuated his big cheeks and dimples. She just bet the move worked like a charm on his mother. Deja, however, was not his mother, so she shifted her weight onto her other foot and frowned at him.

"You know I love stats, right?" he asked.

Deja quirked an eyebrow at him. Jerome loved every class, every subject, every professor. He was naturally inquisitive and enthusiastic. There was a reason he was her favorite advisee. But she knew where this conversation was going because they'd been here plenty of times before.

"What do you think about me double majoring in Sociology and Statistics?" he asked.

Deja stirred her drink, replaced the lid, and straightened her back as she looked up at Jerome because he was nearly half a foot taller than her. She took a deep breath to settle her thoughts, and her eyes wandered around his broad shoulder to Alejandro and Sheila in line.

As soon as her gaze settled on his profile, Alejandro's head tilted slightly, and his eyes found hers. He nodded at whatever Sheila was saying, but his eyes bored into Deja's, making her body warm all over. She imagined that she saw some new warmth in his eyes — maybe even a naked desire that mirrored her own. Big mistake. She ducked her head to look at her toes in her favorite pointed booties and tried to get herself together.

A few seconds passed before she licked her lips and looked back up at Jerome. "J, you're in my office every other week talking about a second major. If you want to do it, bite the bullet and choose one."

"I know," he whined, "but which one?"

Deja took in a large gulp of air and then let it out because they'd had this conversation at least once a semester in the past year and a half. She liked him, she wanted to help him, but she wasn't his mother, and she wouldn't make this decision for him; she couldn't. So instead, she gave him an annoyed look, and he smiled sheepishly at her as if he knew exactly what she was thinking.

Deja took a sip of her coffee and then checked her watch. She still had twenty minutes before the Senate meeting started. That was technically more than enough time to walk across the North Oval, but the competition for seats on the highest tier of the auditorium was fierce because it was the perfect location for bored faculty to open their laptops and grade student work or mess around on the internet without being observed, which was exactly why Deja liked to sit there. If she wanted to get a good seat, then she really only had fifteen minutes max before they were gone.

"I've got a meeting in five minutes in Founders. Walk with me and make a good case for Stats. Then come to office hours tomorrow to talk more about it."

"Perfect. You're the best, Doc," Jerome nodded excitedly.

There was something about his glee that reminded Deja just how young her students were, which made her heart warm, but also made her feel old as hell.

"I know," Deja said, lips pursed for a second before widening into a smile.

As she and Jerome left the coffee shop, she turned to look quickly over her shoulder one last time.

Alejandro's eyebrows rose, and the right side of his mouth quirked up in farewell.

TWO

In the Founders Hall auditorium, Deja snagged a seat in the uppermost tier and did a small dance in her chair at that tiny victory before she came back to herself. She covered her outburst by preparing herself for the meeting, organizing her small slice of the long table. First, she made sure that her paper nameplate was clearly visible to the room behind her laptop — Deja Evans, Sociology — because if she had to be at this meeting, she needed to make sure it was recorded. Behind her nameplate, she placed the neat stack of issue ballots so she could snatch them when necessary. At one of her first meetings, she'd accidentally held up ballot collection digging in her bag for the slips of paper. Her body had practically overheated as the entire room had seemed to turn to glare at her with disdain. She never wanted to be that person again.

She pulled her laptop from her bag and placed it on the table next to her cellphone, both muted. She clutched her coffee cup in her left hand, opened her laptop, navigated to the university's e-campus site, and then sighed at her grading options.

With just a few minutes before the meeting started, Deja knew she had to make this decision quickly, but she couldn't fumble it, because if she chose wrong, she could deepen her boredom, burn with anger, sink into despair or be elated, all while trying to pretend to be paying attention to whatever was happening around her.

All university meetings were long, but the Faculty Senate meeting was so long that it felt like a waste to Deja unless she could check something off her to-do list. If she didn't, she'd stumble out of the auditorium bleary-eyed and even more depressed about her lack of productivity. Like most of the faculty in the room, Deja felt like she was perpetually drowning beneath all the grading she had to complete by the deadlines she'd created, the students expected, and the university mandated. At the top of her list was a batch of essays for her "Race and Ethnicity" graduate course. She'd graded about half of those, and the prospect of whittling down that digital pile was attractive. She also had a stack of short quizzes for "Intro to World Cultures" and short essay responses for "Women, Gender and Societies."

Deja chewed on her bottom lip and considered her options. If she were smart and interested in being kind to her future self, she would choose her graduate essays, but they required a lot of feedback, and she worried her constant typing would be a dead giveaway that she wasn't paying even the slightest bit of attention. Granted, at least half of the room wouldn't be paying attention either, but decorum required the pretense, so she chose the short essays with a smile. That was her favorite class of the semester anyway.

"Working hard or hardly working?"

Deja looked up from her computer to see one of her best work friends, Toni Ward, walking toward her. Her voice rose over the din of over a hundred faculty members and administrators, all trying to find a seat and catch up with one another. Deja wasn't nearly as bold as her friend, so she waited until Toni fell into the empty seat to her left to reply.

"Why, are you the feds?" she asked with a smile.

This meeting might have been the lowlight of Deja's month — every month — but at least it gave her an excuse to see her favorite people.

"Girl, call me the feds again, and I'll keep this muffin I brought you," she teased with a wink.

Deja's eyes widened, and she clapped her hands together excitedly. "You brought me a muffin?"

"Chocolate chip," Toni said smugly as she threw her name-plate carelessly on the table and started digging around in her bag.

Deja snatched the thick cardstock and stood it upright so her name — Antonia Ward, Political Science — faced the crowd.

Toni pulled a plastic container from her bag, pulled the lid off, and pushed the muffins closer to Deja's computer.

Deja folded her hands over her chest and smiled at the baked goods with pure joy suffusing her body as she considered which muffin she wanted — which looked best — when someone reached around Toni to snatch the dish by the closest corner and pull it across the table.

"Bless you," Marie Lau said. Her voice was tired, and not just because she was out of breath. Deja watched as she grabbed a muffin and took a large bite, closing her eyes as she chewed.

"Damn, girl," Toni and Deja said at the same time.

Marie ignored them and continued eating her muffin as her face relaxed with serenity, and Deja watched her with interest.

Marie's hair fell around her shoulders in dark brown waves. Her jagged bangs skimmed her eyelashes, impeccably styled as always, but only because getting her hair done was the only luxury she allowed herself or could reasonably afford. From there, Marie was the picture of exhausted, overworked adjunct. There were dry erase smudges on the heels of her hands, her sweater was bunched in the strap of her crossbody bag, and her ugly but comfortable tennis shoes didn't match her outfit, a faux pas she never would have made normally, but rushing across campus to teach five or six classes a semester mandated comfort over style. All the faculty members on campus were tired, even so early in the semester, but Marie's — and the other adjuncts' — exhaustion was always on another level.

Deja wanted to ask if she was okay, but she already knew the answer. The life of an adjunct professor was as unpredictable as it was unappreciated. Marie normally did her best to weather the storm of her more-than-full load of classes with a smile, but Wednesdays were her longest days this semester, and she looked every bit as tired as Deja knew she was. Besides, Marie shouldn't have had to hide how overworked she was anyway.

"Any word on your application yet?" Deja asked carefully.

Marie shoved the last bite of her muffin into her mouth. Crumbs cascaded down her shirt. "Shit."

Deja reached into her purse and grabbed the napkins Jerome had given her. She pushed the stack toward Marie and grabbed the plastic container to pick her own muffin. She set her treat on a napkin in front of her, deciding to save it until she needed a mid-meeting sugar rush.

She and Toni waited patiently for Marie to answer Deja's question.

Marie fidgeted with her name plate — Marie Lau, Ethnic Studies — for a while before she answered. "Got the phone interview."

"Good," Deja cried.

"Good, my ass," Toni cut in. "She's been teaching *more* than a full load for that department for four years. A phone interview for the job she's already doing is the least they can do." Toni gently nudged the container of muffins back toward Marie as she spoke.

Marie grabbed another muffin and took a smaller bite.

"It'll be 'good,'" Toni continued, "when they start paying her and all the other adjuncts what they're worth, put them on the tenure track, and give them professional development money."

Marie put the rest of her muffin on a napkin and plucked another from the stack to wipe her mouth and hands. She finally pulled the strap of her bag over her head and dropped it on the floor. She shifted in her chair, moving the littlest bit away from Toni and Deja.

They knew Marie was often uncomfortable talking about her job, so they took her silent cue and dropped the subject, but Deja reached around Toni to squeeze Marie's elbow lightly. Marie didn't make eye contact, but Deja saw a small smile on her lips.

The room was louder now as more faculty arrived and chatted before the meeting started. Deja took the time to pull up the essays she needed to grade, ready to get a head start on her work, but she was interrupted when Toni leaned into her side.

"Look who's here," Toni whispered to Deja.

Deja automatically slumped down in her chair and narrowed her eyes, refusing to respond.

"Oh, don't hide now, girl. Your man has arrived," Toni cackled.

"He's not my man. Shut up."

"And with that attitude, he never will be." Marie huffed a

small breath of laughter that sounded so loud to Deja's affronted ears.

Deja could feel her face heating and sweat forming at her hairline, but she refused to look up. Toni and Marie did this to her every month. Apparently, teasing her about her crush on Alejandro was the highlight of the Faculty Senate meeting for them. Meanwhile, every month Deja wished she could crawl under the table and hide, but that would probably only make her friends cackle loud enough to get the entire auditorium's attention, including Alejandro's, and the thought of him seeing her like that made her want to expire and leave this plane of existence behind for good.

"Oh, that's a nice suit," Marie said, leaning into Toni's side and shoving her harder into Deja's body. "Is that a new tie?"

"How should I know?" Deja huffed weakly.

Toni cackled. "Because we *all* know the only person who knows Alejandro's wardrobe better than you is...him. So, is that a new addition or not?"

Deja scowled at her friends' gleeful faces as they waited for an answer or for Deja to overheat and start to melt from embarrassment, whatever came first; they weren't picky, and any form of entertainment — even at her expense — would appease them. She glanced at the clock on her laptop and saw that the meeting was set to start any second. This was her friends' terrible genius. If she wanted to take a good look at Alejandro before the meeting started — and she wanted to do so with the thin veneer of a casual perusal instead of a schoolgirl crush — she needed to do it before the Senate President started the meeting. Even though she'd just seen him in the coffee shop, she hadn't had much time to drink him in like she wanted to. And she did really want to see him, touch him, taste him; a fact that her friends knew all too well.

Deja rolled her eyes, pushed an annoyed breath out of her

nostrils, and sat up in her chair. She tried to play it cool, dipping her head to stare — unseeing — at the screen for a second, before she slowly lifted her eyes to look just over the top of her laptop screen. She could have done a lazy scan around the auditorium, but she didn't have time. Or maybe she just lied to herself about that last part because she was excited to get to see Alejandro again. Pathetic, she thought to herself with a sigh as her eyes settled on him at once.

To be fair, she'd discovered months ago that she could find her crush in any crowd, big or small, with very little effort; a garbage superpower, only eclipsed by her ability to make daily lists of tasks she never completed. It helped that Alejandro liked to sit in the upper tier as well, and usually in a place where Deja — and unfortunately Toni and Marie — had an unobstructed view of him. And what a view.

Alejandro was standing. While Deja watched, he pulled the strap of his artfully worn and stylish leather satchel over his head. Deja swallowed a lump in her throat when his vest lifted the tiniest bit to expose his button-up denim shirt — a look she was certain no one could pull off except him — tucked into his jeans. The fabric pulled taut over his stomach, and she swore she could see each ripple of his abs, or at least the abs she'd imagined there on more than hundreds of occasions. He leaned over to place his bag on the table in front of him, and Deja's eyes lifted to his face. Her fingers flexed on the table in front of her, and then his eyes lifted and crashed into hers. He held her gaze as he stood straight and began to take off his suit jacket, slowly. But maybe this was just Deja's brain once again stretching this moment out so she could take everything in for perfect masturbatory recall later, like tonight.

She didn't know what to make of the fact that Alejandro watched her watching him as he pulled his jacket from his broad shoulders, but she didn't care to dissect it since he looked so good. He had every bit of her attention — and probably half of the room as well — as he neatly folded his jacket over the back of his chair and unbuttoned the bottom button of his vest.

Deja heard someone sigh, and her face heated again. She was certain that sigh had been hers. And then her sex clenched. This was the single most erotic few seconds of her day — hell, maybe even her week — and it was happening in full view of faculty from across campus. This was worse than pathetic.

She should have been ashamed that he'd caught her staring at him twice in less than an hour, but this wasn't exactly the first time that had happened. Thankfully, he never confronted her about her staring — maybe she was better at hiding her lustful thoughts — but god, it was embarrassing, not that her hormones could differentiate between the heat of embarrassment and arousal at this moment.

When he finally looked away to pull his chair out and sit, Deja exhaled long and loud, as if she'd been holding her breath through that entire ordeal. Because she had.

She watched as he set his nameplate on the table facing her — Alejandro Mendoza, History — and turned to the man next to him — Michael Hernandez, Natural Sciences — and struck up a conversation.

Toni grabbed her nameplate and started fanning herself. Marie snatched Deja's muffin and took a bite.

"I need a cigarette," Toni said.

"Oh my god, shut up," she said, ducking her head and swiping at her damp hairline surreptitiously. "The tie is definitely new," she added, licking her lips.

And I want to take it off him with my teeth, she didn't say.

THREE

The next two and a half hours didn't really fly by so much as crawl slowly toward death like a zombie that hadn't gotten a kill shot yet. Or at least that's how Deja thought her twelve-year-old nephew would have described it, but he could find a way to compare most things to zombies.

They'd just handed in their last ballot and were waiting in annoyance as the Secretary read out the final tally of their votes, and then, finally, the end of September's Faculty Senate meeting arrived with a very sedate announcement.

"Motion to adjourn this month's meeting," Dr. Chris Branford, College of Business, Senate President said.

"Seconded," Sheila Meyer, Senate Secretary, replied.

"We are adjourned," Chris said in an unnaturally cheery voice that Deja absolutely related to.

And just like that, the dead quiet of the auditorium burst into the specific kind of excited chatter that Deja only heard at the end of these monthly meetings.

Marie all but sprinted out of the auditorium with a blind

wave over her head to Deja and Toni. She had a class to teach in ten minutes on the other side of campus and not a spare second to waste.

Toni and Deja were already packed up and darted out of the auditorium behind Marie, moving fast enough to avoid getting pulled into conversations they didn't care about with people they didn't like.

Outside of the building, Deja turned to Toni. "I need to go to my office. I left my laptop charger. You coming?"

Toni opened her mouth but then snapped her jaw shut. Deja furrowed her brow just before his voice caught her attention, and not just because his voice was deep and gentle, but also because it was so close.

"Are you going to Mark?" Alejandro asked.

This wasn't the first time Deja had heard Alejandro speak, obviously, but it was the first time she'd heard his voice all day. Normally, they passed each other at least once in the hallways of their building, and he would smile at her and say hi. Sometimes, she heard him speaking to a colleague down the hall, and the deep timbre of his laughter would settle into her stomach. But it was like her body never quite got used to it, and the first time she heard it after a while always unsettled her, but in the most deliciously sensual way. At least in their building, she could shut her office door or hide in a bathroom stall and will her nerves to settle before she had to interact with people again, waiting until she felt less raw with need. Or maybe just until she felt able to better hide the fact that the sound of Alejandro Mendoza's voice had a tendency to make the hair on her arms stand up and her pussy wet. But there was no warning or place to hide in front of Founders Hall, surrounded by faculty from all over the university and her best work friend, and not with him so close.

Deja turned around slowly to see Alejandro smiling at her, his brown eyes big and friendly and also maybe intense.

"I..." She hesitated, licked her lips, watched him watch her lick her lips, and then swallowed. "Yeah, I just need to pick up my charger."

"I'm heading over there too. Can I walk with you?"

Deja was nodding before she decided to say yes, and Alejandro's mouth spread into a soft smile. It was a mild afternoon in early fall, but Deja felt as if she was standing under a midsummer sun, which is to say she was pouring sweat under her clothes. Gross.

"Are you coming as well?" he asked Toni, speaking over Deja's head.

Deja didn't turn to look at her friend at first. She got distracted watching Alejandro's profile, the way the muscles in his jaw moved as he spoke, the faint gray at his temple, his long, dark eyelashes. She had to shake herself to turn to Toni, who was shaking her head and backing away.

"No, thanks. I've got to go feed my cat before he shreds something expensive. See you two later."

Toni locked wide eyes with Deja. Alejandro turned away to say goodbye to Mike, and Toni took the opportunity to mouth "oh my god" to Deja before turning and practically jogging away. Deja watched as Toni pulled a folder from her shoulder bag and began to fan herself.

"Ready?" Alejandro asked, making Deja jump. His hand lightly cupped her elbow, and her mouth went dry.

This might not have been the first time they'd ever spoken, but Deja was certain that this was the first time they'd ever touched. She decided she'd have to have her glass of wine in an ice-cold bath tonight, and then she squeaked out a reply that wasn't much more than a high-pitched suggestion of a word, but it didn't sound like anything intelligible to her own ears. She had no idea what it must have sounded like to him, but he didn't seem deterred, and that gorgeous curve of a smile didn't budge.

He tightened his grip on her slightly and steered her toward the green expanse of the North Oval, leading her across the lawn to their building.

"Are you going home now, or do you have more work to do?" he asked her once they'd separated from the crowd.

Deja had to take a deep breath before she could answer. The word "home" fell from her lips in another squeak. She cleared her throat and continued in a slightly stronger voice. "I mean I have more work to do, but I just want to get off campus. You? Are you heading home?" Those were more words than she'd ever said to him at one time, and her eyes widened in shock.

"I wish," he said. "I've got some grading to do before my graduate class tonight. I'll be here for a while."

"Oh, okay. Sucks," she said, cringing that her PhD hadn't prepared her for more intelligent conversation.

But Alejandro laughed, a deep sultry rumble Deja felt in her bones and the hardening tips of her nipples. "It absolutely sucks."

She turned to look at him, wanting to see the way his laughter changed his face even if only in profile, but he was looking at her full-on, and his laughter kind of brightened his features as if he was lit from within. Or maybe that was her overactive imagination again. Either way, she sucked in a breath as he looked at her. She watched as his crow's feet and laugh lines deepened, and the flash of his pink tongue peeked from behind his teeth.

And then Deja realized that his hand was still at her elbow.

"Ay yo, Professor Mendoza, push back tomorrow's quiz," someone yelled from the East lawn, breaking the moment between them.

Alejandro turned, and Deja sucked in a deep, nervous breath before she looked around him to see a group of boys huddled around a soccer ball.

Alejandro yelled back in Spanish, and they all threw their hands up, laughing and shaking their heads before resuming their game.

"What'd you say?" Deja asked.

"I told them the chances of me pushing back the quiz are as high as the chances of a communist revolution in Argentina."

Deja rolled her eyes and quirked one eyebrow up. "Historians."

Alejandro laughed. "I know, I know. We're very corny. Your eyebrow doesn't have to judge me so hard."

Deja laughed, and they continued strolling, unhurried toward their building. His hand stayed at her elbow, and their bodies bumped together with every other step.

At Mark Hall, Alejandro opened the exterior door for her. She smiled, ducked her head, and brushed past him to walk inside. All the oldest buildings on campus were clustered around the North Oval, and Mark was one of the oldest. It was squat and brick and always a little too cold in winter and too hot in the spring. It had four floors: a student computer lab in the basement, the History Department on the first floor, Political Science on the second, and Sociology on the top floor.

Deja walked up the short flight of stairs to the first-floor landing. "Thanks," she said, turning around to face Alejandro. She wished this moment didn't have to end, but also, she hadn't quite taken an easy breath in a few moments, and that, plus Alejandro's nearness, was starting to make her feel lightheaded.

"Anytime," he said, ducking his head to make eye contact, a small, almost wistful smile on his face.

Deja assumed the wistful gaze she saw there was a figment of her imagination, and she vowed to remember it tonight in bed with her favorite vibrator.

FOUR
OCTOBER

"By now, I'm sure you've all seen the new university home page, with the scrolling personal interest stories..."

Deja tapped her right foot against the table leg in annoyance, ignoring the rest of that supremely dry sentence. Even though she'd seen this item on the pre-circulated meeting agenda, she still couldn't believe the committee was forcing them to listen to — she checked her watch for the fourth time in as many minutes — a twenty-minute conversation from the Head of Information Technology Services about random and unnecessary upgrades to the website. She didn't care — like at all — and she wasn't going to pretend she cared when the campus internet was too slow most days to stream a YouTube video for her lectures. They had bigger issues to attend to, but the tediousness of the Faculty Senate meant there wouldn't be enough time to deal with their slow Wi-Fi when some bored technology manager who'd spent months rewriting the website's code had the floor to giddily tell any and everyone who was willing — or forced — to listen all about it.

Normally, she would have been able to avoid her annoyance by simply ignoring this kind of dry presentation, but her laptop had died, and like an idiot, she'd left her charger in her office. Marie was grading a small batch of quizzes to her right while Toni was tweeting about the latest Supreme Court decision to her left. And all Deja could do was check her email on her phone and watch as that battery died as well.

So, to preserve her cell phone as long as she could, she decided to people-watch instead, and thankfully, the Faculty Senate was full of nothing but personal interest stories. She looked around and spotted a few faculty members watching the presentation with rapt attention. Deja couldn't stop herself from rolling her eyes at their nerve, even if they were only a small fraction, because no one should encourage this kind of boring behavior. Most of the faculty Deja saw were either dozing quietly or working on their computers, and she rolled her eyes at them too because she was jealous of their productivity.

She sighed quietly to herself as her eyes continued moving around the room until she found him. Alejandro's laptop was open on the table in front of him, obscuring Deja's view of his bright white shirt and midnight black tie, both far too well-tailored for this entire campus. By contrast, his computer gave off a much less serious vibe than his clothing. There was a sticker of Rigoberta Menchu on the upper right corner and a Che Guevara decal over the Apple insignia.

Deja sucked her bottom lip into her mouth. She knew she should move her attention elsewhere, but she didn't want to, and if she couldn't grade, she wanted to look at Alejandro for a little bit longer. It wasn't like she had anything more interesting to occupy her time. Besides, as far as she was concerned, there wasn't anything more interesting than his five o'clock shadow, so she gave herself permission to stop pretending and enjoy the view.

Deja wouldn't fully admit the depth of it to Toni or Marie, but her crush on Alejandro was much more intense than they knew, despite the teasing. She'd first met him at a faculty of color mixer a month into her first semester as a newly minted PhD and assistant professor. It had just been a quick introduction and handshake — nothing to write home about — but to Deja, it had been something to remember. And once she knew he existed, she felt like she saw him everywhere; she couldn't escape just a glimpse of him across the Oval or down the hall. Not that she wanted to escape him.

They passed each other on the way to and coming back from their Friday afternoon classes, at the checkout desk in the library, at Black Student Union and Latino Student Association events, and always around Mark Hall. They'd even run into one another at the grocery store late one night when Deja's freezer had been shockingly barren of frozen pizza. She'd thrown a long coat — that looked much too similar to a housecoat — over her pajamas and driven to the store, only to run into Alejandro with a cart full of actual groceries, fresh fruit and vegetables even. She'd felt terrible in her not-a-housecoat coat and satin bonnet and practically ran to the self-checkout line to get away from him, grabbing a bag of spinach on the way. It was one of the worst nights of her life, but she still remembered how sexy he'd looked in his gray sweatpants and sneakers; he never dressed casually on campus.

It sometimes felt as if her infatuation with him grew exponentially each time she saw him, which was unfortunate since she was certain she didn't see anyone with the kind of random regularity with which she encountered Alejandro. And then she'd picked up the Faculty Senate service assignment after one of her colleagues had to take an emergency medical leave, sat down in her chair next to Toni, and looked across the auditorium only to see Alejandro.

For the past year, these monthly meetings gave a kind of structure to their brief encounters. He smiled at her — and Toni and Marie. Sometimes they stopped and talked to him and Mike, and every now and then, he caught her watching him take off his coat, or their eyes met in the middle of a point-less debate about homecoming dates, and he rolled his eyes playfully at her. It wasn't a real friendship, few relationships in the university were, but it fed her immediate attraction, keeping the logs burning on an ill-advised infatuation that her friends loved to tease her about.

He sat back in his chair and ran his hand over the top of his head. Alejandro's hair was that perfect shade of black that was almost blue. He had a thick tangle of waves on top, and it was cut short on the sides. His waves were gelled perfectly in place, but it didn't have that crispy gel look. Deja liked to think of Alejandro's hair as stylish perfection, no hair out of place. And it wasn't just his hair. It was his suits, his nails, his facial hair, everything. Deja tried to dress professionally and fashionably, but sometimes she strolled into her early morning classes with mascara on just one eye, only to find out that her shirt was buttoned incorrectly. But Alejandro was on an entirely different sartorial planet and was always impeccable. Even now, as he frowned at his laptop, he had the nerve to look like a model.

He leaned back in his chair and pressed his fingers against his closed eyes. Deja knew that look of exhaustion intimately, and it made her heart ache and warm at the same time. She was so caught up in sympathetically watching him that she didn't notice when his hands moved until his mouth twitched. Her eyes lifted and met his. Another Faculty Senate meeting, another instance of Alejandro catching Deja watching him like a hawk.

She sighed to herself. His lips quirked at the corners like he was fighting a smile.

On instinct, Deja sucked her bottom lip into her mouth and bit down hard against the rising lust in her body, but she didn't look away. She'd convinced herself that Alejandro couldn't know about her crush, but there was no way he could have missed how she'd just been looking at him. Right?

She watched as his smile faded and his eyes warmed into a banked fire, and even if she'd wanted to look away, now she couldn't. They stared at each other for so long that the rest of the room disappeared. Deja didn't hear any more of the boring report or Marie's annoying mutterings because the sound of her own racing pulse had filled her ears.

But then Robert King, Marketing, cut into their moment.

"So, let me get this straight," Robert said, projecting his voice across the auditorium. "ITS has time to update the website to do things no one needs, but can't figure out why the campus Wi-Fi loads like dial-up? Or why we keep getting all these scam emails? Is this a joke?"

And just like that, the bored, distracted silence erupted into outraged whispers and amused chuckles.

"I'm glad someone finally said it," Toni said, loud enough to be heard by everyone in their small pocket of the auditorium.

Deja and Marie nodded.

Deja stole a look across the auditorium and saw Alejandro and Mike laughing with one another.

This was the most interesting faculty meeting they'd had in a long while.

AS USUAL, Marie ran off as soon as the meeting adjourned, and Deja and Toni walked briskly out of the auditorium to beat the rush.

They made a detour to the bathroom across the hall, making it into the two stalls just before the post-meeting crowd. By the time they were done, there was a line out the door, and they had to practically shove their way back outside.

"Deja," someone called.

She turned at the sound of her name, surprised to find the Dean of Arts & Sciences, Maisie Ward, smiling at her by the door to the auditorium and waving her over.

"Oh lord," Toni breathed. "Pretend you don't see her."

"How? I'm looking right at her?" Deja whispered.

"Don't go over there. Just point at your watch and look apologetic."

"I can't do that. She's the Dean," Deja said.

Toni shrugged and started backing away. "Oh well, don't say I didn't warn you."

"Where are you going?" Deja asked, panicked.

"She called your name, not mine. I'm not getting roped into whatever committee she's about to ask you to join. No friendship is that important to me."

"Toni," Deja hissed, shocked.

Toni shrugged again. She waved and then fled out into the stairwell while Deja looked on in horror.

"Deja," Dean Ward called again.

Deja took a deep breath, knowing instinctively that what Toni said was true. She was also pissed that her friend had abandoned her.

"Deja."

Deja put her work smile on before she turned back toward the auditorium. She walked on stiff legs the wrong way through the crowd.

"Deja, wonderful, I'm glad I saw you," the older woman said happily.

Dean Ward was one of the university's better administrators. She treated her faculty with respect and as fairly as she could, with the little leeway the provost and president allowed, but she was also too ambitious for anyone's liking. She wanted Arts & Sciences to "drive the university" in all areas, which really just meant that the largest College in the university had the most faculty and the highest number of majors, taught the biggest classes, and had the most service assignments. Unfortunately, none of that translated to higher pay. As far as Deja was concerned, it was a prime example of the academic racket; the extra work was taxing and demoralizing, and everyone was overworked, but none of that would matter when she went up for tenure. Deja was heading toward total burnout not even halfway through her probationary period, and even though she tried to hide it, she wasn't that good of a liar. Still, whatever Dean Ward was about to dump into her lap, she couldn't say no, because the Dean wrote her annual evaluations, including the third-year review. She'd also have a large say in her tenure decision when the time came, so staying in her good graces was more important than avoiding yet another work stressor in her life, even if it meant yet another service assignment.

"Hi, Dean Ward," Deja said in her brightest voice.

Out of the corner of her eye, she saw Alejandro and Mike walking from the auditorium. She looked away quickly and focused on Dean Ward's face. But Dean Ward had also spotted Alejandro, and she rested her hand on his shoulder. "Oh, Alejandro, perfect. There you are."

He turned to smile at the Dean and then Deja as he stepped out of the moving human traffic to stand next to Deja. Their arms brushed.

"What's up?" he asked Dean Ward casually. Deja couldn't even imagine being so informal with her.

"I'm putting together a subcommittee on outreach to students of color for the Arts & Sciences Diversity Committee, and I was wondering if you two were interested in being co-chairs."

Deja sucked in a harsh breath. Her brain was whirring as she mentally envisioned her schedule bursting into flames. She wanted to say no. She should have said no because she literally did not have time for yet another service commitment, but of course, she said yes, and enthusiastically at that. She was going to drink two glasses of wine tonight. At least.

Alejandro also said yes.

Fifteen minutes ago, Deja would have been over the moon to be standing so close to Alejandro for any reason, but now she just felt numb. Her brain had decided to stop processing new information, so she didn't hear any of Dean Ward's ideas, not that anyone noticed. Eventually, the other woman patted their shoulders and sped away as if her simple request hadn't just detonated what little control Deja had over her schedule.

Deja stared numbly at the space where the Dean had been for a second before turning toward the exit. She only had enough brain power to make a firm decision that she wasn't even going to pretend to work tonight. All she wanted to do was go home, get into her baggiest sweats, take her two glasses of wine to bed, and try not to cry herself to sleep before she was good and tipsy.

The sky was gray, and the fall air was bitterly cold, but Deja barely felt it because her anxiety was keeping her very warm.

"Are you going back to Mark?"

Alejandro's voice pulled Deja abruptly out of her downward

spiral. She hadn't even noticed he was walking beside her out of the building. She turned to him and was surprised at just how sexy he was, as if she'd never seen him up close before. But she couldn't even really appreciate him because her brain felt like it was covered in a thick fog. She had to think about her answer to his question for a few seconds longer than was probably normal.

"No...I mean yes. I forgot my charger," she finally said.

"Again?" he asked with a smile.

She scrunched her eyebrows together in confusion. It took her a few seconds to realize that he was talking about last month's Faculty Senate meeting.

"Oh, yeah. I guess it's a habit. I'm just so busy and tired," she admitted, her cheeks warming. "I'd forget my head if it wasn't screwed onto my neck. At least that's what my grandfather used to say."

Alejandro chuckled and dipped his head to make eye contact with her. "That's more than relatable." He smiled, and she found herself smiling back. And then he cocked his head toward the Oval. "Walk with me?"

The question made Deja's brain fog lift because that question sounded...different. His voice was softer — an intimate whisper she'd never heard before. His pupils were slightly dilated and warm, inviting even. Also warm was Deja's skin, and not just her cheeks but her chest at first, and then it began to spread across her entire body. She swallowed thickly before nodding at him.

"Don't worry about the committee," he said when they were halfway toward their building.

She let out an exasperated laugh. "How can I not worry? I don't have time for any more service. I barely have time for all the service assignments I have now."

"I know," Alejandro said.

"Do you?" Deja whined, annoyed with herself, but unable to modulate her voice to hide it.

"I do, actually," Alejandro said in a calm voice. "I'm not that far past getting tenure myself."

Deja turned to him, searching his face for something she couldn't even clearly explain to herself. What she found were kind eyes full of sympathy. Looking at him now didn't make her feel hot with desire; it calmed her. Looking at Alejandro looking at her made her feel seen, and it was as welcome as it was uncomfortable.

"How did you survive?" she asked in a small voice.

He smiled at her, and his voice was serious but kind. "The only way any of us survives. I asked for help."

Deja turned away from his eyes, not wanting him to see her reaction. She could feel the sudden and insistent pressure at the back of her eyes, because she didn't have help, and that had been her problem since she'd arrived. She had plenty of senior colleagues who weren't interested in mentoring her but loved to foist their service assignments on her plate. And while she loved Marie, she was just as overwhelmed as Deja. The only help she had was Toni. She was tenured, capable, and always on top of her shit, which is precisely why she was mentoring practically every female faculty member, tenure-track and adjunct, that A&S had hired in the last five years. Deja couldn't bring herself to heap any more responsibility onto her friend's shoulders, so she was rudderless and felt more lost each semester. She didn't want Alejandro to see her like that.

"I'll handle all of the scheduling stuff," Alejandro said, leaning toward her and gently bumping Deja's shoulder with his own. "You just tell me when you're free, and I'll take care of the rest."

Deja looked up at him with wary eyes. "I can't let you do that."

He smiled down at her, with warmth suffusing his gaze. "Let me do this for you," he said in a surprisingly soft whisper.

Her stomach flipped. "Okay," she whispered back.

When they reached the side entrance to Mark Hall, Alejandro pulled the door open for Deja, and his hand moved from her elbow to her back.

She shivered as she walked past him, the warmth of his large body seeming to penetrate the many layers she was wearing. Her legs felt stiff as she walked up the short staircase to the first floor. It almost felt like when they'd done this last month, but different. Deja's dread at the Dean's new assignment was still threatening to choke her, but there was also a crackling of tension between them that she didn't know what to do with except revel in it.

When she reached the first floor, she turned once again to thank him, but he'd already stepped up onto the next staircase, his eyes lifting because he'd been watching her ass. He blushed but then gestured at her to keep walking.

Deja was too shocked to do anything but listen to his directions. She bit her lips shut and walked up the next two flights of stairs with wide, shocked eyes and the heat of Alejandro's presence at her back.

On the top floor, Alejandro reached around her to open the door just as she touched the handle, and their fingers tangled together for a second before Deja flinched away.

"Sorry," she whispered.

"Don't apologize," he whispered back as he pulled the door to the Sociology floor open.

Deja was frozen. Alejandro's chest was a firm presence at her back, and the smell of his cologne had engulfed her, making her feel lightheaded and aroused. She turned her head toward him, and her eyes caught on a delicate gold chain around his throat. She'd never noticed that he wore jewelry before because they'd never been this close before.

She sucked her bottom lip into her mouth, and his Adam's apple bounced as he swallowed. She bit down on the soft flesh between her teeth and let her eyes roam over the perpetual five o'clock shadow on his jaw, his full lips, the tip of his nose. When they made eye contact this time, they were so close Deja knew she wasn't imagining the heat she saw there; she knew without a shadow of a doubt that Alejandro wanted her as bad as she wanted him.

"Can I walk you to your office?" he asked in the softest, sexiest whisper Deja had ever heard from anyone ever. Those few words made her sex shudder in anticipation, and Deja surprised herself with the answering gasp that fell from her lips. She'd never heard herself sound so...soft before. She was even more shocked at how her anxiety had been momentarily burned away by the full force of her desire.

The question was a cover — they both knew it — but the semblance of professionalism felt necessary. They were exposed in the stairwell. Any number of their colleagues or administrative staff could just wander around a corner and come upon them, and the last thing they needed was gossip. Or at least, that was the last thing Deja needed. Alejandro already had tenure and was a man, so he would probably be okay, but she might never recover from rumors that she was getting cozy with one of the university's most eligible bachelors; that she wasn't publishing because she was too focused on dating. The fear of becoming grist for the gossip mill should have made Deja say no. She should have smiled and put some distance between them. She should have made this a moment she remembered fondly — and maybe touched herself thinking about every now and then — because walking away was safer than not. But instead of doing the smart thing, Deja nodded slowly, but excitedly.

Alejandro's mouth curved into a smile, and he tipped his head to the side, urging her on.

Deja stepped into the familiar hallway with shaky steps. The automatic hall lights turned on as they walked past her colleagues' office doors, which meant no one had walked through here for a while. She released her bottom lip and huffed out a sigh of relief that they were more than likely alone.

She stopped in front of her office door and started rummaging through her bag for her key ring. She could feel Alejandro's presence, and just knowing he was there, waiting for her, wanting her made it hard for her to concentrate on the simple task. By the time her fingers finally curved around her keys, her hands were shaking.

Deja jumped when Alejandro's hand closed around the curve of her waist, gently at first, and then his grip tightened.

She shivered when his breath caressed her ear, followed by that sexy whisper again. "Calm down, Deja."

She'd never heard him say her name quite like that before, and the newness of it made her listen to his direction. She took a deep breath, found the right key, and unlocked her office door in slow, measured steps.

Alejandro pushed her door open and urged her forward with his body pressed against hers, all semblance of reserve slipping away.

Deja had never imagined Alejandro as someone who was ever out of control. In her mind, he was always put together and controlled and maybe even a bit bossy. Right now, he was some odd mix of uncontrolled control, and it made all of her shiver. Her future fantasies were going to have a field day with this new information.

The door closed behind them, and Deja felt as if her office

was quieter than it had ever been. She swore she could hear and feel her heart pounding against her chest; it was deafening but drowned out deliciously by the ragged sound of Alejandro's breath in her ear.

When she'd fantasized about what it might be like to finally be with him, she imagined the encounter as frantic, desperate, because she knew she would be frantic and desperate. She couldn't even count how many times she'd dreamt about tearing his suit from his body, buttons flying everywhere, and messy wet kisses ruining her makeup. The reality was so much slower, and not in a bad way.

Deja clutched her keys to her chest as Alejandro's hands bracketed her waist and squeezed, as if he needed to hold her, possess her.

Deja's breathing slowed to match his and then sped up as his thumb started to move up and down her hip, slipping just under her t-shirt and over her bare skin. She could have sworn she felt that movement everywhere; on her inner thighs, across the tips of her tightening nipples, over her clit, inside her sex, everywhere she'd fantasized about Alejandro touching her since the moment they met.

She swallowed a groan as his hand flattened over her stomach in a possessive hold, and then he pulled her back against him. They both groaned as the prominent mound of his dick pressed against the curve of her ass.

"Turn around," he commanded.

Deja shivered with excitement.

FIVE

Alejandro was a patient man. He'd been waiting for Deja for over a year.

A year of watching her out of the corner of his eye across the auditorium at the monthly Faculty Senate meetings. A year of wasting too much time in the hallways of their building in the vain hopes that he might catch a glimpse of her. A year of training his body to recognize the very particular sound of her heels echoing down the hallway. A year of trying to decide if he should sit next to her at the Provost's speeches so he could try to decipher each individual note in her perfume or sit where she was in his line of sight so he could study each microexpression as it flitted across her face. A year of running into her in the student union and then his heart matching the beat of the unconscious and impatient tapping of her right foot — always her right foot — while they waited in line for coffee. A year of wet dreams that made him feel like a pre-teen all over again. A year of waiting for the right moment to ask for so much more.

He'd waited so long that when this moment finally came, he couldn't pretend that he wasn't electrified by the way her small body felt at his literal fingertips. On the one hand, he wanted to savor every small touch, every brush of his skin against hers, the smell of her, the taste of her. Alejandro loved lists, and the one that encapsulated everything he wanted to do with Deja was his longest yet, and he wanted to take his time ticking each entry — each part of her body — off it. On the other hand, his head was light with desire, and his blood was pounding in his veins as it headed south toward his groin, and he didn't want to take his time; there was no more time to waste.

But above all else, Alejandro wanted Deja to set the pace of this encounter. He hadn't waited for all this time just to fuck it up by moving too fast or too slow.

She turned in his arms, and her hip dragged across his painfully hard dick; the sensation was amazing. He just barely stifled a moan, but he couldn't stop the smile spreading across his lips now that he could finally knew for sure what she felt like and didn't have to guess. He let his hands move roughly over her hips and up her ribs and then curled them so he could run the backs of his fingers up her arms and across her shoulders. And then he lightly cupped the sides of her face with his palms. Finally.

Her eyes were on his chest, and she licked her lips nervously.

Alejandro used the small reserve of patience he still had to give them both a bit of space. He wanted to pull her to him, but he stopped and held her face in his hands, waiting for their panting breaths to subside.

While he waited, he took Deja in, watching her with the kind of intensity he normally tried to hide. He'd spent a year wanting more and more of Deja Evans, and he calmed himself knowing that he would get just that soon enough, so he catalogued all the parts of her he hadn't noticed before. The elegant curve and rounded tip of her nose, her fluttering eyelashes, the soft planes of her cheeks, and the slow, wet path of her bright pink tongue as it darted out to taste her lips; Deja never disappointed. He licked his own lips, hungry to follow her example and taste her lips with his own tongue. And then it dawned on him that he could. Alejandro slowly moved his thumb along her jaw to the deep curve of her bottom lip. He caressed it reverently, a silent promise that he would touch her in this exact way if she wanted, if she let him.

Deja sighed softly and finally lifted her eyes to his. He smiled down at her, hoping to chase the nervous gleam in her eyes away, and she sighed again.

Alejandro bent his body nearly in half, moving slowly toward her, giving her time to stop him if she wanted. She didn't. When their mouths were less than a hair's breadth away from finally touching, he stopped again, waiting for her to invite his lips to touch hers the way he'd been dreaming.

A few months ago, just getting this close to Deja would have been more than enough. He would have taken this bit of almost contact and spun it into hours of erotic fantasies to get himself off and to sleep at night, and, on the worst days, he would have conjured the memory of their lips almost touching as motivation to get out of bed in the morning.

This could still be enough, Alejandro thought to himself. If Deja wanted to stop, he would, he could, so he waited for her to make the next move. When she tipped her head back to brush her lips against his, he groaned and finally moved his tongue past his lips to taste the seam of her mouth, and they both exhaled in relief. Alejandro smiled against Deja's lips.

The kiss evolved quickly from a tentative exploration into urgent intensity, as all the months of wanting each other made every press of their lips and the wet slide of their tongues together full to bursting with meaning.

Alejandro had spent a year wondering how Deja would feel in his arms or taste on his tongue. He finally had the answers: just right, and coffee mixed with chocolate. When Deja pressed her tongue into his mouth, Alejandro suckled greedily on it, and she moaned softly into his mouth.

He cupped the back of her head to deepen the kiss just as Deja pulled back abruptly.

"What's wrong?" he asked. His words sounded like a panting groan.

"Shhhh," she said, "I'm not sure who's still here."

Alejandro took a deep breath and nodded. He placed his hands on her waist and walked her backwards toward her desk.

"Wait," she said, pressing her hands to his chest to stop him, but then curled her hands into the lapels of his jacket and pulled him toward her.

He nodded again and smiled as he pressed his lips against hers again. She giggled into his kiss. He had a sudden urge to hear her make that same sound, but while naked.

"Wait," she said again, mumbling against his lips.

Alejandro frowned as Deja pushed him away, gently but surely. He watched as she pulled her purse from her arm, reminding him that his own bag was still slung across his chest, they'd been so eager to touch each other. He blushed and pulled his bag over his head. They smiled awkwardly at one another as they dropped their bags into one of her office chairs.

He grabbed the lapels of his coat, and Deja stopped him with her small hands on his chest again.

"Wait," she whispered again.

He didn't know how she did it, but that one word did something to him that he could barely explain even with all his years of training. Each time she uttered it, his heart stuttered and stopped, his pulse raced, and his desire peaked. No one had ever made him feel that way before.

"Is that all you're going to say to me? 'Wait?'" he asked in amusement.

She looked at him through her eyelashes, with a small playful smile on her face. She sucked her bottom lip into her mouth as she ran her hands down his chest. His abs jumped in surprise at the boldness of her touch. She pressed her palms harder against him as her hands moved back up his chest and slipped inside his jacket to push it from his shoulders. It was the single sexiest thing any woman had ever done to him, and he was rock hard by the time she threw his coat on top of their bags.

In Alejandro's dreams about Deja, this was usually the part when he'd wake up covered in sweat, his dick pulsing and leaking inside his boxers, with his only recourse to take his shaft in hand and close his eyes. He'd stroke himself while he dove back into whatever fantasy he'd been having about Deja, but this wasn't a dream, and in the real world, she was even better than he'd ever imagined.

"I've wanted to do that since the day we met," she whispered, almost shyly, nervously making eye contact. She held his gaze as she backed away until the backs of her thighs bumped into her desk.

"So my plan worked?" he asked with a grin as he followed her as if she was reeling him in, because she was, even if she didn't realize it.

"Your plan?"

"I might peacock a little. For you," he admitted.

Her mouth fell open, and her eyes widened. "This can't be real. I've literally had dreams about you putting on a suit."

"On?"

"And then taking it off," she added.

He burst out laughing. "I'm happy to make that fantasy come true whenever you want."

"Oh my god," she groaned, covering her cheeks and shaking her head in embarrassment.

Her small groan made every muscle in his body harden. He ran his hands down her sides again; now that he'd touched her, he couldn't stop. He didn't want to stop. His hands dragged heavily around to her back and down to cover and then squeeze her ass. And then he lifted her up his body.

She squeaked and wrapped her arms around his neck and her legs around his waist, fitting perfectly against him just like he always knew she would.

"I've had dreams about you too," he whispered against her mouth, tasting her as he spoke.

She swallowed loudly and licked her lips, her tongue just barely grazing his mouth.

It was Alejandro's turn to groan. He squeezed her ass unconsciously as she squirmed against him. He lowered her onto her desk, their mouths close but not touching. They watched each other with hungry eyes as his hands moved to the front of her jeans. Her breath hitched as he toyed with then opened the button and slowly pulled the zipper open. His fingers snaked inside the waist of her pants, dragging along her skin.

"Tell me?" Deja whispered as her arms tightened around his neck. "About your dreams?"

It was a loaded question, Alejandro thought. There were the wet dreams and the other ones, the ones he didn't mention to anyone, not Mike or his brothers because they were too ridiculous, too far-fetched.

Deja rocked side-to-side, lifting her ass from the desk so Alejandro could pull her pants over her hips and down her thighs, just enough to settle his palms on top of her bare legs.

"Do you know how sexy you are when you concentrate?" he whispered as his right hand moved between her legs.

Her brow furrowed. "What?"

"In the Faculty Senate meetings, when you get into a groove on your computer, you concentrate so hard that your shoulders hunch just a little bit, you chew on your bottom lip, and you squint your eyes," he said as his left hand moved to her chin so they could lock eyes again. He wanted to see her face as he got her off.

"And I don't know what it is about it, but watching you concentrate so hard makes me hard."

Deja licked her lips, and he dipped his head to follow the wet path with his own tongue.

"Sometimes," he whispered against her mouth, "I jack myself off just thinking about you watching me with all that intensity, slouched shoulders and squinting eyes and biting your lip." He accentuated that last part by biting her bottom lip gently.

She groaned, and he groaned, and this time, he didn't go slow. He pressed his mouth against hers, pried her lips apart with his lips, and plunged his tongue into her mouth. He pulled the crotch of her panties with two fingers, and they both smiled as his fingers slid along the wet cleft of her pussy.

"Finally," he breathed into her mouth.

Deja tightened her arms around his neck, pulling him closer and kissing him harder. She didn't say it, but he felt the 'finally' in that kiss and the way her pussy quivered around his digits.

THEY KNEW the walls in this building were old and thin. They knew they needed to be quiet, but Deja's office was so silent that every sound seemed to boom. Alejandro's dick pulsed in tune with Deja's soft gasps and strangled groans. She cried out when his thumb circled her clit, and it felt like HD surround sound. He lapped at her mouth, desperate to taste every one of those breathy exhalations.

Alejandro's fingers curled inside of her, and the soft wet give of her pussy sounded obscenely perfect, but then she moaned his name into his mouth, and he nearly doubled over in ecstasy as he pumped his fingers in and out of her again and again and tried to ignore how much his dick wanted to feel her as well. Deja trembled in his arms and around his fingers, and nothing had ever felt so perfect.

Now that he'd had a taste, Alejandro didn't want to stop kissing Deja or touching her, so he did both. He licked and sucked at her mouth and nibbled at her bottom lip while he fucked her pussy with his fingers with increasing intensity.

"I'm close," Deja groaned, her strangled cry making his dick ache.

He moved his thumb over her clit with each press of his wrist. "I've got you," he whispered to her. "Come for me."

And she did. She wrapped her hands around his waist and pulled him closer while she pumped her hips into his hand.

"Fuck," he groaned as the walls of her pussy started to flutter and clench around his fingers.

He wanted to hear her cry out but remembered the thin walls at the last minute, so he grabbed her behind the neck and kissed her hard enough to muffle her moans. He shoved his tongue into her mouth just as she shivered violently against him. She screamed into his mouth as quietly as she could, and he drank up the sound until her body had mostly stilled, and she broke their kiss to pant through the aftershocks of her orgasm.

Alejandro kissed the corners of her mouth, her cheeks, her closed eyelids, her forehead, everywhere he could get his mouth without letting her go.

Deja whimpered when he pulled his fingers from her pussy. Her eyes drifted open, and she watched with rapt attention as he licked her essence from his fingers, with heat in his eyes.

"I think I have a condom in my wallet," he said.

Just as Deja opened her mouth, the familiar sound of the janitor's trashcan rolling down the hallway broke into the quiet of her office, and they both froze.

"Fuck," she hissed and pushed him away.

She jumped from the desk and started to shimmy back into her underwear and jeans.

He tried to help her, but she slapped his hands away. He was offended for a second, but he quickly realized that she was right. If he got his hands near her again, he'd be pulling her clothes back off, not caring if they got caught.

He forced himself to take a few steps back. He snatched his jacket from the chair and pushed his arms into it with maybe a little more force than was necessary. He slung his satchel back over his head and positioned the bag in front of his prominent erection, unsure what else to do with himself.

She buttoned her jeans and then, equally unsure, said, "Maybe you should leave?" It was a question, but it wasn't.

He wanted to tell her that he didn't want to do that, but the sound of an office door opening and closing followed by the trashcan's wheels rolling again filled the silence between them. It wasn't a question, but it was the right thing to do. If he hung around any longer — if they waited until the janitor came and went — soon enough, they'd be right back where they'd just been; his fingers or his tongue or his dick — wallet condom willing — inside of her. And the next time, she might not be able to stay so quiet; he'd see to that.

He nodded sadly at her, a fear settling in the pit of his stomach that, if he left, this would be all there was. And as it happened, they'd passed the point of no return. Now that he'd literally had a taste of her, it wasn't enough. It wouldn't be enough until he had her completely.

Alejandro moved quickly, grabbing Deja behind the neck, and pulled her mouth to his. He tried to sear this kiss onto his brain and hers; the pressure of her full lips, the way she tasted, her mouth, and her sex, and the way her smell clung to him.

She whimpered into his mouth and bit at his lips. She was driving him crazy, and it took all his will to let her go and force himself away. He turned toward the door and threw a lingering look over his shoulder before he left. On the way to his office, he silently promised himself that this wasn't the end, just the beginning. He didn't believe that anything was inevitable, but kissing Deja again was.

It had to be.

SIX
FRIDAY

Deja tried to focus on the student sitting on the other side of her desk, but she couldn't; she'd never wanted to not be in her office more than at this moment.

These weren't her regular office hours, and technically, Deja wasn't even supposed to be on campus on Fridays. She was normally home, puttering around her apartment trying to work on her articles, not making any progress, and then sinking into a comfortable pit of self-loathing just in time to spend the weekend stressed out. Her Friday schedule was usually packed tight with sitting at her computer for half an hour at a time, writing a few words, deleting more words, and then taking hour-long breaks to be self-loathing on social media, or reading a novel, or best of all, having a breakdown about her career while on the phone with her best friend.

The point was that Deja had plans, and she'd rather be at home feeling bad about herself than listening to her student make a case for a grade they both knew he didn't deserve, but this was the only day her student — who came to class so infrequently Deja could place his face but not his name — could meet, so here she was.

They'd been at this conversation for almost half an hour; Deja had been watching the clock very closely. The student kept circling around an issue Deja was certain they'd handled in the first five minutes...but apparently not.

They were barely two months into the semester, and Sheldon — that was his name! — had missed a cumulative two weeks of class and hadn't turned in the first essay that was due over a month ago. He'd ignored Deja's emails trying to find out if he was okay and needed extra help, and when he did come to class, he made sure to skip out as soon as the lecture was over. Deja was on the verge of suggesting that he drop her class when he'd emailed yesterday, desperate to meet. She had been hopeful that the meeting would be productive, in vain, apparently.

Sheldon had shown up with his very late essay in hand and a smug smile on his face that had disappeared when Deja explained that she couldn't, in all fairness, accept a paper so late without a reasonable explanation for its tardiness, nor would she excuse absences without that and some kind of documentation.

After five minutes of a story about how hard Sheldon's other classes were and how he'd thought Deja's intro course would be a "cakewalk", Deja — insulted but still professional — had asked again for explanations for some, or any, of his absences and the extremely late coursework, to no avail. Instead, Sheldon had launched into a story about a math class he'd failed a year ago, and Deja had mentally checked out. She had one eye on the clock on her desk phone and the other on her inbox, waiting for her pre-arranged exit from this conversation and the other reason she was unfortunately on campus this Friday.

At 11:30 on the dot, she sat up straight in her chair and leaned forward, waiting for Sheldon to take a breath. "I'm sorry, but I have another meeting. If you have a reasonable explanation for the missed classes and your late paper from *this semester*," Deja stressed the words, "you're always welcome to come back."

"So..." Sheldon let the word dangle for a second or two, his eyes boring into Deja's. "You aren't going to accept my paper?"

Can a person feel their blood pressure rising? Because Deja could have sworn she felt her blood pressure shooting through her proverbial roof. Her jaw clenched, and she snapped her lips shut to stop from screaming. She was just so tired. Once she'd collected herself, she pulled her mouth into the best smile she could muster and spoke her single word answer slowly and clearly. "No."

Sheldon's brows furrowed in confusion, and Deja took a deep, calming breath. She was about to elaborate — even though she knew that no was a single word answer, and she'd spent the last half hour explaining her simple policy — when a knock at her office door interrupted her. She and Sheldon turned. Deja swallowed the lump in her throat at the sight of Alejandro standing in her doorway.

"Damn," Sheldon muttered under his breath. Deja could absolutely relate.

Alejandro was leaning against her door frame in a light gray suit tailored to fit his body like a glove. And even better, he had a bright smile on his face and a paper coffee cup in each hand. Usually, Deja's fantasies about Alejandro veered on the side of raunchy, but the domesticity of a man showing up at her office dressed like he'd just stepped out of a fancy watch advertisement with a cup of coffee for her? This was a whole new dimension of her erotic fantasies.

"Ale—" Deja cleared her throat and stood, pushing her

chair back hard enough to slam into the wall behind her. She cringed, and her face warmed. "Dr. Mendoza, what are you doing here?"

"We have a meeting," he said, lifting an eyebrow at the same time as he tilted his head toward Sheldon.

"Yeah. Y-yes, right," Deja stammered. She turned to Sheldon, motioning him toward the door. "We're just wrapping up here. Sheldon, I'll see you in class on Monday?" She asked the question deliberately first to remind him that they *had* class on Monday and that she expected to see him there.

Sheldon seemed startled by the question or the way Alejandro's cologne seemed to be filling Deja's office with a delicate, spicy sent that made Deja's mouth water.

"Um, yeah, sure," Sheldon mumbled as he left.

Deja sighed sadly.

Alejandro backed into the hallway to make room for her student to leave, but he kept his eyes on Deja. She, in turn, watched Sheldon's back, stalling for time. She took deep breaths through her nose, trying to slow her rapidly beating heart. It wasn't working. He was clear across the room, and yet, Deja could feel his body heat or the heat from the intensity of his gaze, something.

When Sheldon was gone, Alejandro stepped into her office with deliberately slow steps.

Deja sucked a deep breath in through her mouth this time and swallowed nervously. It was a mistake. She tasted the bitter smell of coffee mixed with his cologne as he stepped closer, and now, her mouth was really watering, and her pulse wasn't the only thing pounding.

"Are you going to invite me in?" he asked in a low and intimate whisper that reminded her of the last time they'd been in this office together. She felt hot, and it wasn't from her malfunctioning heater.

"Maybe you shouldn't come in," she said in halting words.

Alejandro stopped and lifted both eyebrows, a small, playful smile on his face. "No?"

Deja swallowed again. "The last time you were here, things went...haywire," she whispered.

"Haywire?" he asked thoughtfully. "That's not a word I would have used to describe that..." His voice trailed off, and somehow, that silence made Deja's nipples hard. "I thought things went really well until we were interrupted."

He took a few more steps into her office and whispered across the space between them. "Invite me in, Deja. I promise to keep my hands to myself."

Deja took a deep breath and clutched one hand in the other. Nervous excitement wracked her body. It felt like static ghosting over her skin. She nodded slowly.

Alejandro kicked the door closed with his right foot as he walked inside.

Deja jumped at the sound of the door closing, and her mind conjured the memory of his lips on her. She tried to keep her breathing even as he neared, anxious and a little bit terrified to see what he would do. She was worried that this was a mistake and even more worried that she wanted to make it.

Alejandro kept his distance — to Deja's disappointment — and leaned his back against the door. She watched him watching her like they had so many times across the Faculty Senate and student organization meetings, but now that she knew how his fingers and mouth felt on her body, his eyes on her felt like the feeling of his fingers digging into her soft hips.

"I brought you coffee," he said in a husky voice. "Latte, extra shot, two sugars."

Her eyebrows rose. "How do you know my coffee order?"

Alejandro's cheeks turned a bright red, and he ducked his head to smile. "I might have asked Toni," he admitted.

"Of course, it was Toni." She rolled her eyes and then smiled shyly at him. "Thank you."

He pushed from the door and walked toward her in those slow, deliberate strides. He stopped on the other side of her desk and offered her the coffee cup in his right hand. "You're more than welcome."

She rocked back onto the heels of her boots, feeling even more flustered now that he was so close. She sucked her bottom lip into her mouth and tentatively reached for the coffee cup. The tips of their fingers brushed around the cup, and Deja felt the brief touch deep in her core. She dropped her eyes as she took a sip of her drink. She could feel his eyes on her as she hummed in happiness.

Alejandro coughed as he dropped into the chair Sheldon had vacated.

"What's wrong?" Deja asked, sitting down as well.

He smiled and shook his head as he crossed his legs. "Nothing, I just... If I'm going to keep my hands to myself, I should keep my mouth shut and stay over here. And you should definitely stay over there."

Deja's mouth fell open, but she had no idea how to reply to that confession besides the tiniest smile on her face that she tried to hide by taking another sip of her coffee.

"I'm sorry," he said after a few seconds of heated silence.

It took a second for Deja to process his words because she was so focused on the way his voice slithered under her clothes and across her skin. She tried to hide her labored breathing with another sip of coffee.

"Sorry for what?" she eventually asked.

He took a sip of his own coffee and uncrossed his legs. Deja's hand tightened around her coffee cup to make sure her eyes didn't dip to his groin, a feat.

He bent forward to rest his elbows on his knees. When he

looked up at her, his eyes were no longer playful; they were as serious as the set of his mouth before he spoke.

"I don't regret what happened on Wednesday," he said in a quiet voice. "I've been waiting for that moment for over a year. But if I could go back and do it again, I wouldn't have put you in that position. Not in your office."

Deja sucked in a shocked breath at his words and then exhaled loudly. Her shoulders slumped, and a weight she hadn't quite realized she was holding on her shoulders lightened.

She knew that her family thought the life of a professor was cushy, a few classes a week, and weekends and summers off. She'd given up on trying to correct their assumptions about her life because she quite literally didn't have time. But being on the tenure track had been hard for Deja in ways she sometimes struggled to even admit to herself. She'd expected the long hours outside of class and the heavy teaching load. She'd even been prepared by her mentors for the lack of mentorship, to a certain degree, but she hadn't expected the uncomfortable ways she'd folded under the weight of all those pressures.

And she couldn't have imagined three years ago that she'd be so reckless as to let a man she'd been crushing on for over a year get her off in her office. But she had, and as she looked at Alejandro across her desk with a look of sexy contrition — because apparently, that was a thing — on his face, she understood why. She was lonely and starved for the tiniest crumbs of attention and affection. So lonely that she'd let a man who was realistically a complete stranger fingerfuck her where anyone could have heard, risking the job that had become her entire world, whether she liked it or not.

And the worst part was that she'd do it again — she knew she would — and that made her so sad. It also made Alejandro even more attractive today than he'd been on Wednesday.

There was so much riding on Deja succeeding at her job and getting tenure, personally and professionally, and yet, when she tentatively looked into his eyes, she could feel the sad pit of loneliness she'd been avoiding since graduate school. It had become all too easy to avoid how she felt with her schedule because she had almost nothing else going on in her life, but the minute she was presented with a brief reprieve from that loneliness — like the opportunity to let Alejandro touch her again — she knew she'd fold, even if it cost her so much more than she could realistically give.

Her department had a lot to lose if she wasn't all they'd hoped she'd be when they hired her. She was their first tenure track hire in nearly a decade, part of a campus-wide diversity initiative meant to bring in marginalized faculty, and it would certainly reflect poorly on the department if she didn't receive tenure; not as badly as it would reflect on her, but still, not great. That was partially why Deja had so many service commitments; her department needed to make sure that she was seen, a constant reminder that the Sociology department wasn't full of old white dinosaurs. Not anymore, at least.

Common sense might have led another department to protect Deja, mentor her even. If she stayed, received tenure, and excelled, the university could reward them with another tenure track line and their department — small and overtaxed — might rehabilitate their position in the College. But as her mama always said, common sense ain't common.

Instead of supporting her, her department didn't mentor her in her new position, even though she came directly from graduate school and had no idea how to be a faculty member and had no time to learn while running from class to class to meeting. Her colleagues didn't consider keeping her workload regular and manageable; they didn't give any consideration to what it was like for her to be the only woman of color in their unit. And worst of all, more than one of her senior colleagues had reminded her that just because she was new, with a higher teaching load than any of them had had when they were at her level, had more service and was still fledgling in her career didn't mean they would cut her any slack when it came time to vote on her tenure dossier. The honesty was useful and completely demoralizing. It didn't matter that the last time they'd voted on a candidate, the university was still recovering from the Y2K scare; all that mattered was that Deja work harder and longer than they did without any recognition for it.

The overwork allowed Deja to avoid confronting the loneliness, and her crush on Alejandro had allowed her to imagine there might be a time when she wouldn't feel so lonely, and her job wouldn't rule her life. Something about him reminded her that she wasn't just harried assistant professor Dr. Evans, she was also Deja: young, single, and very much horny.

But when she looked at him now, looking at her with a face full of contrition, it seemed to open the lid on all the sadness and loneliness she'd been avoiding, because she felt as if he could see it too. Now that they weren't sitting on opposite ends of the auditorium, he was closer; he'd gotten closer, and she had to fight the urge to push him away like she had on Wednesday. But it also felt nice to see him seeing her. She'd assumed that she'd have to explain to Alejandro why Wednesday was such a huge mistake because she'd expected that he would be like her colleagues, not fully understanding the stakes she was up against. But he saw her, and the force of the relief she felt made her want to cry.

"Thank you," Deja replied after a too-long pause. "Thank you."

Alejandro smiled at her, tilting his head to the right, peering at her as if he was trying to understand the weight of those two words. "You're welcome," he said simply. As she watched, he scooted forward in his seat. He put his coffee cup on her desk and then splayed his hands out, palms down, in front of her.

Her eyes flickered down to look at them involuntarily. She shouldn't have done that, because as soon as she did — as soon as she saw his thick, stubby fingers against the sickly gray color of her metal desk — she remembered what they'd felt like inside her. She remembered how free she'd been in the throes of her orgasm and how strong his arms had felt as he'd held her through the reverberating quakes before they were interrupted. It had been so long since anyone had held her like that or at all.

"I want you to know," he said, butting into her trip down erotic memory lane, "that when I've dreamt about touching you, it was never here." He smiled at her, dirty and seductive and playful.

Deja's entire body began to warm again.

He shrugged and corrected himself slightly. "Well, sometimes we were here or sneaking around on campus. But those were the PG dreams, I promise," he laughed. "A little making out, nothing too risky."

Deja felt lightheaded. No man should be this charming and smart *and* dress so well. She was way out of her league. "You've been dreaming about me?" she croaked.

Alejandro's eyebrows lifted and then furrowed. "Of course, I have. You really didn't know I was interested in you?"

Deja shook her head. "I thought you were just being friendly."

He stood up and leaned fully across her desk. Those hands moved to either side of Deja's coffee cup, and his mouth was right there at eye height, tempting her.

Deja wanted to grab his face and pull him closer, but she couldn't do that — not again — so she fisted her hands in her lap instead.

"I promise you, I'm not that friendly," he whispered to her.

Deja felt every word of that sentence across her skin. His voice made her sex clench, her heart pound, and her temperature rise, and all she could think was that it should be illegal for anyone to make her feel so good with such little effort. She licked her lips, and his eyes tracked the movement.

And there was that little ethical dilemma again. She wanted to lean forward and kiss him. She wanted to taste his coffee order on his tongue and feel his five o'clock shadow against her skin, but if she did that, she could guarantee that in a few short minutes he'd have her sprawled across her desk, naked from the waist down and gleefully letting Alejandro play her like a fiddle. Literally. Again. And this time, someone would absolutely hear.

She sucked in a harsh breath. A groan slipped past her lips as she pushed her chair back from her desk, away from the temptation of his mouth.

Once again, Alejandro's eyes softened in understanding. "Don't worry. I made a promise. I won't touch you."

She huffed a laugh. "I'm more worried about myself right now."

He straightened, that sexy smile back on his face. "Good. Have dinner with me tonight?"

The past few minutes had been a lot for her to process, especially on a day when she usually only tried to think and failed. But as it happened, she didn't need much energy to think about her answer. In fact, she didn't need to think at all. She bit back a smile and nodded.

A look of relief washed over his face, as if he'd really thought there was even a sliver of a chance she'd turn him down. Just the thought of that made her smile widen.

"Alright, I'm going to go before I do something rash," he announced, standing up straight and smoothing a hand down his tie and then adjusting his belt buckle. Deja followed the path of his hand and licked her lips. "Yep, I need to get out of here."

She nodded absentmindedly, still watching his belt buckle.

He walked around her desk and leaned over her to dip his head. He brushed his mouth along hers in a chaste kiss.

She closed her eyes briefly and lifted her chin toward him as he pulled away, a small whimper falling from her lips. When she opened her eyes, he was smiling down at her. The man never stopped smiling, and she loved it.

She cleared her throat. "You said you'd keep your hands to yourself," she whispered.

He moved his head to brush his lips along her cheek to her ear. "I didn't say anything about my mouth," he whispered to her.

Deja's blood was pounding in her veins as she watched Alejandro snatch his cup from her desk and walk to the door. He turned to her, one hand on the doorknob, and winked before pulling the door open. He lifted his cup to his mouth to hide his smile, once again leaving her speechless and panting.

She slumped back in her chair with a foolish smile on her face.

SEVEN

FRIDAY NIGHT

Deja had been on pins and needles all day. She'd spent the faculty meeting that had actually pulled her onto campus on her day off, pretending as if she was paying attention to her colleagues fighting about next semester's enrollments, but really poring over Alejandro's brief email telling her that he'd pick her up at seven. She'd carefully sent him her address, looking seriously at her laptop screen so her colleagues might think she was taking notes on the meeting. And then she'd spent a solid twenty minutes trying to remember if her favorite little black dress was still at the back of her closet and if she could still fit into it.

When the meeting was over, instead of hanging around and listening to her colleagues' continued complaints or heading back to her office to grade, she practically ran home to her small apartment. And then, instead of spending a few hours walking in small circles around her home office, talking to herself — but not typing — she pulled every hanger out of her closet so she could try on every dress she owned. By the time she was done, she'd discovered that she could just fit into her favorite little black dress and had a trash bag full of clothes she couldn't or no longer wanted to wear. She took the rare opportunity to rearrange her entire wardrobe and stepped back with a brief satisfied smile. It wasn't a finished and submitted article, but a clean closet soothed Deja's jumping nerves.

She wasted an inordinate amount of time shaving and moisturizing herself from head to toe. How long it had been since she'd been on a date? Too long, was the closest she got to an answer.

How long since a man had taken her out for dinner and a movie? How long since someone she was attracted to told her she was beautiful while running his fingers along the circumference of her wrists with the lightest touch? Opened doors for her? Put his hand heavily at the small of her back after a glass of wine? Leaned in close so his cologne enveloped her? Looked at her with soft, enamored eyes like he couldn't think about anything else but kissing her?

Too. Damn. Long.

She mentally replayed an expedited version of her love life in the past few years alone and was bored. Her mood sagged as she shimmied into her dress and resisted the urge to change into something that covered her cleavage or didn't hug it so...tight. She did her makeup and refreshed her curls. When she stood back to look at herself in the full-length mirror hanging on the back of her bedroom door, she thought she looked like a version of herself she hadn't seen in Too Damn Long.

When Alejandro pulled up to her apartment, Deja wasn't watching him through the curtains in her living room window, but she wasn't *not* watching from the window. But since she was looking, she watched him stand from his car and sucked in a harsh breath.

He was in a casual suit...she thought. She didn't actually

know much about menswear except that Alejandro had always looked immaculate. This suit was dark blue, and once again, tailored within an inch of its life. The white shirt was so white it was either brand new, or he was using some kind of bleach normal people couldn't buy. He also wasn't wearing a tie, which made him seem less like a professor, and she appreciated that subtle change. And he capped it off with a pair of brown dress shoes that Deja normally wouldn't have bothered noticing except these seemed to accentuate that this man had big feet. Her eyes went to his groin briefly before she looked away.

Each step he took up to the front door of her apartment building was slow and measured, which meant she had plenty of time to appreciate the way his muscles rippled under his clothing. But when he was at the front door, bent over at the intercom system to look for her name, she saw that he had a nervous smile on his face, and that made her smile.

The buzzer rang, and even though she watched him press the button, she jumped.

She ran to the intercom. "Hello?" she squeaked.

"Deja? It's Alejandro."

His voice sounded amazing, even through the crackling intercom speaker that was at least thirty years old.

"I-I'm coming," she said.

"Take your time," he said, and her stomach burst into a nest of butterflies.

She took a deep breath as she stepped carefully into a pair of eggplant purple suede pumps that she hadn't worn in so long Too Damn Long didn't feel long enough. She grabbed her small wallet on a chain and threw it over her arm and grabbed her favorite pea coat before she opened her door.

She locked her apartment door and then turned to see Alejandro looking through the long pane of glass at her. She froze, caught off guard by the hunger in his eyes as he looked her up and down. She felt self-conscious for a second before his eyes lifted and he looked her in the face.

"Come on, Deja," he said with a smile.

She walked slowly to the front door and pushed it open a bit.

Alejandro pulled the door open fully for her, and he didn't even try to hide his interest as she walked out into the cool evening air.

"You look amazing," he said wistfully.

"It's just an old dress," she said, clutching her coat to her stomach.

"I can see why you kept it," he mumbled.

Deja's entire body was warming again. Apparently, Alejandro just had that effect on her. "You look great too," she whispered, too nervous to look him directly in the eyes.

He stepped forward, and his right hand settled on the small of her back. Deja sucked in a surprised breath. Alejandro leaned forward, and his mouth brushed her cheek and then moved to her ear. "Good. I dressed up for you."

Deja didn't know that a man telling her that could be erotic, but it absolutely was.

"Come on," he said, his hand flexing at her back, the weight of it sure as he led her to his car.

THE THING about being at a small university in a small Midwestern town like Centreville was that the closest good food, or museums or good stores, or bars or good music venues could be anywhere from thirty minutes to six hours' drive away, and that was the case for Deja's university.

In hindsight, she would have preferred a job in a slightly bigger city with more than cheap pizza joints within walking distance, but she'd only had one job offer, so she hadn't even had the chance to be picky. But the fact that Centreville was so small and students were everywhere had only deepened her isolation, and even though she could drive to more interesting places, she almost never did; she always had too much work. Those were at least the excuses she used to keep herself from actually getting a life, so when Alejandro hopped on the freeway to head out of town, she grinned so hard, her cheeks hurt.

They didn't talk much on the way to Port Wayne, the closest medium-sized city. Alejandro played some jazz, and Deja listened, sinking into the quiet and his soft leather seats. It should have been weird not to talk on a date, but she'd spent so much time not talking to Alejandro that it felt comfortable. The twenty-minute drive let her sink into the realization that she, Deja Evans, was on an actual date with Alejandro Mendoza.

By the time he pulled into a parking lot, just behind a stretch of bars and restaurants Deja always told herself she'd come to but didn't, she was still nervous, but not so much that she was worried the butterflies in her stomach might riot if he touched her again. He walked around his car to open her door and offered his hand to her.

She bit her bottom lip as she took it. His palm was warm, and he helped her to stand with a comfortable strength. He closed the door with his free hand and then stood in front of her, so close she had to tip her head back to make eye contact.

"Do you think I need my coat?" she breathed.

He smiled. "I volunteer to keep you warm," he said, and she believed him, she was already hot at his touch. "There's a little bar that I like here. I thought we could get a drink. And the best Mexican restaurant in like fifty miles is next door. How does that sound?"

It sounded great to Deja, but as he spoke, Alejandro had

stepped forward, backing her against his car with her body. She groaned instead of answering.

He laughed and moved his hand under her chin, gently tilting her head farther back and her mouth closer to his.

"We can go somewhere else if you—"

"That's fine," Deja breathed. "Kiss me?" Her voice was a throaty, husky whine. She'd never heard herself sound like that before or asked a man to kiss her.

He licked his lips. "Gladly."

Deja felt like she was in a whirlwind. A week ago, kissing Alejandro felt like an impossibility. Four days ago, letting him get her off in her office hadn't even been a thought in her head. And three hours ago, imagining that this kiss could be better than their first wasn't even in the realm of possibility, but it was.

His head dipped forward slowly. He brushed his mouth against hers gently, side to side and up and down, just letting their lips touch. And then he moved forward again, pressing his lips against hers and prying them open. He didn't hesitate to slip his tongue into her mouth, licking inside, tasting the moan he'd pulled from her. Her free arm flew to his waist, and she pulled him forward. He smiled against her mouth, tipping her chin up a fraction of an inch more with his hand to kiss her deeper, but still soft.

She wanted this kiss to last forever, all night, but all too soon, he pulled back. He swiped at his mouth with his thumb, smearing the trace of her lipstick from his mouth before wiping it away. There was something about her makeup on him that made Deja's blood pressure rise.

"Yeah," Alejandro breathed as if he knew every dirty thought in her head in that moment or maybe every dirty thought she'd ever had about him. "Come on." He pulled her gently forward by their still clasped hands and laced his fingers through hers in a tight grip.

He walked her slowly across the cobblestoned pathway toward the street, never rushing her and always with care. The entire night was like that. In the bar, he sat her at a table before grabbing their drinks. They sipped slowly and talked — steering as clear of work as possible — and he kept his hand at her back, rubbing slow circles over her spine. When their knees brushed, Deja flinched, but Alejandro simply scooted forward so his knees knocking hers every so often.

When they finished their drinks, he helped her carefully from the stool, and they walked next door. They didn't have to wait for a table even though the place was packed.

"I know the owner," he said, just as the hostess took them to a quiet booth in the back of the restaurant. Instead of sitting across from her, Alejandro slid onto the bench beside her, their knees brushing again. They read the menu together as he whispered his favorite dishes to her as if they were a love poem, his right hand resting on her thigh. She let him order for her, something she never normally did, simply because she liked the way his voice sounded in Spanish, and she liked the way he made her feel cared for.

Alejandro was the most eligible bachelor on campus not just because he was attractive and perfectly groomed but because he seemed unattainable, completely out of everyone's league. Deja had made a fantasy of him, imagining that he would be as perfectly calm and cool as he was on campus, but he wasn't quite that at all. He was a lot like the restaurant, actually; beautiful aesthetics but warm and unpretentious, and she found herself sinking into him. They talked and ate, and their legs rested together — her left kneecap to his right — and she forgot to be nervous as she came to know Alejandro as a person, not just a figment of her fantasies.

He paid for dinner, frowning at her suggestion that they go Dutch. He grabbed her hand again as they walked back to his car. The night was cooler now, and she leaned into his side for warmth. The skirt of her dress fluttered in the gentle wind, and she smoothed it with her free hand. Alejandro pretended not to notice the flash of her thighs, but she saw him lick his lips, and she leaned into him just a bit more.

It might have been too damn long since Deja's last date, but Alejandro obliterated the fuzzy memory of the last man she'd gone out with. Whatever that date had been like, this was better, and it was over too soon. Alejandro opened the passenger door for her, and as soon as her butt hit the seat, her mood started to plummet. She didn't want it to end.

Instead of taking the freeway back to Centreville, Alejandro took the slightly slower path home on the state road. It was a straight shot on a dark road with no lights, deer hazards, and whiteout warnings in the winter, and something about the darkness enveloping them soothed Deja's sadness at the end of their date. Alejandro held her hand over the center console as he drove, a wistful smile on his face, and more light jazz on the radio.

She turned in her seat to face him and moved their connected hands to her lap. The skirt of her dress slid up her thighs, and he took advantage at once, sliding the soft pad of his fingers along the inside of her knee. Deja shivered as goosebumps erupted on her skin.

At a red light, Alejandro turned to her. The headlights from an oncoming car illuminated a silver streak just at his temples and the beautiful angles of his face briefly.

"We're going to your place, right?" Deja suddenly blurted out. When she processed what she'd said, her eyes widened, and she licked her lips nervously.

Alejandro's hand covered her right knee as he barked out a laugh that Deja felt in the pit of her stomach. "I was trying to figure out how to invite you over," he chuckled. "So yes, Deja, we're definitely going to my place. Or we can go to your place if that'd make you feel more comfortable."

As he spoke, his hand flexed and gripped her leg. His thumb went back to caressing her skin, his touch calming and exciting at the same time. A moan escaped her lips before she could stop it.

He smiled innocently at her.

"Definitely not my place," she said in a strained voice. "My neighbors are all old and *very* nosy. As is, they'll be asking me about the 'nice young man' who picked me up." Her voice was light, but she actually hated how uncomfortably on display she sometimes felt living so close to campus. But when it came time to look for another place to stay, she struggled to find a place she liked and could afford, and that wouldn't add at least an hour of commute time to her day. Her apartment was just one more thing she hated about her life and felt unable to change.

But she didn't want to burden Alejandro with those feelings, especially not on their first date, so she buried them and smiled wider at him.

"Okay, my place it is," he said, pulling her from her sad thoughts with an easy shrug. "My neighbors are always high. They'll forget you were there almost immediately."

She laughed and relaxed into her seat with a soft smile on her face. As Alejandro's car accelerated, Deja watched his profile with slightly drooping eyelids as her hands moved over his forearm, and his hands caressed her legs.

She shivered under his touch. "I like that. I like you."

The car slowed. Alejandro's face reflected the glare of the bright red light at the intersection. As soon as the car stopped, he turned toward her. His smile was gone, but the look on his face was even better; sexy, seductive, promising. He leaned over the console toward her.

She wanted him to kiss her before the light changed, but

she also wanted him to take his time, and he did. His free hand wrapped around the column of her neck, and she let him pull her mouth to his. Before their lips touched, he took in a deep breath through his mouth, tasting the humid air between their lips. Alejandro shoved his tongue into her mouth as soon as their lips crashed together, and they both moaned.

Deja whimpered, tasting the promise of that kiss, even though it was over all too soon.

When he pulled back from Deja's mouth, he was smiling again. "I *more* than like you," he said, and then he turned forward to ease his foot off the brake as the light turned green.

IF ALEJANDRO HAD KNOWN that Deja was going to come over to his apartment, he would have hired a cleaning service or spent the afternoon straightening his apartment at least. He wished he could have left her on his front doorstep while he did so, but that only happened in movies, otherwise it was rude as hell. Thankfully, he wasn't a slob. He said a silent prayer of thanks that his mother sent him off to college with sage advice. "What woman wants to date a man who can't put his dirty boxers in the laundry basket, mijo?"

No woman. That was the answer she'd drilled into his head, and he'd learned by watching his college roommates' girl-friends scrunch their noses at their messy apartment, so he always kept his apartment presentable. Sometimes in the middle of a terrible semester, it got a bit chaotic, but this semester wasn't terrible, just regularly busy.

He held his breath as he opened his front door. He ushered Deja inside, exhaling nervously as he entered his apartment behind her, waiting for her to turn to him with a scrunched nose or judging eyes. She didn't.

Deja slipped out of her heels and walked slowly but curiously into his living room.

Alejandro toed off his shoes — something he *never* did — and followed behind her. "Do you want something to drink? I've got water, wine, beer. I can make you coffee if you want," he offered.

Deja turned toward him. She was holding her hands against her stomach, something he'd noticed she did when she was nervous. "Water's fine," she said in a soft voice.

He nodded and turned to the kitchen. He poured them each a glass of water and then closed his eyes, taking a couple of deep breaths to calm his nerves and his galloping heart. When he walked back into the living room, Deja was gone. Alejandro frowned. "Deja?"

"In your bedroom," she called back. His grip on each glass tightened, and his eyes widened.

The carpet muffled his steps down the hallway, but he felt each one as a boom in his ears. He took a deep breath before turning into his bedroom doorway and swallowed a moan when he saw her.

She'd dimmed the lights, bathing the room in a warmth that seemed to bounce from Deja's dark brown skin in brilliant swatches of orange that made every plane of her face and shoulders and calves seem severe and soft at the same time. Not for the first time since he'd met her, Deja's beauty slapped him in the face. Deja was the kind of beautiful that hurt.

Alejandro's heart pounded against his chest.

She was sitting at the foot of his bed, chewing at her bottom lip. She'd crossed her legs, and her right foot was bouncing in that familiar way he loved. Her eyes tentatively lifted to meet his gaze. "I was going to undress for you," she said quietly. There was just the slightest hint of a Southern drawl in her voice. He'd never heard that before, and it made his dick jump with interest.

"Why didn't you?" he rasped.

She licked her lips. "I thought that it would be more fun if you did that."

"Shit," he groaned.

Alejandro set the water glasses on top of his dresser and walked toward his bed, toward Deja. "I had no idea this date would end like this," he admitted in a shaky voice. He wondered if she could hear the need in his words.

"Me neither," she said, laughing nervously. "I-I hoped, though."

He smiled as he sat next to her, and his bed dipped a bit. "Yeah," he said, lifting his hand to brush a lock of her curly hair behind her ear, "I did too. This week has been..."

She smiled at him with wide eyes and dilated pupils, "The best fucking week I've had in a long while."

"Yeah. Me too."

Alejandro's hand lingered on her skin. He caressed her earlobe and then down her neck. She sucked in a harsh breath as his fingers moved along her collarbone, and his thumb dipped into the small depression at the base of her throat. He felt her swallow, and it made his balls ache.

"We can stop or slow down," he whispered.

"Is that what you want?" she asked, looking up at him through her eyelashes.

"I want what you want. I want you," he admitted.

She exhaled at those three words, and her eyes closed briefly.

"Fuck, you're beautiful," he said, his fingers ghosting over her décolletage, dipping just under the fabric of her dress to caress her cleavage.

"I don't want to stop," she breathed when she opened her eyes.

He was so relieved, and his dick began to swell, and then she stood from his bed. He watched her with eagle eyes as she stood in front of him, her hands going to her stomach. He opened his legs in a clear invitation.

She smiled down at him and moved between his thighs.

His face was level with her breasts, and his mouth watered at being so close to tasting new parts of her. She tentatively placed her hands on his shoulders and squeezed. He interpreted that small movement as a request for him to take control. He'd been waiting for that all night. He moved his hands to the backs of her knees.

Deja jumped. "I'm ticklish," she admitted.

"Noted," he said with a smile.

She swallowed loudly and started to pant softly. Alejandro watched her chest rise and fall as his hands drifted up the back of her legs. Her skin was soft and warm, and she trembled under his touch. She was perfect as far as he was concerned.

When his hands stopped at the back of her thighs, and he squeezed, she let out the sexiest whimper he'd ever heard, and he squeezed again.

Her hands moved over his shoulders before her fingers sank into the hair at his nape. Alejandro shivered and continued his exploration under her skirt.

He palmed the soft globes of her ass, and he squeezed her as well. "I like this dress," he whispered into her cleavage. "You never wear dresses to work."

Her fingers tightened in his hair. "You noticed what I wear?"

"I notice everything about you, Deja," he said, licking a path over her left nipple which had protruded slightly through her dress.

She shivered and moaned, and her fingernails scraped his scalp.

But when he looked at her, her mouth had turned down at the corners in an adorable frown. Her eyes skirted away from his as she spoke. "When I was a grad student, I wore a dress to class once. It was a hot as fuck spring day, and the building I was teaching in didn't have any air-conditioning. It was my favorite dress, professional, not too tight or short or anything. I had to give that lecture again the next week because all my male students spent the entire class staring at my legs like I had four of them or something. I haven't worn a dress on campus since."

Alejandro sighed and shook his head. He moved forward and pressed his mouth against her chest. "I'm sorry," he whispered against the fabric of her dress.

"You don't have to apologize," Deja said lightly. "But thank you."

He moved his hands from underneath her skirt and then smoothed it down her legs reverently. He placed a tender kiss on her shoulder and squeezed her waist, and he noted a small metal zipper at her left hip. He nudged it with his index finger and lifted his eyes to Deja's face.

She smiled shyly and nodded. "God, yes," she breathed.

Alejandro kept his eyes on her as he moved his index finger up the zipper until he found the pull, and then he moved it down her body. Her breathing got heavier, and her nipples seemed to get harder as the teeth of the zipper separated, and her dress loosened.

He nudged her backward as he stood. His hands moved toward her neck, and he slipped the straps of her dress over her shoulders. He dug just his fingertips under the fabric and groaned as he pushed her dress down her torso and over her hips until it fell in a heap at their feet.

Once she was standing in front of him in just her bra and lace underwear, Deja giggled and covered her face with her hands.

Alejandro grabbed her wrists gently and placed her palms against his chest. "Don't hide now. Where's the girl who invited herself over and into my bedroom? I liked her a lot," he teased.

She groaned when his hands moved to her ribcage as he leaned down to suck her bottom lip into his mouth.

It was his turn to groan as she dug her short nails into his pectorals before circling her arms around his neck and pulling his mouth closer. He smiled against her lips and kissed her in deep, strokes of his tongue with firm pressure from his lips as his hands moved around her back to the clasp of her bra.

Deja licked into his mouth and smiled back, tightening her arms around his neck, encouraging him to keep going.

He undid her bra with sure, warm fingers.

She let go of him just long enough to let her bra fall down her arms and fling it carelessly away. As soon as they were free, Alejandro cupped her small breasts with his hands, feeling the hard points of her nipples in his palms.

Goosebumps covered her skin, and she pulled his mouth to hers just as another moan escaped her lips.

He licked after that sound, wanting to taste every inch of her, planning to taste every inch of her. Before they could sink back into that kiss, he moved his hands back to her waist and spun her in his arms. He pulled Deja's body back against his and couldn't help but grind his growing erection against the curve of her ass. He'd been hard all night. Hell, he'd been hard since Wednesday, and just feeling her soft ass against his dick made him groan right into her ear.

She shivered and cupped the back of his head, keeping his mouth at her ear.

He moved his hands up her sides slowly, focusing on touching every bit of her skin.

"Fuck," she whispered.

"Soon," he breathed back with a smile against her cheek.

When his hand flattened on her stomach, they both tilted their heads to look down her body. They watched as his hands moved up to cup her small breasts, holding them, squeezing them, circling her areolas, teasing her, getting her off.

"Touch me," she pleaded.

"I am touching you, Deja."

She growled and whimpered in frustration, and he loved that unique mix of demanding submission. He rewarded her by moving his thumbs and index fingers to pinch her nipples, and she moaned so loud he felt it ripple through his body from the ends of his hair to the tip of his dick.

She squirmed in his hold as he alternated between pinching and rolling her nipples, grinding her ass back into him in desperation.

"Can you come like this?" Alejandro asked in a husky voice.

She shook her head quickly, desperately.

He nodded and kissed her softly on the cheek. He released her nipples, and she gasped for air with a whimper. Alejandro sank back onto the bed, pulling Deja into his lap. She tried to sit demurely, legs together, but he shook his head and clapped his palms against her thighs gently, but with enough force that the sharp sound filled the room. He pushed her legs open to bracket his thighs and then spread his own legs to open her further.

Deja squirmed in his lap and smiled excitedly.

Alejandro had spent so many nights thinking about what he would do if he ever got Deja Evans in his bed, and now that she was, he didn't want to miss a single opportunity. He wanted to feel every shiver and shudder, taste every moan, swipe his tongue along every part of her, and feel her wet excitement on his fingertips. Alejandro wanted to savor her after so long waiting.

He wrapped an arm around her waist and held her steady in his lap, and they both watched as his other hand charted a path between her breasts, over her ribs, and down her stomach. They watched as he swirled his index finger around her belly button.

Deja huffed out a breathy laugh.

"I didn't imagine you had an outie in my dreams," he said, absentmindedly.

"Guess you'll have to correct that the next time you dream about me," she panted.

His hand started to move again, playing with the edge of her underwear before he cupped her sex roughly.

She was grinding in his hold, and he reveled in the feeling of her weight on top of his dick as she rolled her hips, trying to press her pussy against his palm. "Please," she begged.

Alejandro could feel her wet pussy through her underwear, and he pushed his index finger into the wet fabric, between her folds, before finally moving the damp fabric aside. He kissed her shoulder as he ran two fingers up and down her sex. They were immediately coated in her juices.

Deja watched as he brought his hand to his lips and sucked them into his mouth.

"God, you're sexy," she moaned as she leaned forward to lick his fingers and lips, pulling a groan from his throat.

When he moved his hand back down her body, he was done going slow. He pushed those wet two fingers inside her at the same time as he sucked her tongue into his mouth. Her pussy shuddered around his digits as he pumped in and out of her with deep strokes.

She cried out when he added a third finger and ground the heel of his hand against her clit. Alejandro watched her face intently as he fucked her with his fingers. He drank in her cries and rubbed his fingertips against her soft, wet center when she began to quiet down. He wanted her loud and desperate. He wanted her to finally let go.

And then she did. "Fuck. Oh fuckfuckfuckfuck," she screamed in breathy whispers and then a final high-pitched moan.

He held her as she whimpered and shuddered and then went limp in his arms.

Alejandro squinted down at her. "Deja?" he said, pulling his fingers from her sex. "What the fuck?" he breathed into his quiet bedroom, Deja's soft snores rumbling from her chest.

EIGHT

Deja bolted awake, nearly naked and disoriented in a strange, but comfortable bed.

"Calm down, Deja," Alejandro whispered, reminding her of where she was.

She grabbed handfuls of his comforter and clutched it to her chest as she turned to him. Her brain was still sluggish from sleep, but it booted up quickly once she saw him reclining against his pillows next to her. He had a stack of essays in his lap, and a blue ink pen clutched in his right hand. While she was unconscious, he'd changed into a pair of gray sweatpants and a simple white t-shirt that hugged his pectorals and surprisingly built arms. She'd never seen him look so casual, not the one time she'd run into him at the grocery store and not even in his "casual" date attire. He was always so well put together that seeing him without a button-up shirt, or at least a crisp tailored pant made him look almost like an entirely different person; still fine as hell, but not quite so unattainable. But it was the glasses that did her in. She'd seen him in glasses before, every now and then, but somehow, in the soft light of his bedroom, in his white t-shirt and sweats, the thick black frames seemed to accentuate the soft planes of his cheekbones and his adorably round chin. They made his stubble seem darker, and his lips look fuller. The whole image made her want to crawl into his lap and gently take them from his face before she kissed the daylights out of him. The fact that she was waking up to that image of him in his bed didn't hurt either.

"How long was I asleep?" she asked in a small voice as she tried to calmly smooth her hair.

"Not long. About forty minutes," he said casually, putting the cap on his pen.

"Forty minutes. Fuck, I-I'm sorry. I don't usually fall asleep after foreplay. Or in stranger's beds. On the first date." She looked at her watch. "Before ten p.m.," she added, embarrassed.

She watched as he turned to place the essays and pen on the nightstand next to him. The muscles in his back moved deliciously under his t-shirt, and she realized that her mouth was dry. When he turned back around, he held a glass of water out to her.

"Drink this."

Her fingers brushed his as she took the glass from his hand. "Thanks."

"You don't have to apologize, by the way," he said. "It's been a long week. I had to take a nap after my last class to even be able to take you out to dinner, so I get it. We're old."

Deja swallowed water down her windpipe as she tried to laugh and swallow at the same time only to dissolve into a coughing fit.

Alejandro managed not to laugh at her as he took the water from her hand and rubbed her back, but his smile was adorable. "Sorry, no more jokes while you're swallowing." His voice was dry and teasing.

She rubbed the tears from her eyes and frowned. "Oh my

god, I'm a train wreck," she rasped. "I'm not usually this terrible a date." She looked at him with big wet eyes but then frowned. "Actually, I'm not sure that's true. I don't *think* I've ever been this bad before, but it's been a while. Maybe I'm rusty."

Alejandro's smile widened as Deja tried not to start coughing again and word-vomited about how sad her life was. And when she was done making a fool of herself — hopefully — he handed the glass back to her.

She took slow sips of water this time and refused to meet his eyes.

"This is the best date I've had in a while," he said, pulling her eyes back to his.

"That only makes sense if it's your first date ever," she quipped and then shook her head. "No, please don't respond to that. I don't actually want to know about your dating life. I'm not trying to pry. It's too much. Too soon."

"That's fine. We have a lot of time," he offered carefully. "But if you are ever interested, I'm an open book." The mattress depressed by Deja's right hip under his fist and the weight of his shifting body. Her eyes moved to his hand, so close to her bare leg, and she shivered. "In the meantime," he whispered, letting that sentence dangle between them. The air crackled with tension and possibility.

Deja lifted her eyes to his slowly. She felt self-conscious and unsure, but not in the way she normally did; feelings fed by loneliness and insecurity. No, the goosebumps slowly erupting on her body — starting on the hip closest to Alejandro's hand — were about anything but insecurity. If anything, when she locked eyes with Alejandro and saw the naked hunger in his gaze, and the almost casual, but deeply suggestive, smile on his face, she felt powerful for the first time, in ways she hadn't in years. And oddly enough, that power was more disorienting than feeling weak.

"Why don't you wear your glasses more often?" she blurted out.

"I prefer contacts," he said with a shrug. "Glasses make me look..." He let the sentence trail off with a sheepish grin and another shrug.

Deja's brow furrowed, and she tilted her head to the left, peering at him with disbelief. "Hot? Is the next word you were going to say hot? Or fine? Or beautiful? Sexy?"

A warm blush spread across his cheeks, and he bit his bottom lip to stem the laughter she could see building in his chest.

She was equal parts exasperated at him for insinuating his glasses weren't literally the equivalent of makeup on an already beautiful woman and charmed as hell by the shyness she'd never seen on his face before.

"No one's ever called me beautiful," he said, shifting that hand closer to her leg. He started rubbing circles on her skin again. She'd never been with someone so casually affectionate. She liked it, a whole fucking lot.

"Bullshit," she said in an airy whisper.

Alejandro chuckled lightly, and Deja's stomach clenched at the brief flash of his tongue between his lips. She lifted her hand to his face, settling her palm against his left cheek. Alejandro's laughter slowly petered away, and he rubbed his stubbled jaw against her palm.

"You changed without me," she whispered to him.

"I would have waited, but you were knocked out," he laughed. "You snore, by the way."

"Shut up. I wanted to undress you." She was never normally this forward, but at least this time, she'd meant to say those words, and Alejandro didn't make her regret them.

"I'm wearing clothes, and you're more than welcome to

take them off me." His hand moved over her thigh and slid down toward her hip.

"I wanted to take off your cufflinks and unbutton your shirt slowly, one button at a time. Sometimes that's all I can think about when we're in the Faculty Senate meetings, how I want to undress you painfully slow, so you'll fuck me the same way." Her face was hot with her admission. Deja had never been the type to talk dirty, but she liked to tell the truth. She meant every word she'd said to Alejandro, and there was more where that came from.

Alejandro's pupils slowly dilated as she spoke. "Next time," he croaked in a rough voice dripping with arousal.

"Promise?"

He swallowed, thick and loud, and then nodded. "I might have had that fantasy too."

Deja smiled and sat up on her knees, letting the covers fall from the vice grip of her left hand. Her nipples pebbled as the cool air hit her skin, and Alejandro's eyes widened as they did. Yeah, she felt powerful and wanted, and she never wanted this feeling to end.

"Stand up," she whispered.

Alejandro practically leapt to his feet in excitement.

Deja laughed and shook her head and then bent over to crawl to the edge of the bed toward him.

He groaned and cursed under his breath.

She slipped her hands under the hem of his t-shirt and slid her palms over his abs and up his ribs and his chest. She straightened to pull his t-shirt over his head. She kept her eyes on his as she bent forward, lowering her mouth to his stomach. She placed soft kisses on each of Alejandro's ridiculously defined abs and then moved her mouth up his chest. She let her tongue move through the hair dusting his chest until they were face to face.

She watched him as she pushed his sweatpants down his legs with a smile. It was his turn to pant in anticipation, although he didn't beg the way she had. At least, not yet.

He wasn't wearing any underwear, and she sat back on her heels with an appreciative smile and a groan. She'd never had a better view.

"Deja," Alejandro said in a choked voice. It wasn't a plea, but his voice sure was strained.

She didn't look at his face, couldn't tear her eyes away from his thick dick as it slowly grew before her eyes like magic, like intensely lustful magic.

When looking would no longer suffice, she gently cupped his length from underneath, cradling it in the palm of her hand as if it was precious, squeezing him gently. And then she leaned forward to run her tongue over the head and up the top of his shaft.

Alejandro hissed.

As she licked him from tip to root again and again, his legs tensed, and his body began to shake. She had no idea what any of these muscles were, but watching them spasm as she used her tongue to tease him was a definite highlight of the night. She finally lifted her eyes again so she could watch his face when she sucked just the head of his penis into her mouth.

"Dammit," he hissed, grabbing onto his head as if he were falling apart.

"I really hope you have condoms," she whispered against the mushroom crown of his shaft.

"I bought two boxes after Wednesday," he admitted in a rush.

"Gotta love a man who's prepared," she said, sitting back on her heels.

Alejandro laughed and pushed her onto her back, gently but still urgently, covering her body with his.

Deja moaned at all their skin connecting, and his tongue in her mouth. He kissed her until she was squirming underneath him and scratching at his back and circling her panty-covered pussy against his groin.

He tore his mouth from hers just long enough to pull open the drawer in his bedside table with a bit too much force. He lifted onto his knees and tore the box of condoms open while Deja shimmied out of her underwear, accidentally kicking Alejandro in his side to get it over her knees and off one leg.

"Oof," he huffed.

"Fuck, sorry," she said.

His only answer was laughter and to push her legs apart again so he could look at her slit as he rushed to roll the condom down.

She found that she liked his eyes on this part of her body and moved her hand between her legs, touching her sensitive folds for their pleasure.

His hand tightened over the head of his dick as he tried to stave off a release, and she slipped her middle finger into her warm pussy for the opposite reason.

"Fuck, Deja," he whispered.

"I love it when you say my name like that," she breathed.

He grabbed her right thigh, squeezed, and pushed it down toward the bed, opening her fully to him. "Like what?" he asked.

"Like I'm making it hard for you to stay calm," she said as she moved her wet finger along her lips to circle her clit just as the tip of Alejandro's dick tapped at her opening.

"Fuck!" Her moan was a shouted, surprised, but satisfied cry.

"That's exactly how I feel," he said and then pushed inside her in one long, slow press.

When he was in her to the hilt, he grabbed her other thigh and squeezed, pushing her thighs to the bed.

The spread hurt deliciously. She'd never felt so exposed or so full as she did in that moment. "Shit," she breathed.

"Yeah," he whispered back to her, and she could hear that he was as far gone as her.

"Keep touching yourself," he demanded, his eyes shifting between her face and between her legs where he was filling her up.

Deja was more than happy to obey. She gently rubbed at her clit as Alejandro began to pump into her as slowly and deliberately as he seemed to do everything else.

She felt every inch of him enter until his balls rested against her ass and then retreat, her own sex pulsing and clenching at him to keep him inside. Deja hadn't had bad sex before him per se, but she'd never had anyone work her over so thoroughly before. It was exquisite.

But she wanted to feel his weight on top of her again. She moved her finger down her lips, and then, when he was almost fully inside her, she grabbed him at the base and squeezed.

"Holy fuck," he hissed and doubled over her. His fingers dug into her thighs, and she wondered if it would bruise and how she might feel about that.

Next time, she thought to herself and pulled him on top of her.

His hips jerked, and he started fucking her from this new angle, not as deep but harder. She slipped her finger into his mouth so he could taste her pussy. When he released her finger, she cradled the back of his head — scratching gently at his scalp — and pulled him into another kiss. She didn't think she'd ever get sick of kissing him.

Alejandro's lips slowly caressed Deja's mouth, and his

tongue massaged her own as he rocked his hips against her in hard thrusts that made her moan each time.

They fucked each other slowly for what felt like hours until their bodies were covered with sweat, and their moans mingled in their kiss, and Deja's body was shuddering with her coming orgasm.

"You're close. I can feel it," he groaned against her mouth.

She was too incoherent to do anything but nod.

Alejandro wedged his hand between their bodies and settled his thumb over her clit. Deja broke. This orgasm was no less intense than the last; there had been too much wanting and waiting between them, and one orgasm wasn't enough; there might never be enough to sate over a year of need. So it was a good thing he never let up. He fucked her through that release, groaning as her pussy fluttered and clenched around him, enjoying the ripples of her climax. And when she seemed to be coming down, he moved harder against her and increased the pressure of his thumb on her clit until she came again. And then he went through the whole routine again, fucking and teasing her until she came and then spinning her back up again. She couldn't do anything but scream and scratch at his back in desperation.

When he was close, though, he shoved his hands between her ass and the mattress. He grabbed a cheek in each hand and squeezed as he started to fuck her harder than ever, using his hold on her to jerk her hips into his.

Deja hadn't thought she could fall apart anymore, but she did. She became a screaming mess as he chased his release inside her. She wrapped her arms around his shoulders and pulled his mouth to hers again. Their kiss was sloppy and full of her cries and his grunts and teeth and tongue as he came apart on top of her.

She locked her ankles behind his ass, in no hurry to break

the embrace. She liked the feel of his damp body on hers and his dick inside her, but most of all, she loved the way his heart was pounding so hard and fast she could feel it in her own chest.

Deja knew they'd have to get up eventually, at least to throw the condom in the trash. But when Alejandro's body relaxed, and he settled his full weight on top of her, she knew that she wouldn't be the one to force them to do it. She'd never felt safer than she did with Alejandro on top of her and his mouth ghosting over her cheeks.

NINE

THE MORNING AFTER

Maybe other, better-adjusted people could wake up the morning after finally hooking up with their crush and feel energized, ecstatic, maybe even horny.

Deja was not one of those people.

Her eyes blinked open, and her vision filled with Alejandro's shoulder and bare chest. She was painfully near-sighted without her glasses or contacts, and she could feel her contacts sticking, dry and painful, to her eyelids. She knew she'd pay for having slept in them just as soon as she got home, but Alejandro was close enough to her that she could see the trail of brown freckles across his right shoulder. She watched as his chest rose and fell in deep, slow breaths and unconsciously calibrated her breathing to match his. She had the urge to run her fingers over those freckles and through the soft hair across his chest and then down his stomach, followed by her mouth, but she stopped herself, suddenly unsure.

She'd been single for so long that she'd deluded herself into thinking dating would be easy once she tried again. She'd spent years spinning yarns in her head about what it would feel like when she met the right person, romantic fantasies that grew more elaborate and unrealistic as the rest of her life became more and more stressful. The point wasn't to prepare herself to date again, her fantasies that were distractions; Deja didn't believe the right person existed. That's why it had been so easy to pour her desires into Alejandro; he was a walking fantasy, but apparently, he was even better in person, even better than she, Toni, and Marie thought.

But the insecurity that seized her wasn't about Alejandro; it was about herself. He might have been a great dresser, smooth talker, down-to-earth, amazing kisser, and damn good in bed, but she was just regular old, overworked, burnt-out Deja, and in the sunshine coming through his bedroom window, she knew that she was punching way above her weight with him.

Instead of touching or kissing Alejandro like she wanted to in the first gasp of consciousness, Deja started inching toward the edge of the bed, ready to run. She didn't have a concrete plan, but if there was anything she'd become adept at since graduate school, it was winging it. That's what she did when she had to lecture about a topic she didn't know much about or had to teach a class she'd never taught before. The trick was that she only had to know more than her students and to speak clearly and authoritatively, and she only needed to be a week ahead of them in the readings on the syllabus. And if she failed...well, she'd failed a lot, and it had become a familiar state of being.

There wasn't a syllabus for slinking out of her crush's bed the night after great sex, but she could scoot out of bed with determination; that seemed like a good start. All she had to do was get out of bed, find enough of her clothes so she didn't get arrested for indecent exposure, slip out the front door without waking him up, run half a block away, and call a cab. Easy. She could do that, she thought, and then she fell halfway out of bed and banged her knee on the hardwood floor with a loud yelp.

Failure again.

Alejandro grunted awake and sat up, rubbing his eyes. "What's happening?" he asked to no one in particular.

Deja sighed. He was adorable with his hair mussed from sleep and just curling at the ends. And his voice was a solid A+ first thing in the morning and made her sex quiver, battling her aching knee in intensity.

"I was trying to sneak out," she admitted, still half-hanging out of bed. She rested her chin on the mattress and frowned.

He grabbed his glasses from the bedside table and shoved them onto his face. Deja looked away; he was too much.

"Were you trying to sneak to the bathroom, or were you leaving?" he asked with a serious frown on his face that he probably used when asking his students why they hadn't done the assigned reading.

"Leaving," she mumbled.

"Were you going to leave a note?"

She shook her head.

"That's cold, Deja."

She bit her bottom lip. "I think I freaked out a little... A lot. I freaked out a lot."

"And then you fell out of bed?" he asked. She could hear the laughter in his voice.

"This is very typical pathetic behavior from me," she said.

He grabbed her hand, and she let him slowly pull her back onto the bed.

"Ow. I hurt my knee," she whined, rubbing at it once she was sitting on the bed again.

Alejandro lost the battle not to laugh at her, and she smiled. It was funny. And pathetic.

He brushed his fingers over her kneecap. "Just so you know,

I sleep like a rock most of the time. You could step on me, and I won't wake up, but loud sounds...yeah, that wakes me up."

Deja sighed again. "Good to know."

He leaned over and kissed her temple. "Next time," he whispered, and her stomach flipped. She turned to see him smiling at her. "Stay here. I'll get you some ice."

She nodded mutely and watched as he stood from the bed. The covers fell from his body, and he didn't bother to cover his nakedness as he looked around the floor for his sweatpants. She was almost sad to see him dressed, but he looked so sexy with the pants hanging low on his hips and his muscled body covered in a light dusting of dark black hair everywhere. The heat of shame and failure burned away as the desire to touch him washed over her again.

He stopped in the bedroom door and turned back to her. "I don't think you're pathetic, by the way."

"I do," she shot back.

"Don't. If you feel the need to run again, just leave a note. Please," he said quietly and winked at her before leaving the room.

"Fuck, he's perfect," she breathed.

"I'm really not," he called from the hallway with a laugh.

"You heard that?"

"These walls are thin as fuck."

Deja's entire body warmed, and she buried her face in the closest pillow.

Alejandro wasn't just as great as she'd thought; he was better.

TEN

NOVEMBER

"Alright, there'll be a special faculty meeting to go over the applications for the job candidates. I'm sorry to have to schedule this during finals week, but we really don't have much time before the semester is over, and we don't want to do this through email," Sheila said.

Alejandro didn't groan, but he sympathized with whichever one of his colleagues had. "That week is a scheduling nightmare," he said, giving voice to the tension filling the room.

"I know, but it's either this or ask you all to either stay in town for or video conference in during your winter break."

"Not an option," Marcus Ford said to Alejandro's left. "I'm posting my final grades from the airport, and then it's a complete technology blackout until two days before spring semester. Marriage retreat. Sasha and I have been looking forward to this all year," he said with a wide smile on his face.

"Why?" Alejandro asked with a laugh.

Marcus shoved his shoulder playfully.

"I agree. I've got a ten-hour drive ahead of me after my last exam. Schedule the meeting, that's fine with me," Rachel

Bloom said. "As long as I don't have to postpone my trip home, I'll agree to anything."

Even though everyone was annoyed at adding one more meeting to their schedules, this was the best-case scenario. Alejandro nodded at Sheila just as his phone vibrated. It was a reminder for *yet another* meeting. Normally, he hated days like this, where he had to rush from meeting to meeting with barely enough time to think or breathe, but when he shoved his laptop into his shoulder bag and stood from the conference table, he felt a frisson of excitement shoot up his spine.

How could he feel any other way? He was about to see Deja.

Never mind that it hadn't even been a month since the last Faculty Senate meeting, and they were already gathering again just so the university could waste one more afternoon in the most boring way before the end of the semester. Never mind that he still had three final exam sheets to write and a stack of quizzes to grade and return, he still couldn't help feeling a kind of ridiculous excitement at knowing he'd have two uninterrupted hours in a room with Deja.

They'd been dating for a few weeks, even though they hadn't called it that yet, but they'd only had time to properly go out on a date twice since their first, and each time they had, they hadn't been able to go farther than the burger joint down the street from campus; the one that the faculty and graduate students preferred, not the undergrad dive. Alejandro was somehow chairing three different committees in his department, sitting on the Faculty Senate, and teaching three classes; he was the faculty advisor for the Latino/a/x Student Union and secretary for the faculty union, and that was before he'd agreed to co-chair a committee with Deja, which would put who knew how much work on his plate next semester. It wasn't that they didn't want to go out more, it was that they didn't have time, so they made the most of every minute they could be together, including the Faculty Senate meeting.

He rushed to the student union with the goofiest grin on his face. As soon as he stepped into Go Brews! to grab an espresso before the meeting, he saw Deja. She was last in line, her cell phone in her hands, fingers flying across the screen, looking stressed. Deja always looked stressed. Now that he was around her more, he realized that she tended to fill every down moment with work. She woke up early some mornings to grade, even if she hadn't gotten enough sleep the night before or she never went to sleep at all, she worked through weekends unless they had plans together, and she responded to student emails while waiting in line for coffee, and all he wanted to tell her was that she could just...not. She could let an email sit in her inbox for an hour or two, or twenty-four if it wasn't urgent. He wanted to tell her that it was okay to prioritize her mental health and give herself some slack, but she was pre-tenure and sensitive about any feedback on her job performance or ability to cope with the demands of the job, even though she knew the demands were sometimes outrageous. And Alejandro had been struggling to find the right balance between concern and over-bearing and figure out the best way to support her the way he wanted.

He rushed into line behind her. He wanted to wrap his arms around her and kiss her, but she'd hate that, and he'd promised to keep his hands to himself after last month. They'd agreed to be discreet while on campus, yet another reason why it had been difficult to spend time together.

He looked around to make sure that he didn't see anyone that he readily recognized before clasping his hands behind his back and leaning over her shoulder.

"Te extrañé," he whispered into her ear and felt her shiver.

She turned to him with wide eyes, and it made his blood

rush. It had only been a month, and that wasn't enough time for the excitement at finally being able to flirt with her the way he wanted to fade, even if he still couldn't touch her in public.

"I don't know what that means," she whispered.

"It means I missed you."

She bit her bottom lip to try and hide her smile. It didn't work. "Someone might see us," she mumbled.

He stood up straight and shrugged innocently. "We're just talking."

She bit down on her lip, and he had to look away, or else they wouldn't just be talking. "Line's moving," he coughed.

It took Deja a second to register his words, and when she did, she ducked her head and stepped forward. Alejandro snaked his arm around her side and squeezed her waist quickly. He hoped he'd moved fast enough that no one had seen, but if they had... Touching Deja would always be worth it.

"Let me buy you coffee," he said as the line inched forward.

She shook her head.

He rolled his eyes. "Colleagues buy each other coffees and lunches all the time. No one will think twice about it."

"But..."

He raised his eyebrows at her, and she smiled shyly.

She chewed her bottom lip for a few more seconds. "Fine."

"Doc," someone said. "Excuse me, Doc."

Alejandro and Deja turned to see Jerome Miles standing next to them in line.

"Oh, hey, Dr. Mendoza, what's up?"

"You two know each other?" Deja asked.

"Yeah, I've been to a couple LSU discussion forums as the BSU rep," Jerome said.

"Jerome always has great contributions," Alejandro said and watched as the student smiled and ducked his head. "How do you two know each other?"

Jerome's entire face lit up. "Doc's my advisor. She's the best."

Alejandro looked down at Deja. "Yeah, she is," he said, unable to keep the wistful notes from his voice.

"Next," the cashier called.

"That's us," Deja said, clearly desperate to change the subject, as she always was when there was too much attention on her.

"I got you," he said. "You and Jerome go ahead and talk."

"Alright, bet," Jerome said.

Deja frowned at Jerome. "Boy, what now?"

Alejandro shook his head and laughed as he walked away to order, but he turned back to see Deja, her entire demeanor changed.

She'd crossed her arms in front of her chest and was looking up at Jerome with skeptical eyes. Her demeanor was stern but playful as she gave her student her full attention. Alejandro wished Deja could see herself the way he and her students did.

———

DEJA WASN'T nervous so much as freaking the absolute fuck out as she and Alejandro walked across campus to Founders Hall. Together. If it weren't for Jerome talking her ear off and giving her something to focus on, her legs might have just stopped moving. They'd been...doing something for a few weeks, and she was too nervous to name it even in her own brain, but she knew that just being near him made her heart race. Under normal circumstances — i.e., not on the campus of the university where they worked or in the college town where they lived alongside their colleagues and students — kind of dating a man who made her heart race would be a great thing, but it wasn't. Every time she saw him, she had to bury the urge to touch him the way she wanted or even look at him for too long just in case someone else might see desire written all over her face. Or maybe it was that Deja's fatalistic personality wouldn't let dating Alejandro be a great thing because she couldn't let herself be happy, as Toni had suggested. Either way, Deja felt like every eye on the University Oval was on her as they walked to Founders, and it was nerve-wracking.

Thank god for Jerome.

"So, what if I did a double major in Sociology and Statistics and a minor in Communications?" he asked her after a very long preamble that she hadn't heard this time but assumed was the same as the other major-minor configurations he'd presented to her for comment. Lots of sophomores struggled with their academic path, and Deja's job was to help gently guide them toward a decision and then to the administrative building to submit the paperwork. Usually, she wanted to tear her hair out when confronted with students who hadn't given their majors or minors much thought and just expected her to tell them what to do with the rest of their college careers and sometimes their lives. That *wasn't* her job, and she didn't want that kind of responsibility ever.

Jerome also made Deja want to snatch herself bald but because he was giving his majors and minors *too much* thought. She hadn't even known that was possible, but it seemed he was in her office every other week with the idea of picking up another major or two minors or a certificate program and on and on and on, and asking Deja to run through the next two years of class schedules and help him research post-graduate career paths. It was frustrating and inspiring. Deja knew Jerome wanted to make the most of his time in college. He didn't want to miss a thing, and she wanted to make sure he didn't, but she also wanted him to settle on a second major or minor or whatever so he could finish his prerequisites and not add another semester or year to his time there. She also wanted him to leave her alone about this, but she couldn't say that.

"Stats will add another year of math," she reminded him. "You can take some of them over the summer at a community college, so this might affect your ability to work when you go home. Also, you need to rest as much as you can between semesters. I keep telling you this."

"I know, Doc, but I gotta save money for books and stuff," he said, his face scrunching in concentration as he tried to figure out how to process this new information.

They walked in silence for a bit. Deja understood Jerome's position well. Like him, she'd been a first-generation college student. She'd worked a part-time job during the semester and a few part-time jobs in the summer to save money. She'd spent all her free time in the library reading her assigned work and more because she was terrified that one day in class her professors would make a reference to something — a book, an author, a concept — that she didn't know but all of her classmates would, and she'd be crushed by the weight of her inadequacy. She understood Jerome's impulse to take every class, do everything, read everything, see everything, but she also knew what would happen if he spent the next three, five, or ten years with that kind of frenetic desire.

He'd turn into her.

And even though he *thought* she was amazing, she felt anything but. She missed the kind of passion for her work Jerome was still cultivating. She missed feeling like she was learning things that would help the people she cared about and the communities she lived in. She missed when she didn't need a pot of coffee to feel as if her brain was firing on almost all cylinders. She missed not having to pay extra to thin her glasses lenses. She missed not feeling tired all the time. She missed feeling like herself, whoever that was these days. And if she only did one useful thing this academic year, she wanted to save him from a fate like hers, but he wasn't making it easy. After months of trying to explain why he needed to dial back and make time to rest because those things were important — maybe even more important — than choosing the perfect combination of majors and minors, she was still struggling to get through to him.

"What do you want to do when you graduate?" Alejandro asked.

Jerome looked sheepishly at Deja and shrugged.

"He's not sure yet," Deja answered for him.

"Good," Alejandro said, and Deja and Jerome turned to him in shock.

He smiled and shrugged. Jerome's shrug had made Deja think of her nephew, the way he shrugged when his parents asked him if he understood why he was in trouble. But Alejandro's was from a completely different realm; his movements were languid and unpretentious, and the smile on his face was effortlessly charming.

Oh, she thought to herself, this is way more than a crush.

Alejandro smiled at Jerome for a brief second before his entire demeanor shifted from affable colleague to professor.

"The minute you get here, we tell you that you have to have the next four years planned out, and two years after that would be even better. It's not really fair, but if we're being honest..."

He leaned across Deja toward Jerome, and she felt like a small child since they were both nearly half a foot taller than her. She rolled her eyes and shook her head.

"You can't tell anyone I said this," Alejandro continued, "but it's really not necessary to be *that* prepared. Take whatever classes you want. You can change your major as many times as you want to. There's no penalty. But you want to have a plan. Declare a major, look at your degree audit, see what classes you still need, and if you won't have room for the things that matter to you like BSU or your work schedule or study abroad, if you want to do that, then maybe that's not the degree path for you." And then he smiled at Jerome again. "It's actually not a secret, you can tell all your friends."

"That's what Doc's been saying," Jerome said, even though he was nodding his head and looking at Alejandro as if he'd never heard any of this before.

"Glad to know you've been listening to me," she mumbled.

"I listen," Jerome said with a sheepish grin, "but it's just hard not to feel like I'm wasting time and not doing enough, you know."

Oh, Deja could relate to every part of that sentence. She felt her face scrunching with concentration.

"The thing to remember about college is that this isn't your entire life, it's just one phase of many," Alejandro said. "You're here to learn as much as you can and not just in the classroom. Sometimes the thing you need to learn is balance. You can take all the classes and double, even triple major if you want to, but when you're burnt out at graduation and can't even enjoy all the things you've accomplished, you'll regret it."

"So, what do I do?" Jerome asked.

"Give yourself the rest of the academic year. Don't make any decisions until the summer. Until then, take classes in your prereqs with majors you *might* like without commitment. Then, when the year is over, and you're back home and *resting*," he said, his eyes flicking mischievously to Deja, "then you can decide what you want your majors and minors to be."

Deja had said some version of this to Jerome before, and she held her breath, waiting to see if this time it would stick. She watched Jerome's face scrunch again. They were almost at Founders Hall, and they really needed to get into the auditorium to get good seats, but if Alejandro echoing advice she'd been giving Jerome almost weekly was enough to make it stick, Deja would be late. Happily.

In front of Founders, Deja stepped onto the first step so she could be almost at eye level with Jerome and Alejandro.

"What do you think, Doc?" Jerome asked.

There was a part of Deja that just wanted to mother her students, especially her Black students who had no idea how to navigate the university. She wanted to wrap them in a blanket and fight all their battles, but she couldn't do that. Most of them had mothers to do that, and most crucially, mothering wasn't her area of expertise. Her job was to advise them and prepare them as best she could for the world off-campus, which meant she couldn't make decisions for them. She could support them in making these decisions for themselves but no more, and sometimes, it was hard to keep that boundary.

"I think," she said and then took a calm breath, "that Dr. Mendoza and I have a meeting right now, and you have to get to the Writing Lab."

Jerome checked his watch, and his eyes widened, but he didn't rush away. Instead, he looked back at Deja as if waiting for her to dismiss him. He looked so amazingly young in that moment.

"How about you think about what Dr. Mendoza recommended, and then come to my office hours *next week* to talk," she said; otherwise, Jerome would be at her office hours the next day with a pros and cons list.

He smiled at her and nodded. "Alright, I can do that. I've got a paper to write this weekend, anyway."

Deja smiled, "Good. Now go, before you're late."

"Bye, Doc," he said, already turning. "Bye, Dr. Mendoza."

"Bye," Alejandro called after him.

"Put a hat on," Deja yelled, shivering as the wind blew, and flurries started to fall. Okay, maybe she could give them a little mothering.

Jerome didn't turn around, but Deja watched as he dug his beanie from the pocket of his winter coat and shoved it onto his head.

She sighed in relief and then turned to find Alejandro watching her.

"You're good at this. You know that, right?" he said.

Deja shook her head and started up the steps. "This is the job," she said, deflecting.

Alejandro chuckled and jogged up the steps to open the door for her. "We both know that not everyone would care what Jerome majored in or about his mental health. This *is* the job, but not everyone's doing it."

Deja avoided his eyes as she walked through the door. She knew he was right, but she couldn't accept it — she couldn't accept the compliment — because at the end of the day she was worried that it wouldn't be enough; no one would care that she cared about Jerome's sleep schedule and if he wore a hat or about all the hours she spent career planning with him or her other sixty advisees. They both knew that Deja could be the best academic advisor and teacher — she wasn't, but she could be — and the university could still deny her tenure because she hadn't published nearly enough articles. Teaching and advising and service were most of her job but not enough to guarantee that she could keep it, and that incongruity was at least eighty percent of her stress.

A part of her wanted to round on Alejandro and tell him that this wasn't the pep talk she needed. As much as she enjoyed Jerome, her colleagues would argue that she should spend less time mentoring, and more time writing, as if it was that easy. She wanted to tell him that she needed to hear that she was a good academic, not a good mentor, but she didn't, because none of this was his fault, certainly not her inability to write. But she also kept her mouth shut because she was terrified that if she exposed her anxieties to him and exposed how overworked and unproductive she was — and how much anxiety it was causing her — he wouldn't be able to give her the pep talk she needed. It was one thing to see pity in Toni or Marie's eyes, but it would undo her to see it in Alejandro's. Deja knew herself, and she knew that if she saw even a flicker of pity in his eyes, that one look would overwrite all the other flirtatious and dirty looks he gave her, and she wasn't ready to lose that.

So she kept her mouth shut as they walked up to the auditorium. They snatched their name tags from the table by the door and walked toward the seating area. They weren't as early as Deja liked, but there were still a few seats in the top tier. She tried to find three seats together that she could grab for herself, Toni, and Marie when Alejandro's hand cupped her elbow.

"Mike saved us seats, come on," he whispered to her.

She felt that whisper and his touch through all her layers of clothes and her winter coat in the warm room, and it slowed her response. By the time she could think to remind him that she always sat with Toni and Marie, he was already pulling a seat out for her.

"I...um...maybe I shouldn't," she mumbled.

He was pulling his winter coat off, and the movement made his tight button-down shirt pull taut over his abs. Abs, she remembered in that moment, she still hadn't traced with her tongue.

She had to look away quickly before she did something reckless. She started searching the crowd for her friends, thinking maybe she could slink off to sit with them before the meeting started.

She spotted Toni's big braided bun bobbing through the

crowd and then saw Marie trailing behind her. She watched as they snagged the last two seats across the auditorium on the highest tier, and they pulled their coats off. Deja willed them to look up at her, and then Marie did. Deja watched as Marie whispered to Toni, who looked up, searching the crowd before her eyes met Deja's briefly. Her gaze slid to Deja's left, where Alejandro was just sitting down, chatting with Mike. Deja watched as Toni smiled mischievously and then turned back to Marie, speaking quickly.

Deja couldn't hear her from so far away, but she could guess what that conversation was like, and she slumped down in her chair, feeling suddenly like everyone was looking at her and Alejandro.

"I HATE THIS," Deja said, watching her friends whisper to each other across the room as they shared a tin of what looked like a batch of Toni's oatmeal cookies. Deja's favorite.

"I know," Alejandro whispered to her. "No one really cares about the directory, but once a year, we really have to have an entire discussion about it, and nothing even changes."

Deja turned to him and squinted in confusion. "Huh?"

He smiled at her, also confused, and then gestured at the podium at the front of the auditorium.

Deja followed the direction of his hand and frowned. She rolled her eyes when she saw Gerald Lehman at the podium. Every year, he showed up to ask the Faculty Senate to get rid of the faculty and student directories in a long meandering speech about privacy issues, and every year, someone would explain how it was an emergency response issue or something, and he would get voted down. As soon as Deja saw his name, on the schedule the Senate secretary had emailed two days ago, she'd blocked it out of her brain. Too boring.

"Not him," she said, turning back to her friends. "Them."

It was Alejandro's turn to follow her direction. "What's wrong?"

She looked at him and rolled her eyes again. "They're over there with cookies, and I'm over here, without cookies."

His shoulders relaxed, and he smiled. "I've got a granola bar in my bag."

She wanted to roll her eyes one more time, but his smile was adorable and so earnest that it made her heart clench. "We can share it," she said.

"Deal." She watched as he bent over to rummage in his bag.

Her phone lit up with a text message. It was Toni. Of course.

CUTE. A. F.

Deja's face warmed, and she flipped her phone screen down on the table. She lifted her head to glare at her friends until Alejandro bumped into her arm.

"Sorry," he said. "I've got good news and bad news."

She sighed. "No granola bar?"

He slid a granola bar onto the table. "Granola bar is the good news."

"Then what's the bad news? Is Gerald going to bust out another PowerPoint?"

"That would be the worst news. No, the bad news is that it's broken," he said, shaking the package a few times to illustrate his point. He cringed at her. "Sorry."

She reached for the package, and the tips of their fingers touched. She carefully opened the wrapper, splitting it down the foiled seam, and then placed it on the table between them.

"It's easier to share this way," she whispered, tilting her head so no one — Alejandro, Toni, and Marie, especially — could see her smile.

Alejandro leaned back in his chair, raised his eyebrows at her, and leaned over to press his arm against hers. "Look at you, being optimistic," he teased. Deja laughed and then bit her lips shut. Alejandro bent over and whispered directly into her ear. "I like the way this looks on you."

She frowned and dropped her chin to her chest to look at her boring gray sweater and blue jeans.

"Happiness," he corrected. "I've always loved the way you smile."

Deja sucked her bottom lip into her mouth as he pulled back and smiled down at her, his own bottom lip clenched between his teeth.

Deja heard her phone vibrate against the table, but she ignored it. Unfortunately, they couldn't ignore Alejandro's friend Mike, who sat on his other side.

"Is that a communal granola bar?" he asked, leaning into Alejandro.

"No. Bring your own snacks," he said, pushing the granola bar closer to Deja. "I tell you that every month."

Deja grabbed a shard of the granola and popped it into her mouth. She reached for her cup of coffee and then plucked up the nerve to check her phone again, not surprised to see another text message, this one from Marie.

GET A ROOM! ;)

ELEVEN

SATURDAY

Alejandro didn't believe in working through the weekends. Ever.

He'd done enough of that during graduate school to know that it wasn't worth it; his brain needed time to reset. He'd had to bend the rule every now and then while he was on the tenure track, but now that he had job security, he never broke that embargo; he finished all of his grading and class prep before he left campus on Friday afternoon, or it got pushed to Monday.

But then he started dating Deja.

She was still in the thick of the journey to tenure, and she was a classic case of all the worst parts of that endeavor. She worked too hard and only rested when she crashed. She sometimes fell asleep while they were on the phone. She struggled to differentiate between the most important items on her checklist for tenure and the things that felt pressing because they were immediate. She was always tired and rushing around campus. She never just let herself breathe. It was hard to watch when he hadn't *really* known her and had only suspected that she was running herself ragged, like most junior faculty often do, but seeing it up close was growing more difficult by the day.

He remembered what the tenure track felt like — the insecurity, the anxiety, the manic spurts of writing for hours or days at a time, and then months where even getting a paragraph on the page felt like a feat. Alejandro wanted to save Deja from making the mistakes he had or that he'd witnessed, but he also didn't want to step on her boundaries when their relationship was so fragile and new. Besides, Deja clearly had a hard time prioritizing the things that made her happy, including him. There were things she wanted to do and see and experience, but she avoided them all because she didn't have time — she didn't make time — and he was secretly worried that if he pushed her too hard, she'd stop making any time for him.

So, he worked on weekends.

He pulled his car into the first parking space he saw. He checked his hair in the rearview mirror and made sure he looked casual, not too thirsty, and ready to work. He felt the exact opposite of all that, but if he showed up looking like he wanted to throw Deja over his shoulders and go back to his house to watch movies or spend the rest of the day in bed, he knew she'd clam up.

When he was satisfied that he looked less needy for her attention than he felt, he stood from his car and grabbed his satchel from the backseat, which was much lighter than normal since he'd left his laptop at home. He didn't want to do any real work, so he'd thrown in a book he needed to read for a graduate class he was teaching next semester, figuring he could read unhurriedly while Deja worked. He just wanted to spend a little time with Deja before the semester ended, and he flew home for Christmas and the new year, and they were separated for over a month.

As he walked toward his favorite coffee shop, he realized it was much colder out than he'd thought. He dug his hat from his bag and pulled it down over his ears, frowning at having to ruin his hair just to stay warm. He walked faster and hoped he could minimize the damage. When he rounded the corner onto Main Street, he smiled at Deja's back. He jogged a few steps and tapped on her right shoulder. She jumped and turned to him with bunched, angry eyebrows that relaxed once she saw him. And then she smiled.

It was pathetic how happy it made him to see her entire mood change for him.

"It's cold," she whined.

"I know. Sorry, I didn't think it'd be this bad when I suggested meeting up."

"This is why I stay home," she said with a laugh.

God, what he wouldn't have given to be at the stage in their relationship where they could spend the weekend just hanging out in one of their warm apartments. If they had been, he'd have invited her over and not let her leave his bed until she *had* to teach her first class on Monday, but they weren't. More importantly, when he'd suggested they spend the weekend together, Deja had immediately started to list all the grading she had to get through before exam week, so, he'd pivoted quickly, and suggested a work date.

He pulled the front door to the small and trendy Il Café, completely out of place in Centreville, but a nice alternative to the Starbucks where all the undergraduates congregated, especially before midterms and finals. This café was a little pricier, much more pretentious, and mostly populated by faculty and a few grad students. It was the perfect place for them to work if they had to be out, although Alejandro was a little worried they might run into someone they knew, which might freak Deja out.

"Why is this place so packed?" she asked as soon as they stepped inside and in line to order.

They started peeling off their layers.

"It's always packed on Saturday." He pulled his hat from his head.

Deja opened her mouth and then smiled up at him. "Your hair," she said, lifting onto her toes and reaching for him.

Alejandro instinctively bent down and closed his eyes as she plunged her fingers into his hair to smooth it back into place. Feeling her touch him, even in such a benign way, felt intimate, especially after a week when they'd barely seen one another off campus, and on campus, Deja was always very careful not to touch him. He suddenly didn't care what his hair looked like, only that she kept touching him.

She eventually finished fixing his hair, and her fingers trailed over the outer shell of his ear, a featherlight touch.

It took all his self-control not to physically shiver under her touch or kiss her. But he opened his eyes slowly and didn't hide the desire he felt from her. He bit his lip and let Deja see just how much he wanted her, even if he wouldn't act on it just yet.

Her eyelashes fluttered, and her lips parted on a soft pant.

"Better?" he whispered.

The left side of her mouth lifted into a grin, and she nodded as her eyes dipped to his mouth.

His hands clenched at his sides.

Just then, the café's front door opened. Deja pulled her hand from him, and the cold air from the open door only accentuated the loss.

"You want to go find a table?" he said, straightening. "I'll get your drink."

"You don't have to," she said, eyes darting side to side, and her hands clutched over her stomach.

He sighed and smiled at her calmly, hoping it would put her at ease. "This again?"

"I don't want anyone to think, you know…"

"That I might buy a friend a cup of coffee?"

"You know what I mean," she said.

"I do, and I think you're worried about nothing. But if you're really worried about people noticing that we're…you know," he said with lifted eyebrows and a wink. She rolled her eyes but chuckled lightly. "Then maybe you shouldn't run your fingers through my hair like that. Very unprofessional."

She licked her lips.

"Or look at me like that," he added.

"Like what?"

"Like you want me to kiss you."

She licked her lips again. "I'll go find a table," she said and then rushed away.

Alejandro smiled and watched her walk away.

FOR THE PAST FIFTEEN MINUTES, Deja had been trying not to yawn and failing.

"Alright," Alejandro said, closing his book, "let's get out of here."

She shook her head. "No, I can't. I only have two more essays to read, and then I'm done," she frowned at her laptop screen, "with that batch."

"Do them tomorrow," he said.

"I have a whole different stack of essays to start tomorrow. If I don't finish these today, I'll be behind."

Alejandro looked at her with soft, warm eyes. "Deja," he said, and she knew she wasn't going to love what he said next. "I know you have a schedule, and you're terrified about falling behind, but I promise you that working yourself to exhaustion is not the way to stay on track. Isn't that basically what you told Jerome?"

"I know, but I—"

Alejandro shook his head. "You work too much. You need to give yourself a break."

Deja's face warmed, and she slumped in her chair.

Alejandro slid his hand across the table so his fingers could brush hers. No one would even notice they were touching if they weren't looking, but it was enough to make Deja start to sweat. She tried to bite back a smile, but it didn't work.

"I wasn't ready to be told the truth. Can I get a warning next time?" she said, trying to sound playful even though she felt so exposed; he'd inadvertently poked at a sore spot.

She always told her advisees to do as she said, never as she did because she knew much better than them that hers wasn't a path to emulate. If they wanted to be happy, fulfilled adults with a good work-life balance, they needed to prioritize themselves and their needs better than Deja could. And even if they didn't yet know they wanted to be well-adjusted adults, she wanted it for them and never let them forget it. Unfortunately, she never listened to her own advice.

But apparently, Alejandro was prepared to step in where she couldn't. He leaned across the table toward her. "I'll always tell you the truth, Deja. And I'll always want you to be nicer to yourself. You can take that as a blanket warning if you like."

Deja's lips hurt from trying not to laugh as hard as she wanted.

"And until you figure out how to be nicer to yourself, you can let me take care of you sometimes," he said, focusing on her as if there wasn't anyone else in the crowded room. His fingers moved between hers on the table, stroking hers noticeably.

"I let you buy me coffee," she said.

"Step one."

"What's step two?" she whispered, hoping it was sex, or at least kissing, even though those seemed like big leaps from coffee. His eyes darted around them. She thought there was a chance she wasn't far off, and that made her heart race.

"Let me cook you dinner," he offered out of the blue.

Deja's mouth fell open. "You cannot be this amazing."

His eyebrows lifted. "It's just dinner," he said.

"You have no idea how terrible men are to date, do you?"

Alejandro leaned back in his chair with a bark of laughter. Deja could see people turning to look at them out of the corner of her eyes, and it took a great deal of effort to not look away from the sight of Alejandro laughing or snatch her hand away from his. She deserved to see and feel these things, she thought. She deserved him, didn't she?

"Alright, alright," Alejandro said after a while. He wiped tears away from his eyes with his free hand and nodded. "You could be right about that."

"Could?" she asked and shook her head. "Am. The bar is on the floor, but you're..."

"I'm...?"

Deja had to bite her lips again. "Amazing," she whispered.

He leaned over the table toward her again. "Take a break and let me take care of you tonight," he whispered to her.

She knew by the way his whisper was deeper than it had been and the way his hand covered hers that he wasn't just talking about dinner.

She licked her lips, and he boldly licked his own as he watched.

"Okay," she said, turning her hand over so their palms touched.

Alejandro sat back in his chair, the look of happiness and

relief so clear on his face that it made Deja feel something she still wasn't ready to name, but she knew that she liked it. She liked so much about every minute she spent with Alejandro.

TWELVE

He and Deja decided to split up for a few hours. She needed to do a few loads of laundry, and he needed to drop some suits off at the dry cleaners before they closed. He also needed to go to the grocery store because he'd somehow thought it was a great idea to invite Deja over for dinner when just this morning, he'd opened his fridge and closed it because there wasn't anything in there besides a few stray bottles of beer and kombucha. He also needed to call his brother, because Alejandro couldn't cook.

Alejandro preferred to go grocery shopping between eleven at night and two in the morning on weekdays because he was often so busy that was sometimes the only time he could make it there and when undergrads were less likely to be buying energy drinks and frozen burritos. He never went to the grocery store in the middle of the day if he could help it, not because it would be packed, but because if he did, he usually ran into someone from work and was unwittingly dragged into a fifty-minute-long conversation about fall enrollments; a subject he didn't give a single fuck about.

But for Deja, he'd take the risk.

After the dry cleaners, he pulled into the parking lot and parked. Before he got out of his car, he put his earbuds in and called his younger brother, Angel.

"I'm busy," Angel said by way of a greeting.

Alejandro rolled his eyes and hopped out of his car. "Then why did you pick up?" He grabbed his reusable grocery bags from the trunk and then headed toward the grocery store entrance.

"To tell you I'm busy. Obviously," Angel laughed.

"I need your help," Alejandro said, ignoring him.

"I agree. There's so much wrong with you. Where do you want to start?"

"With dinner," Alejandro said irritably. "I need you to tell me what to make for dinner."

"I'd ask if this was a joke, but this is pathetic, even for you. Make whatever the fuck you want to eat."

"I have a date," Alejandro said with an annoyed sigh. He had to whisper those words just in case he passed someone he knew. He worked hard to keep his personal life away from his professional life, and even though Deja was firmly in the latter, he wanted her in the former enough to blur a few lines to make it happen; but everyone didn't need to know that.

"And you're cooking? Do you not like her?"

"Shut up, I can cook," Alejandro exclaimed, even though they both knew that was true only in the most basic sense.

"I mean...you get by," Angel conceded. "You haven't killed yourself, at least. But cooking for someone else is a...step."

"Right. That's why I'm calling you. I need you to suggest something I can cook in like an hour or less that I can absolutely make and is going to impress her."

"I'm not your personal chef," Angel said. Alejandro could imagine him rolling his eyes because being mildly annoyed with each other was the bedrock of their relationship.

"But you are a personal chef."

"Yeah, and people pay me to do this. They also give me more than half a second's notice to plan."

"I actually have about three hours before she comes over, but I need to clean my apartment and shower and all that. Also, I don't want to waste time cooking on our date."

"When you could be sexing," Angel added. "Got it. Smart."

"Shut up and help me," he spat as he threw his bags into a shopping cart and maneuvered inside the grocery store.

"Strange way to ask for help."

"This has been the longest week, Angel. I'm tired. Please, just help me," Alejandro said in a weary voice.

There were a few seconds of silence on the line before Angel spoke again. "So, you *like her* like her," he exclaimed. "Does mami know?"

He sighed. "Kind of."

"Need more information."

"I might have told her that I had a crush on someone, but not that we've gone out."

"Ooooh, 'cause you *really* like her," Angel teased. "This is cute. Okay, I'm emailing you a recipe now."

"Thank you," Alejandro said, his shoulders slumping in relief.

"Yeah, whatever, no big deal. But if it gets you head, consider that when you get my Christmas present."

Alejandro hung up on Angel without another word.

DEJA WASN'T SO MUCH nervous as petrified, which kind of didn't make any sense since she'd already been over to Alejandro's place and had dropped her panties for him embarrassingly easily. What did she have to be nervous about now? Probably nothing. But she was, nonetheless.

"I don't know if I can do this," she said to Toni, clutching the microphone part of her headphones in her hand and holding it up to her mouth.

"Yeah, you can," Toni replied nonchalantly.

"What if I screw it up?"

"How? Also, just pop a titty out if you do. Instant reset."

"What is wrong with you?" she hissed.

"Nothing. I'm actually being a great friend to you right now. I'm trying to get you to accept the many blessings this fine ass man is trying to bestow upon you. A home-cooked meal and dick? Girl! You a lucky bitch and you don't even know it."

"I like him," Deja whined.

"Even better! I'd fuck a man I didn't like if he could cook. No lie. I'm not proud about it, but it's been a couple years since I got some good dick, and my standards are dropping embarrassingly fast. Anyway, enough about me and my neglected love life. Make sure there's no lipstick on your teeth and get into that man's apartment."

"You should be a life coach," Deja said sarcastically.

"No lie, I've considered that if this whole academic scam doesn't pan out."

"Thanks for nothing," she muttered.

"More than welcome. Feel free to repay me in leftovers or a decent bottle of wine."

Deja hung up on the sound of Toni cackling at her.

ALEJANDRO HAD MAYBE BITTEN off more than he could chew.

"Okay, I might be burning this," he said.

The sound of his brother's laughter filled his ears. He would have ripped his earbuds out, but he didn't have a free hand since he was currently trying to gauge if it was time to flip the pieces of salmon sizzling in the pan or not.

"Angel, help me," Alejandro said.

"Fuck, I wish I had recorded that. Flip."

"Now?" Alejandro asked, panicking.

"Yes. Duh."

When he did so, he didn't feel any less nervous. "Did I burn 'em?"

"Do they look burned?"

"Kinda?"

"Send me a picture," Angel said, clearly judging his older brother.

He wiped his hands on the dish towel over his shoulder and then took his phone from his pants pocket. He took a quick picture of the fish filets and took pictures of the couscous and salad, which he hadn't burned, and sent them over, waiting with bated breath.

"They look alright. A bit sloppy but good. She there yet?"

"If she was here, I wouldn't be on the phone with you."

"So you'd just be burning this fish in front of her? Bold."

"You said it wasn't burned," Alejandro panicked, and then his doorbell rang. His chest actually hurt from his heart hammering against it.

"Shit, she's here."

"Take the fish off," Angel said nonchalantly.

"Why? Fuck."

"Because it should be done by now. Take it off and let it rest. You're gonna have to eat now, though."

"Oh, okay. Okay," Alejandro said, turning in a small circle, unsure what to do with himself.

"Damn, bro, you sound nervous as fuck. Send me a picture."

"Of what? Me freaking out?"

"Ugh, no. I know what that looks like. Send me a picture of her. I want to see what she looks like since she got you sounding like a teenager. I mean, if you ever answer the door."

"Shit," Alejandro spat. He moved the fish from the hot pan, turned the burner off, and rushed toward the door. "Bye," he said quickly to Angel before tapping his earbuds and cutting him off.

His doorbell rang again. "Coming. Sorry," he called. He stopped to take a deep breath before he pulled the door open, and even though he'd pushed all the air from his lungs, Deja still took his breath away.

DEJA HAD BOUGHT this dress two years ago, thinking it would be a great dress to wear on a date, and then she hadn't gone on a single date since. She had lots of items in her closet like that, things she'd bought on deep discount with the intention of wearing them out to all the social engagements she might one day have on her empty calendar, and then shoved at the back of her closet, unworn and forgotten. This velvet A-line spaghetti strap dress with an intricately laced back that exposed more skin than it hid had cost her more than she'd normally spend on a single item — even on sale — but when she'd seen it in the clearance section at Nordstrom Rack, she hadn't been able to stop touching it. It had taken almost an hour roaming around the store with the dress clutched to her chest before she convinced herself to just bite the financial bullet, never thinking it would take two years to have a reason to wear it.

She tried not to imagine how much money she'd wasted

over the years on occasion wear without any occasion each time she pulled out the same jeans and sweaters to head to work or the grocery store and then home again. Reaching into that forgotten corner of her closet to get dressed for tonight had felt like a triumph as if all that money hadn't actually been a waste at all. And then Alejandro opened his door, Deja's heart skipped a stuttering beat, and she knew she hadn't wasted a single cent.

His hair was curling at the ends again, still wet from a shower, she guessed. He was wearing a pair of simple blue jeans, and a white t-shirt that looked soft as butter stretched over his muscles.

He invited her inside, and when she stepped in, the sweet, salty scents of cooked food engulfed her. She was impressed just as she realized that she was also hungry as hell.

Before she got out of her car, Deja had thrown her coat on and clutched it closed with a gloved hand to dart to Alejandro's front door. She hung her purse onto one of the hooks on the foyer wall and then turned to face him, letting her coat gape open.

Alejandro's eyes widened to the size of small saucers. "Can I take your coat?" he asked with a reddening face.

She nodded silently, not that he noticed since he was busy devouring her cleavage with his gaze. She turned slowly and pushed her coat from her shoulders, smiling at the sound of Alejandro's sharp intake of breath as he took in her bare skin. His fingers skimmed over her skin, raising goosebumps in their wake as he took her coat.

Deja shivered.

He clutched her jacket in his hands as she turned around, his eyes on her in this dress she'd only ever worn for him, even if he didn't know it. She tried not to fidget under his gaze but couldn't stop herself from smoothing her hands over her hips.

His eyes followed the movement, and he licked his lips. "You look..." he said, his voice trailing off as a smile formed on his lips.

She swallowed nervously. "What?"

His eyes slowly moved up her body, and Deja felt as if all the muscles in her stomach clenched at his attention.

"You look fucking perfect," he finally said as he made eye contact with her. "Beautiful."

She ducked her head and smiled, a small part of her brain wishing she could see herself the way he did.

THIRTEEN

"I can't believe you made this," Deja said for the second, maybe even the third time.

"Men can cook," Alejandro replied with a chuckle.

"Not many. Certainly none of the losers I've dated."

Alejandro watched as she cringed at her words before taking another dainty bite of salmon and chewing, determined to move on from that admission. He ducked his head to hide his smile at her adorable admission and that simply letting his brother annoy him for a few hours had produced that result. But he didn't want to deceive her; he liked her too much for that.

"My brother's a personal chef. He basically told me how to make all this, and I was terrified that I'd burned the salmon as soon as I put it in the pan," he admitted in a rush.

Her eyes lifted to his, and she swallowed before smiling. "But you still cooked it. You didn't try and convince me you made Burger King burgers even when I could see the wrappers in the trash."

"Wait. What?"

"You didn't offer me a selection of top ramen."

"No," he whispered.

"Or bust out the Cheez Whiz for hors d'oeuvres."

"Please be making this up," Alejandro groaned.

"I once dated a dude who burnt minute rice."

He barked out a breath of laughter. "No."

"Yes."

"How?"

"Great question. I asked him more than once and never got an answer that made sense. It was a weird reason to break up with someone," Deja said with a shrug. "But it literally tells you how long to cook it on the box. It's in the name!" she exclaimed, and Alejandro could tell that she told this story often, always annoyed at the memory.

Alejandro dropped his fork, doubled over in laughter. There were tears in his eyes when he turned back to Deja, who was smiling at him. "I can't believe..."

"Neither could I," she said with a smile. "Like I said, the bar is on the floor, but you really are amazing." She smiled down at her plate for a second and then raised her head. "If you aren't careful, I'm going to develop standards for men again."

The laughter died on Alejandro's tongue, and his smile faltered. "Good," he said, his stomach swirling with a mix of annoyance and happiness. "You deserve to be with a man that can do so much more than just barely cook a pot of rice. This isn't even a question. You know that, right?"

Her own smile fell into a rueful grin. "Men always say stuff like that, as if women want to be dating useless men. As if so many men aren't useless and great at hiding it. As if so many of us don't either settle or stay single."

"Is that what you've done?" he asked.

She sucked in a quick breath and swallowed. "Yes," she admitted quietly. "I settled all through college and grad school for men who sometimes remembered Valentine's Day was the same day every year and could be bothered to pick up a card. But then I moved here."

"And then what happened?"

"There's literally no one to date here," she said. "Look at the demographics. This place is sixty percent female during the academic year and fifty-five percent female when the students are gone, which is also Centreville's median age during the summer. There are no men to date unless I want to drive an hour, at least, just to see a movie."

"I'm here," he said impulsively. His chest warmed when she ducked her head briefly to smile.

"Yeah," she breathed. "You're here, and until a couple of months ago, I didn't think you'd ever..." She shook her head in disbelief. "Best believe, every single woman on campus has a crush on you, straight or queer. Some of the married women, too. Maybe even some of the queer men, I don't know."

"You're exaggerating," he said, blushing.

She scoffed. "And you're oblivious, apparently. You, Mike, and Johan in Physics are the single male avatars of the College of Arts & Sciences. You three could have any woman on campus if you wanted."

"I just want you," he said.

She sucked her bottom lip into her mouth. Her white teeth flashed as she bit down, the smile she was trying to hide lifting her cheeks.

Alejandro's stomach was tight with lust and anticipation. His heart was racing, and it was suddenly just a little too warm in his dining room. He'd been waiting for this moment all day, all week even. He stood from his chair and walked around the table to her. He put one hand next to her dinner plate and the other on the back of her chair. His thumb brushed the tantalizing bare skin that her dress exposed, that he hadn't been able to stop thinking about since she'd arrived. And then he bent down to face her.

Her lips fell open, and his balls ached at the thought of all the things he wanted to do to her mouth.

"I just want you, Deja," he said and watched her shiver.

He relished the effect he had on her, but he couldn't help but wonder if she realized the effect she had on him.

***

WHAT HAPPENS AFTER DINNER?

Alejandro hadn't thought that far. He'd only wanted to spend a little more time with Deja and take care of her a little bit. Okay, that wasn't true, he'd been thinking about what he'd do when she came over again — if she came over again — since their first date, but their schedules had been so packed as the semester sprinted to a close. So, he continued dreaming about her, jacking himself off to fantasies of her and coming more forcefully these days because now he knew how she felt, and tasted, and the noises she made when she came.

Now that she was in his apartment again, he was wearing his self-control thin, stopping himself from leading her to his bedroom. But it was hard to sit across from her at his dining room table and watch her lips slide along the tines of her fork, or see her nervously stroking the stem of the wine glass in her hands, or even flip through the photo album on his coffee table, turning the page with her index finger, and think about anything else but how much he wanted to touch her and for her to touch him.

"These pictures are beautiful," she whispered, and the softness of her voice made his balls ache.

He shifted closer to her on the couch. Their sides touched.

"Thanks. I don't have much time to take pictures these days, but I try."

Her hand stilled, and she turned to him. "Wait, you took these?"

"Yeah."

"They're amazing."

He shook his head. "They're okay. It's just a hobby."

"That you're great at," she corrected.

"I used to be okay at it," he hedged. "Like I said, I don't have much time to shoot." He swallowed and leaned to the side to press into her again. "I'd like to take pictures of you, though."

Her eyes widened, and she shook her head. "Oh my god, no. I hate pictures. As soon as someone aims a camera at me, I just freeze up."

Alejandro moved his right hand to Deja's knee. He pushed the hem of her dress up so he could stroke her inner thigh with his fingertips. She took the most elegant intake of breath, and his composure slipped away. He slowly pushed his entire hand between his legs, waiting for her to stop him or open her legs and invite him inside. When the tips of his fingers touched the place where her thighs met, they both stilled and inhaled sharply.

Alejandro's gaze was on her mouth, stained with the remnants of a wine-colored lipstick. He licked his lips and then met her eyes. He watched as she placed the wine glass onto his coffee table, and then leaned back, getting comfortable on his couch. And then she spread her legs for him.

He groaned and started moving his hand again, and his dick hardened in his pants. She moaned softly as he possessively cupped her mound with his hand. She was shaking. So was he.

"Would you really freeze if I took the pictures?" he whispered to her.

"Probably," she said in a breathy moan. She squirmed, spreading her legs wider as her eyes drifted closed.

He couldn't look away. He loved watching as the small wrinkles over her brow began to disappear as she relaxed under his touch.

Alejandro had spent a year memorizing the contours of Deja's face in pieces, new little details he memorized about her as they passed one another around campus, but he wanted more than glimpses. Alejandro wanted Deja completely; he wanted to touch and taste her and know that it wasn't a fleeting thing, but it was too soon to be thinking that let alone to ask her for it, so he moved his fingers into her underwear and started stroking her sex. He said with his hands what he couldn't say with his mouth. Not yet, at least.

"I don't think so," he whispered in a hoarse voice as he reclined next to her and teased her opening with his index finger.

"What?" she groaned, and those wrinkles returned.

"I think you'd be okay if I took pictures of you," he said, pressing his middle finger inside of her. "I think I could relax you."

She shifted her hips with a groan, trying to pull him deeper inside her.

He pulled his finger back, teasing her opening again before pressing two fingers inside of her this time. The wrinkles softened and faded.

Deja whimpered, and Alejandro couldn't resist the urge to kiss her anymore. He wanted to taste that sound.

She smiled against his mouth and spread her lips. The tip of his tongue swiped across her bottom lip before she sucked it into her mouth. He groaned, finally breaking and giving her what she wanted.

Alejandro pushed his fingers into her with hard pressure

and made sure to drag the pads of his fingers along her g-spot as he retreated. She cried out in his mouth, and so he did it again.

And again.

And again.

After a month of barely contained need, Alejandro let himself go, fingerfucking Deja as she suckled on his tongue. His dick was so hard it hurt, and he was humping himself into her hip. When he moved his thumb over her clit, her head fell back, and she screamed aloud, spasming around his digits and shuddering underneath him.

Alejandro smiled against the soft rounded point of her chin as he moved his hand between her legs.

"Let me take pictures of you," he said. Alejandro wasn't the kind of man to make demands, but he could get very close if motivated, and Deja was the best motivation. He hadn't ever thought about dusting his camera off, but now he couldn't think of anything he wanted more than to aim it at Deja, to take pictures of her so she could see herself the way he did.

"Oh, fuck," she said, wrapping her arms around his shoulders.

"Pictures, Deja," he said again.

"Yes. Okay. Fuck. Right there," she groaned.

He covered her mouth with his again and focused all his attention on getting her all the way off. They were moving so forcefully that the poster of Los Angeles above his couch was shaking. He hoped it wouldn't fall, but he wasn't willing to stop. He kissed and fucked her until she screamed into his mouth, and her pussy clenched around his fingers, and then gushed warm and wet into his palm.

He wrapped an arm around her waist and held her close as she shivered. And then he moved his fingers to his mouth and sucked them clean.

Just the taste of her was too much. He couldn't have known

that or else maybe he wouldn't have tasted her, but he did, and then he came in his pants.

"Fuck," he said as he buried his face in the crook of her neck.

HE WAS EMBARRASSED, and Deja thought that only made him sexier. She couldn't believe it was possible, but red-faced, sweating Alejandro was somehow even better than starched-shirt-buttoned-under-his-chin Alejandro.

"I can't believe that just happened," he muttered to himself, refusing to look her in the eyes as he stood from the couch.

"It's a compliment," she said, standing to follow him.

"Is it?" he asked skeptically, heading toward the bathroom.

"Very."

She followed him, the post-orgasmic euphoria making each step lighter than the last.

At the bathroom door, he turned to stop her. "Let me just... clean myself up," he said.

"What about me?" she asked innocently.

His eyebrows furrowed. "What do you mean?"

"Don't I get to clean up?"

"Oh," he said. "Yeah. Sorry, I'll be quick."

She shook her head and placed her hands on his chest. She tried to lean into him, but he backed away, hips first. She had to bite her bottom lip to stop from laughing. He was so adorable.

"What if we cleaned each other up?" she asked, not as innocently.

His eyebrows furrowed. She waited patiently for him to get the hint. When he did, his eyes widened, and he started to blush. "Seriously?"

"Unless you don't want to."

"I want to," he said. "But I thought...I don't want to rush you at all. I can change, and we can just, like...watch a movie or something."

"We've already had sex, Alejandro," she teased.

"I know, but I don't want you to think I just invited you over to have sex again."

Deja sighed. "This is why everyone has a crush on you. You know that, right?"

He ducked his head, and she could feel the heat of his body as he warmed up, and she warmed right up with him. "Are you going home over winter break?" she asked.

He lifted his head and cringed, the answer in his eyes before he replied. "Yeah. I bought the tickets this summer before we..."

He sounded apologetic, and she hated that. He didn't have anything to apologize for, though his answer did make her sad. "When do you come back?"

His frown deepened. "The day before spring semester starts."

She had to force herself not to frown with him. "It's okay," she said, even though it wasn't. She pressed her hands into his chest and moved them heavily over his shirt, around his shoulders. "Want to take a shower with me before you leave?" she whispered against his lips.

Alejandro's expression transformed from sad to excited so quickly that it made Deja's heart race. His smile was intoxicating. So were his arms as they wrapped around her waist and pulled her tight against his body, no longer worried about the wet stain on his pants.

"Yes," he whispered as he kissed her and backed into his bathroom. "Yes," he said again as he slid his hands under her dress and pulled it over her head. He swallowed hard and nodded as he unclasped her bra and slid her underwear down her legs. "Yes. Fuck," he groaned when she pushed his hands from her body and started to undress him in return.

Contrary to what her students and family believed, most days, Deja felt like a weak, disorganized mess and lived in terror that people would see her for the fraud she was. But every minute she spent with Alejandro made her feel powerful and capable and beautiful, something she didn't know she was missing. It had only been a few weeks, but Deja felt desperate to stay in the bubble of her time with him, and now that she knew she couldn't — that he would be heading home soon — she was determined to revel in the way he felt and the way he made her feel. She wanted to savor every inch of his naked skin and his red face as he helped her pull his boxers quickly down his legs.

"I swear I don't always come that fast," he said.

"We'll see," she teased as she turned toward the shower.

She giggled when he wrapped his body around her from the back, pressing his face into the crook of her neck. She shivered at all the skin-to-skin contact, the way the hard planes of his muscled body felt against her soft curves.

"Condoms are in the bedroom," he whispered into her ear, following the words with his tongue.

Deja groaned. "We'll get there."

Deja normally spent Saturday and Sunday trying — and failing — to get her life together. She spent hours catching up on grading and course prep while cleaning her apartment and washing her clothes. She didn't rest, though, and when she did, she usually felt terrible for it, or she was sick and had no choice.

But as she and Alejandro stepped into his shower together, she did something her parents and sister and mentor and friends had all been trying to convince her to do for years: she gave herself permission *not* to work. If she only had a week or so before Alejandro left for over a month, she wanted to spend as much time with him as she could. She wanted to fill her mind with as many memories as she could, hoping they might hold her over while they were apart.

It had been far too long since she'd given herself permission to put herself first, and her anxiety spiked for a second, but then Alejandro's hands began to knead her breasts, and suddenly, there wasn't any room to mentally berate herself. There was only Alejandro.

WINTER BREAK

FOURTEEN

Deja liked to spend the first day of winter break cleaning since she usually had to give up keeping her apartment in order right around final exams. But it was the first day of winter break, and Deja had other, better things to do. Alejandro had a red-eye flight home tonight, and he and Mike were heading to the airport in three hours, so they were making the most of their limited time together.

"Fuck," Alejandro hissed and then moaned.

Deja smiled as she tightened her hand around the base of his dick and concentrated on lowering herself onto him as slowly as possible. She wanted to ride him until their emotional wheels fell off, and based on the way his muscles strained and trembled underneath her, he wanted that too, but Deja had given this a lot of thought while grading her final essays and exams and taking in all the last-minute extra credit assignments and fielding the angry and sad emails about grade changes, and she had decided that if the two of them were going to spend a month and a half apart, she wanted to make sure he remembered her. A lot could change in six weeks, and she didn't want one of those things to be Alejandro's feelings for her. So she lowered herself onto his dick, squeezed her pussy tight around him — gritting her teeth because he felt so good — and then lifted just as slowly, only to repeat it all again.

Even though they only had a few hours left, Deja forced herself to pretend as if she and Alejandro had all the time in the world, and she fucked him slower and slower until they were both one entwined, sweaty, shivering mess.

"Deja, fuck," Alejandro said before muttering a string of Spanish at her.

She was happy that she was riding him reverse cowgirl with her hands on his shins. If she'd been facing him and could see that adorable way he bit his lip when he was trying not to come, she knew she wouldn't have been able to stick to her plan.

He grabbed her waist and pumped his hips upward, desperate to get deeper and deeper inside her. "Not yet," she moaned, circling her hips to accentuate the point.

"Deja, just fuck me. Please," he begged.

It was music to her ears. Maybe if they really had more than a few hours, she would have continued to torture him — and herself — and ignored that outburst, but the reality of their time constraints and the pull of her own need made her crumble. She laughed, ground her pussy down on him, and then moved her hips up and down in short jerking motions.

"Deja!" His hiss was delicious.

"I'm fucking you," she giggled, her breath giving out in a weak rasp at the last word. "This is what you wanted."

"Faster," he said, accentuating that word with a jerking pump of his hips that made them groan in unison.

Deja's head fell back, and she shivered as he slid a hand up her sweaty back.

If he wanted, Alejandro could have flipped her onto her stomach and fucked her into his mattress. He'd done it more than once. But just as much as she wanted him to remember her, he seemed to want the same.

Deja turned her head to look at Alejandro over her left shoulder.

He was doing that lip bite thing as he watched her ass bounce up and down on his dick.

She shivered and clenched around his shaft, pulling a moan from his lips. He hadn't shaved in almost a week, and his five o'clock shadow had grown into a thick starter beard. She wished that she could watch it grow longer over the break, to feel it over her naked skin, especially between her legs, at its different lengths, but she couldn't, so she focused on the here and now. And right now, she loved the way it accentuated his perfectly angular jaw and his inky eyelashes.

When he turned his eyes to hers and dug his fingers into her waist, she loved the way his new dark beard made the flash of his tongue stand out even more.

"Baby," she whispered to him.

"Yeah?" he grunted.

"Do you want me to go faster?" she purred, rolling her hips above him.

He rolled his eyes. She tightened her pussy around him. His head fell back to the pillow and groaned from deep in his soul. "Yes. Fuck. Yes."

"Say it," she whimpered, damn close to coming herself. She rolled her hips again.

Alejandro bit back a high-pitched moan as he nodded desperately, "Okay. Fuck. Fuck me faster. Please."

She smiled down at him, not that he noticed because his eyes were clenched shut. "Okay," she said and turned forward, ready to really get to work.

She moved her hands from his shins to the bed for better purchase and then circled her hips in a wider circumference.

Alejandro's sharp intake of breath spurred her on, and she moved above him faster and faster, harder and harder.

His fingers dug into her waist, and then he huffed out a relieved breath, followed by a long, desperate moan. Deja kept moving her hips, and Alejandro's hands started to guide her on top of him. Her pussy stroked and clenched around his shaft until their grunts and moans met the wet slapping of their bodies coming together over and over again.

When Deja's orgasm came, she lost the rhythm of their sex as her hips stuttered, and her thighs shook.

Alejandro picked up the slack.

He thrust up into her with shallow strokes, letting her ride out the waves of her release on top of him until her body's spasms began to slow, and then he eased her onto the bed. He turned her onto her back and swept the curly tendrils of her hair from her face.

She reached up and wrapped her arms around his waist and spread her legs wide to pull his hips closer.

He stroked her cheek with one hand and used the other to guide his dick back inside her. And even though he'd just been begging her to fuck him faster and harder, he fucked her in long, achingly deep, slow strokes. And even better — or worse — his eyes never strayed from her face. Deja had nowhere else to look but back at him as he made love to her tenderly until the force of his own orgasm made him bury his face in the crook of her neck.

She felt his shouted release against her skin as he filled the condom between them.

Six weeks was a long time, but Deja wanted to believe that it wasn't too long. She wrapped her arms and legs around Alejandro and held him close, hoping for the first time ever that winter break didn't last too long.

FIFTEEN

WEEK ONE

Deja was sitting in her home office at the desk she rarely used to write and mostly used to stress about writing. She had a small stack of books piled high on her right — books she'd started reading but hadn't finished yet — and a folder of earlier iterations of the first and hardest chapter of the book she was really trying to write on her left. She opened the latest version of the chapter on her laptop and forced herself to take slow, even breaths.

Her most frequent writing advice to her students was that a messy first draft was your friend because it was always easier to revise than confront a blank page. She fundamentally believed in that advice, but over the years, she'd started to wonder if that advice could work for everyone else but her. But she knew that couldn't be true because she remembered writing those chapters of her dissertation and feeling a kind of freedom. Sure, she'd camped out in the grad student computer lab in her alma mater's main library at the computer in the far south corner for nearly ten hours a day, every day for close to three months, but she'd loved it. She'd been certain that her brilliance was hitting the page in a way that would change the field of Sociology, and she'd felt so hopeful about the rest of her career.

Her dissertation wasn't perfect, but her committee believed in the cheesy adage that "the best dissertation is a done dissertation," and they believed in her and her work. She'd walked out of her dissertation defense certain that she had a damn good basis for that groundbreaking book she knew she was writing. Nearly three years later, she couldn't even fathom what had made her think that at the time. When she looked at her dissertation now, all she could see were flaws she didn't know how to fix and holes in the research she didn't have the expertise to fill, and it made her want to cry.

Toni would have said she'd developed a phobia about her research, and she needed to see a therapist about it and talk to her mentors. Marie would have agreed but then reminded them of the last time they'd all tried to find local, culturally sensitive therapists covered under their insurance. Then they'd all be sad.

Deja knew Toni was right, but she had no idea how to scale the wall she'd mentally built between herself and her writing, and her current coping mechanism for it was to just run away. The only problem was that with her third-year review looming, she didn't have anywhere else to run. When she turned in her portfolio next fall, she needed to be able to say that she'd made some progress with her book and had at least a couple of articles under review at journals in her field.

Her phone rang.

She thought she'd put it on do not disturb, but apparently, that was yet another thing at which she'd failed. Her low self-esteem didn't care that it was an accident. She grabbed her phone from the desk as a new self-loathing mixed with her insecurity briefly before dissipating when she saw Alejandro's name.

"Hi," she breathed into the phone.

"Hi," he breathed back.

In the background of his call, Deja heard what sounded like a party and then the click of a door closing and then quiet.

"Are you busy?" he asked.

Deja's eyes skittered to her laptop. The answer was yes. She should have said yes. She knew that, but she silently pressed her laptop closed. "Nope," she said. "What's up?"

It sounded like he sighed, and Deja was certain that she could hear a smile in his voice. Or maybe she just wanted to hear that. "I needed to hear your voice."

"Yeah?" she asked.

"Definitely. I miss you."

Deja had to bite the inside of her cheek for a bit to stop from screaming. This man couldn't be real. "I miss you, too," she mumbled.

"How much?"

"What does that question mean?" she asked with a laugh.

"What are you wearing?"

"Really?"

"Sí. Sí. I've been dreaming about you," he said in a husky voice that reminded her of the way he sounded first thing in the morning, memories of the few times they'd spent the night together. Her sex responded immediately, clenching around air in a wet rush.

Deja stood from her desk chair and headed toward the door. "What kind of dreams?" she asked, her own voice a bit deeper as well.

There was a smile on her face as she flicked the lights off and pulled her office door closed behind her.

SIXTEEN
WEEK TWO

All academics lie. Period.

Sometimes, they lied as a matter of course. For instance, at some point in every semester, Deja said to her students, "You know more than enough to pass the exam." Technically, that wasn't a lie outright. For students who came to class and did the work, she was telling the absolute truth. But for the thirty to sixty percent of the students in each class who didn't come to class and didn't do the reading, she was lying; they *didn't* know enough to pass her exams. Of course, she couldn't tell her students that because she didn't want to freak them out so much that they dropped the class for fear they couldn't pass. So, it was a kind of lie of omission.

Sometimes, professors lied without even thinking about it, like when they had their annual goal-setting meetings with the chairs of their departments. Every year, Deja told her boss that she planned to finish her book, and she meant it. The problem was that she had the best intentions, but no time.

But the biggest and worst lies were the ones professors told themselves.

Every year, Deja promised herself that she would rest during winter and summer breaks. She promised herself that she'd catch up on all the sleep she'd missed during the semester. She vowed to cook real meals, go for walks, and rediscover herself during the holidays. She made herself the most solemn promises — usually in the middle of the night while scrambling to get graduate research papers back on schedule and with copious feedback — that she would actually take a break during the break.

She also simultaneously told herself that once the semester was over, she'd get all the research and writing done. By the time the semester was over, she usually had a notebook of half-formed ideas she wanted to turn into academic articles, notes on revisions for a book chapter or two, and a stack of books to read in just six short weeks.

How was she supposed to get all that done while resting and course prepping for the next semester? Well, that was the lie: that she'd find a way. Every break that she didn't magically find a way to do all the things she'd planned to do made her feel worse. And when she walked into the next semester less rested and more stressed, the worst part was that she'd believed her own fairy tales.

On some level, her students knew she was bullshitting about how easy her exam was. They knew their attendance grades and if they'd barely passed the reading quizzes, assuming they took them at all. They'd also been on ratemyprofessor.com, so they knew how many other students said she was a hard grader, a bitch, a mess, unqualified to be doing her job. Her students knew she was lying, just like the chair of her department knew she wouldn't finish her book this year even as he nodded solemnly at her and wished her luck. But Deja believed that she would do all the things she'd planned and more, even with all evidence pointed toward the fallacy. She had to believe because it was about the only way she could trick herself into believing in herself.

So she wasted the first week of her winter break studiously checking books out from the library, printing out academic articles, and organizing her notes. She didn't read or write anything, but she got herself in order. She deep-cleaned her apartment, she washed all the laundry she hadn't had time to do, and she made many, many lists. And at the end of the week, she Skyped her family on Christmas Day.

"I wish you could have come home, sweetheart," her dad said, his face too close to the laptop, as usual, so all she could see were his eyebrows, forehead, and thinning hair line. It made her smile.

"Me too, dad, but I—" Deja stopped speaking to take a few breaths. She didn't want to cry on the Skype call because then her entire family would start crying. Again. They'd been here before, and after years of staying away to finish her work — to try to stay afloat — her family was used to her missing all the holidays, even if they hated it. "I just have so much work to do, dad. If I can just get my book in good shape, I really think I can submit it to presses next year. I do."

Deja tried to ignore the pathetic naïveté she heard in her voice. She sounded like a used car salesperson, but she didn't know who she was trying to convince; herself or her father. Either way, it was so sad.

"I know you will, baby girl. I have faith in you," her dad said. He'd heard all this before, and Deja didn't know if he believed her or not, but she did know that he was always in her corner, and that mattered a whole hell of a lot.

"Open your present," Deja's mom called. "Franklin, turn the computer toward the tree. Let Deja see what we got the baby."

Deja's dad grumbled and started turning the monitor. Deja

swiped at her eyes while no one else could see, and then she put on her biggest smile to watch her nephew open the zombie Lego set the entire family had pitched in to get him, even though Deja's sister still wasn't sure if it was smart to encourage his zombie obsession.

When she closed her computer a few hours later, she saw a text message from Alejandro wishing her Merry Christmas with a picture of him in the corniest Christmas sweater she'd ever seen. She smiled at her phone and texted him back.

She waited a few minutes for a reply, but it didn't come, and that was okay, she told herself. He was with his family, getting the break she'd denied herself, and she wouldn't begrudge him that.

She padded into her kitchen and found a frozen meatloaf dinner. She popped it in the microwave, opened a bottle of wine, and sank deeper into a depression because this was her life.

Three pages!

Deja had written three new pages on an article she'd dug out of her files, and she felt like a rock star. The article wasn't anywhere near complete. Actually, chances were high that when she looked at it in a few days, she might decide that she hated those three new pages and delete them and more, but she'd worry about that another day. Right now, she just wanted to be happy that those three pages existed. It was New Year's Eve, and she wished she was doing something more interesting than saving and backing up the latest version of an article she'd been writing for almost a year, but she wasn't, and a lesson she really wanted to learn next year was how to be grateful for where she was and what she'd accomplished instead of always only focusing on the things she still needed to do.

It was a sad fact to realize that she didn't have lots of strategies for celebration. Even worse to realize that she'd arrived at this conclusion before. In fact, that was something her and her old therapist had been interrogating, the fact that Deja didn't have coping skills for being happy for herself. She didn't know how to reward herself for a job well done, but she had lots of destructive methods for wallowing in her failures. How pathetic, she often thought to herself, with no idea how to break that cycle.

But right now, unexpectedly, she wanted to celebrate.

She thought about calling Toni and Marie, but they were still out of town. Marie had gone to visit her family in New York, and Toni was at an all-inclusive resort in Barbados for New Year's. Besides, what she really wanted was to go somewhere, to do something, and be with someone. But since that wasn't a possibility, she decided to do the next best thing: talk to the person she was desperate to be with.

Alejandro picked up on the second ring.

"Hey," he breathed.

"Hey. You busy?"

"No. Not at all."

"You sure? Sounds loud."

"My family's loud. We're getting ready for a party, but I have time," he said quickly. "Let me just...hold on."

Deja listened to Alejandro breathe — trying to ignore how much she liked even that sound — as the background sounds on his end of the line began to fade. She heard a door snick closed.

"Okay, what's up?" he breathed.

Deja was sitting in her office chair, looking at the Word file, but she didn't feel nearly as excited about it now. She felt so pathetic, actually. Here she was, alone on New Year's Eve, excited that she'd written three probably crappy pages while everyone she loved was hundreds and thousands of miles away. And she'd chosen this. She'd wanted to share the joy in those three pages with Alejandro, but now that she had him on the phone, she was second-guessing herself.

"Um...I just called to say hey. I figured I probably wouldn't be able to talk to you later."

"Why? Did you think I wasn't going to call you at midnight?"

Deja's face warmed, and she bit back a smile. "You don't have to do that," she mumbled.

"Yes, I do," he said forcefully. "And I want to."

She shivered at the simple declaration in his voice. She loved the way he made everything seem so easy in a way she couldn't. It made her feel secure, and she knew she'd get used to it if he kept at it; she probably already had.

"I wrote three pages today," she blurted out. "I mean, it's not a lot or anything, but—"

"Congratulations, Deja," he said, cutting her off. His voice was bright with excitement, like real excitement, and it made the happiness she'd snuffed out earlier come back to life. "I'm really proud of you. I just wish I was there so we could celebrate together."

"It's just three pages," she said, dipping her head to hide her smile even though there wasn't anyone else in her apartment.

"There's no 'just' when it comes to your CV, you know that. I know that. Hey, when I'm back, we'll celebrate your three pages and whatever else you write, okay?"

Deja felt so pathetic because she was on the verge of tears, not just because Alejandro wanted to celebrate with her, or because he knew how important this was, but because he thought she would write more pages. She didn't know if she believed him, but knowing that he believed in her was everything. She stopped biting her lips shut and let the smile that wanted to form spring fully to life.

"I miss you," she admitted quietly.

"I miss you, too. So, what are you wearing?" he asked in a playful voice.

"Boy, shut up," she laughed and stood from her chair to walk out of her office.

"I'm just saying, I have a few minutes. Just in case you wanted to Facetime me or send me a picture or something. For good luck."

Deja giggled as she walked into her bedroom, the warm feeling in her chest spreading as she pushed her pajama pants over her hips.

EIGHTEEN

Week Four

"I'm not hungry, mami," Alejandro called through his bedroom door.

"Why not?" she yelled up at him. "You need to eat more."

Alejandro rolled his eyes. He ate enough. He'd learned in graduate school that sometimes the only thing he could control about his life was what he put in his body and how he treated it, so he tried to eat a healthy diet, he worked out a few times a week, he drank lots of water, and ever since he'd gotten tenure, he made sure that he got as much sleep as possible. He did the best he could.

But still, the minute he'd walked through the front door, his mother had hugged and kissed him and then frowned. "You're so skinny," she'd exclaimed.

He wasn't.

In fact, now that he was past thirty and spent more time

sitting at a desk than playing sports with his brothers or working out, he'd gained weight and spent a small fortune last spring getting his favorite suits re-tailored. He knew his mother expressed her emotions through food, and at any other time, he would happily sit at his parents' old beat-up Formica table and let her feed him all the menudo and tamales she wanted.

But not today. Not right now. He had a date.

Alejandro closed and locked his bedroom door behind him. But then he remembered how many times his younger brothers had burst into his room when they were teenagers, even when he was certain he'd locked it, and he started searching for something heavy enough to keep them out. It took a bit more effort than he remembered, but he managed to push the heavy wood dresser he'd had his entire life in front of it and prayed it would be enough.

Once that was handled, he excitedly grabbed his laptop from his old desk, settled onto the full bed that had been too small for him since middle school, and logged into Skype. He smiled when he saw the small green button next to Deja's avatar and pressed the call button.

Alejandro had to force himself to breathe evenly while the call rang out and rang out and rang out. He frowned at his computer screen and then snatched his phone from the desk. He checked the time. Six o'clock. They said they'd talk at six his time, eight for her. He checked his text messages, just in case he'd missed a message saying she couldn't make it.

He hadn't, and his frown deepened.

He was just about to call Deja, his finger hovering over her name in his cell phone contacts when she picked up on Skype.

"Sorry, sorry, sorry. I'm here," she said.

His eyes drifted back to his laptop screen, where he had a great view of her light pink comforter and white pillows against the light rattan wood of her headboard. Even though he was happy she'd picked up, he was annoyed because he hadn't called to see her bed, even though he'd never actually been over to her apartment, and a few weeks ago, he'd have killed to know what it looked like. But it had been weeks since he'd left Centreville, and he wanted to see her, desperately.

"Deja?" he said, and then a soft, fluttery gray silk something fluttered into the frame of the camera.

Alejandro's entire body froze when he saw Deja's leg rest onto her mattress.

"I'm here. I'm here," she said, "just give me a second."

He nodded and stared at the soft crease of her bent leg. The past three weeks had gone by in a flash, so fast that it was only in this moment that he processed that it had been three weeks since he'd run his hands and lips up that thigh. Three weeks since he'd sank balls deep inside her. It wasn't that long, considering how long they'd crushed on each other, and yet, it suddenly felt like an eternity.

He absentmindedly reached for the bottle of beer on his desk and took a swig, his eyes drinking in Deja's brown skin while he waited for her to come fully on-screen.

"Okay," she huffed as she bounced onto the bed and in line with her laptop's camera.

Alejandro groaned. That soft, fluttery gray silk was a robe draped over Deja's obviously naked body. He swallowed the swig of beer in his mouth and licked his lips at the sight of her adorably perky breasts moving freely underneath that slip of fabric. He was especially interested in the way her nipples disturbed the drape of the silk. He took another sip of beer.

Deja was sitting in front of her laptop with crossed legs, and the robe, unfortunately, covered her sex, but much like the sway of her breasts, there was something so erotic about seeing her but not seeing her. If this was his reward for her being a few seconds late, he would have waited an hour for this, not that he wanted to.

But then he started to feel terrible. "I'm underdressed," he mumbled.

Deja squinted at the screen and then tapped at her keyboard. Alejandro watched an adorable smile form on her face, and then her chest swayed softly with laughter. "I'd say you're overdressed."

He looked down at the basic black trackpants and white t-shirt, for all intents and purposes his uniform when he was home and didn't have to dress up to teach or go to a meeting or to impress Deja.

"I didn't know what to wear to a Skype sex date."

"Me either," she said as her hands moved to the belted knot at her waist.

Alejandro's hand tightened around the bottle of beer as he watched her elegant fingers deftly and slowly undo the scrap of silk and slide up the lapels of her robe to pull it open. Just that flash of her chest made all the blood in Alejandro's body rush determinedly toward his dick.

"I thought naked made the most sense," she said, pulling her robe over her shoulders to pool at her waist.

He nodded numbly, even though his dick was very aware of her. "Yeah. I should have thought of that."

Deja licked her lips slowly. "You can always catch up."

Alejandro's eyes widened, and he spilled his laptop onto his bed in the rush to stand. He accidentally slammed his beer down on his desk, and it foamed up the spout. "Shit," he said, looking around for a towel. He didn't have one, so he ripped his shirt from his body and sopped up the liquid — it was coming off anyway — and threw it in the laundry basket.

Deja's giggle filtered into his bedroom, and for a second, Alejandro imagined that she was there with him.

"You've got a great ceiling."

"Shit. Sorry," he said, righting the camera so she could see him.

"Okay, now we're talking," she exclaimed. There was a glass of wine in her hand, and she was rocking side-to-side on her butt with excitement. Even when she was naked and getting ready to have virtual sex, she was still the most adorable person he'd ever met.

Alejandro's hands moved inside the waistband of his pants and underwear, and he pushed them down his legs. He didn't want to waste any more time.

"Four out of ten," Deja said. "Not the best strip show I've ever seen, but I have faith in your ability to improve if you're willing to put in the work."

Alejandro laughed as he crawled back into bed. "Next time I'll Magic Mike you, I promise."

"God, I hate that movie," Deja mumbled.

"So, the only place to go is up," he said.

He pulled his laptop in front of him, angling the camera so Deja couldn't see how hard he already was. When they were both settled in front of their laptops, naked, they stopped for a second just to stare.

Deja had a wistful smile on her face, and she took another sip of wine.

"You ready?" he asked softly.

She licked her lips and nodded before turning briefly to put the glass on her bedside table. When she turned back, her hands drifted to her breasts, and she pinched her nipples softly. She visibly shivered.

"Three weeks is a long time," he breathed, palming his dick.

"I've gone much longer without sex," she said. "That was before you, though."

He could tell by the angle of her eyes that she wanted to see him, so he adjusted his laptop screen so she could see him stroke himself.

A soft whimper fell from her lips, and she squeezed her right breast.

"How do you want to do this?" Alejandro asked.

Deja smiled shyly. "I don't know. I've actually never done this before."

"Neither have I," he rushed to reassure her. "Let's just... keep it simple, yeah?"

"Meaning?"

"I just want to watch you come."

"Ditto," she whispered in the husky voice he recognized so well.

"Okay, then," he breathed and grabbed the lubrication he'd picked up specifically for this date. He squirted some lube into the palm of his hand and started stroking his dick more seriously this time, in slow, rhythmic flicks of his wrist. His hand felt amazing, and he was very used to getting himself off, but he didn't groan at his own touch. He groaned at the sight of Deja's legs splayed open around her computer, putting her pussy front and center for the webcam and for him.

"Jesus," he breathed, squeezing the head of his aching dick.

"Yeah," she said, pulling a long purple vibrator into view and rubbing her own lube along the shaft.

Alejandro slowed his hand to match the pace of hers coating over the toy. It was the best he could do with the thousands of miles between them.

"Ready?" It was her turn to ask him and his to nod in return.

She scooted back on the bed, putting her pussy even closer, not close enough to touch and taste but close enough that Alejandro knew he wasn't going to have any problem getting off.

"You have no fucking idea," he breathed.

The soft hum of her vibrator made Deja moan, which made Alejandro's balls ache. He watched as she rubbed the vibrator up and down her lips, teasing herself.

"Your clit," he panted as precome started leaking from the tip of his dick like a river.

She groaned loudly and squirmed as she followed his direction.

He moved his hand to the base of his dick and squeezed himself tight while she teased herself, trying to stave off the aching in his dick and balls and entire body, actually. Deja was like a shot of premium liquor; it didn't take much of her to get him up and ready and off in no time. It was embarrassing, but he could deal with that emotion later; right now, he didn't want to wallow in his quick orgasm when flashes of Deja's pink pussy were on his screen.

"Fuck, Deja," he groaned, looking up her body for the first time.

Her nipples were hard peaks, and she was pinching and turning her left nipple between her fingers.

"Ready?" she asked again.

He could only grunt in response as he stroked his dick faster. His eyes moved back to her pussy just as she started pressing her vibrator inside. Her stomach clenched, and her thighs began to shake. "Go slow," he said in a hoarse voice.

She didn't answer, but she did as he asked. Once again, he matched the movement of her hands and began to pump his dick at the same pace as she pushed her toy inside and out. Those flashes of her pussy's deep pink became a constant, and Alejandro's entire world shrank to the small rectangle of his laptop screen.

They were breathing heavily and moaning. Alejandro's

muscles tensed slowly, winding tighter and tighter as he watched Deja fuck herself with her vibrator.

Alejandro had been looking forward to this all day. They'd first started talking about some kind of phone sex just after Christmas, but finding a time when his parents' house was empty or at least when he thought no one might hear him beating his meat with his girlfriend on Skype was near impossible. They'd spent two weeks trying to find the perfect time until finally, Alejandro just gave up; he didn't want to wait any longer.

Alejandro could almost laugh that they'd spent two weeks planning for barely fifteen minutes of sex, but he was preoccupied. "I'm close," he moaned.

"Oh, thank god," she moaned. "Me, too."

Alejandro huffed a laugh and began to pump his palm up and down his shaft faster and faster with one hand as the other gripped his tip.

Deja was fucking herself faster with one hand and circling the sensitive nub of her clit with the other. And even though she was thousands of miles away, he could tell that she was trying to keep her groans to a minimum, but he knew she'd lose that battle eventually and thankfully had the wherewithal to turn the volume down on his laptop. For safety, he should have silenced it all together, but he couldn't bear to. He wanted to hear her come. If he couldn't touch her or taste her, at the very least, he needed to hear her.

And when she finally did press the vibrator deep inside herself and scream out her release, Alejandro was surprised that he'd hung on that long. He licked his lips as her wet release leaked out around her vibrator, and it sent him completely over the edge. His toes curled, and his back tensed, and finally, he came with a sharp gasp and a long, deep grunt as his semen splattered along his thighs and stomach in hot spurts. It was dramatic, but he was out of breath and thought he saw stars. He'd had penetrative sex with women that hadn't made him come so hard.

"Fuck, I miss you," he breathed in a satisfied shudder.

"Three weeks," Deja groaned back as she sat up in bed. "Just three more weeks."

Alejandro's laughter was weak from exhaustion and satisfaction.

"I can go again," Deja said, shocking Alejandro's eyes back to the screen to see her circling her clit with the vibrator.

He wheezed. "I'm old. I need more than a minute."

"Whenever you're ready," she said happily. "I'm just happy to be here."

He shook his head with a smile. "Don't wait for me. I don't mind watching."

Deja's eyes widened behind her eyeglasses. She licked her lips, "Yes, sir, Doctor Mendoza."

Alejandro grabbed his pants from the floor beside the bed and started cleaning himself up while Deja started fucking herself with her toy again.

"Three weeks," he mumbled to himself in a bone-deep hunger to be back in Centreville, to be with Deja. They could survive that. So long as the internet connection held.

NINETEEN
WEEK FIVE

Deja always said she was too old for all-nighters, and then went
ahead to have at least one all-nighter a semester. When she was
a college student, it was easy. She'd work all night, write a half-
decent essay, catch a power nap, wake up, run a spellcheck on
her essay, shower and run to class. Now that she was a college
professor, every night with less than six hours of sleep made her
feel as if she'd aged a decade overnight. When she slept poorly
or for not enough time, she felt it in her sore back and neck and
could see it in the dark circles under her eyes that she didn't
have enough energy to hide with concealer. And as reliant as
she'd become on coffee to get her through the day, if she slept
poorly, there wasn't enough coffee in the world to make up for
the lack of sleep.

Each time she was forced to pull an all-nighter, she always
promised herself that she'd never do it again, and then she did,
because without it, she wouldn't have been able to find the time
or motivation to revise an entire article and submit it to the
Journal of Comparative Sociology barely a week into the new
year. She was awake for twenty straight hours, but it was worth

it. It was a small thing, and she couldn't stop herself from catastrophizing as she pressed submit, but she'd submitted an article at the top-tier journal in her field.

She knew deep in her bones that it would probably be rejected because she couldn't believe that it was good enough; she never could. But when she started preparing her third-year review files in the summer, she'd have one more article to list as under review in her anemic publications section. Toni would have told Deja to "focus on the good shit, cause the bad shit never stops coming," and she was right, so she showered, put on a fresh pair of pajamas, and crawled into bed.

She slept for nearly eighteen hours.

When she woke up with bleary eyes and a full bladder, she had to rush to the bathroom. She sat on the toilet, tired and confused at her entire existence. She also felt so grimy that she flushed the toilet and climbed directly into the shower. If this was how the rest of the year was going to go, she was nervous, to say the least.

Deja felt like an entirely new person after her shower. She wrapped herself in the thick terrycloth robe her parents had given her as a Christmas present her first year in graduate school and walked into her bedroom to peer at her phone. She pushed her glasses up her face as she read through the list of text messages and missed calls.

She was just typing a text to her older sister when Toni's face popped up on her phone screen.

"Hello?" Deja croaked, her voice dry and hoarse from disuse.

"You sound terrible," Toni said.

"I just woke up."

"Oh, look at you resting! I'm proud of you."

"Shut up," Deja said and rolled her eyes.

"Anyway, bitch, I'm back in town!"

Deja's face lit up. "Yay! Welcome back to nowhere."

Toni sighed. "Yeah, yeah, yeah. When was the last time you left your apartment?"

Deja's brain was still moving at the speed of molasses, but that wasn't why she took a handful of uncomfortable seconds before she answered Toni's question. She stalled because she knew Toni was about to light into her when she did. "I'm not..." Deja started and then turned to the kitchen with a suddenly dry mouth. "I can't remember, actually."

"Jesus, Deja," Toni breathed.

"I've been writing and resting and cleaning. You should have seen how messy my apartment was after finals."

"Girl, you need fresh air and some time away from work. You shouldn't be holed up in your apartment all day, every day, it's not healthy. That's how you get burned out."

"I've been burnt out; it can't get any worse."

"Yes," Toni said, "it can. You have no idea how many of my friends have bounced from job to job because they can't produce, or they just leave academia itself. This is no joke, and your department does not care if they burn you out. We've been over this."

They had, and Deja knew Toni was right, but it was one thing to hear her say the words and nod along with them; it was an entirely different thing for her to figure out new strategies. She was convinced that the only way to accomplish that was to become a new person altogether, and she was too embarrassed to admit to Toni that she thought of herself as a lost cause.

"I know," she whispered into her phone. She pulled open her fridge and grabbed the water pitcher from the top shelf. She poured a large glass of water and gulped half of it down in a few swallows.

Toni sighed again, and Deja forced herself to drink the rest of her glass of water while she waited.

"Okay, look," Toni said after a few seconds. Her voice sounded softer, a forced chipper that made Deja feel worse somehow. "I just got back, and I'm jetlagged. But I'm about to put a load of laundry in the washing machine, power nap the fuck out of my afternoon, and then you and I are going to happy hour at Burger Barn."

Deja groaned, "I hate Burger Barn."

"No, you don't. You hate running into your students at Burger Barn, but you love their onion rings. That's why we have to go now before the kids get back. So, get your life together, and I'll meet you at the barn house at 7 on the dot. Deal?"

Deja sighed this time. "Fine."

"Sound happier, please," Toni directed.

Deja laughed unexpectedly. "Fine," she said in a happier tone.

"Great. See ya," Toni said and then hung up before Deja could respond.

DEJA DRESSED UP.

It was kind of pathetic because she literally just walked fifteen minutes to the roadhouse-style burger joint that was usually full of students and loud enough that some nights she could hear the commotion from her apartment, especially during homecoming weekend and right before spring graduation. But she hadn't left her apartment in an indeterminate amount of time, and she wanted to celebrate the occasion.

She pulled her favorite black skinny jeans on and put on a pair of leather riding boots and a slouchy sweater that draped to show a little shoulder. Granted, she then covered that naked shoulder with her winter coat, wrapped her thickest knit scarf around her throat, and grabbed a hat and gloves on her way out the door, but it was the attempt at style that mattered.

The walk to the restaurant was brisk, in her pace and in the air, but it was nice to be out in the fresh air. Deja hated to admit it, but Toni was right; she really needed to leave her house more, and not just to run errands. Deja wasn't going to tell her that she was right, of course, because no one loved being able to say "I told you so" more than Toni. Still, Deja spent the short walk realizing that she needed to stop treating herself so poorly.

By the time Deja arrived at Burger Barn, Toni was sitting at a table with a margarita in front of her and a bright smile on her face. Her face lit up when Deja walked in the front door, and she waved her over.

Deja began unwrapping her scarf from her throat as she walked through the dining room, and the closer she got, the more she noted just how rested Toni looked. Her vacation braids were piled messily atop her head in a cute style, her eyes were bright, no concealer needed, and her skin had a sun-kissed glow, because she, unlike Deja, had taken a break instead of working over the holidays.

"Hey," Toni said when Deja was within earshot.

"Hey. You look amazing,"

"I feel wrecked. Ten hours traveling to get here, and I only slept for like four hours."

"Oh my god, why didn't you cancel?"

Toni squinted at her. "Why the hell would I do that?"

"So you could rest," Deja replied with a frown.

Toni rolled her eyes. "Girl, please. If I hadn't come, I wouldn't have done anything besides wash some more clothes and eat that last microwave dinner at the back of my freezer. But this way, I get to have a good old gross and greasy American hamburger to welcome me home, I get your hermit ass out of the house, and this margarita is about to put me straight to sleep."

Deja lowered into her chair with a smile. "You always have a plan."

"It's my superpower," Toni said with a cheeky smile and a long sip of her drink. "Now, let's get down to business."

Deja's hands froze over the menu in front of her. She felt the icy dread that often overtook her when the chair of her department just happened to "drop by" her office to "see how she was doing," which Deja always understood to mean that he was making sure Deja was being productive. The thought that Toni was about to ask her about the exact word count of her writing over break terrified her, even though she'd submitted the article to the *Journal of Comparative Sociology* barely forty-eight hours ago. That one article submission wasn't enough. She knew it, but she didn't want Toni to tell her that for real. She also didn't want Toni to ask her how many books and articles she'd read or if she'd even started working on her syllabi for the upcoming semester, because Deja knew that no matter her answer, it would never be enough.

She stopped breathing as Toni pinned her with a laser stare.

Toni's lips curved into a Cheshire cat smile as the words spilled from her mouth. "You talked to Alejandro during the break?"

Deja hadn't expected that question, and she hadn't expected that just hearing his name would affect her. She felt as if she was still wrapped up in her coat and scarf and dabbed at her forehead, certain she was sweating. She tucked her chin against her chest to hide her smile, and the instinctive move was the only answer Toni needed.

"Aw yes, bitch! Somebody's got a man!" Toni leaned

toward her over the table. "Please tell me his ass is as good naked as it looks in his suits."

"Toni!" Deja shrieked.

"What? Oh, you must have it bad. You spent all last spring semester staring at that man's booty, but now, it's too scandalous?" she teased. "That means it's even better naked. Ugh, I knew it." She took a long sip of her margarita.

"Shut up," Deja giggled.

"Mmmmhmm. Thought so."

TWENTY

WEEK SIX

Classes started in four days.

Deja was trying not to think about the vast distance between what she'd planned to do over winter break, what she'd needed to accomplish, and what she had actually completed, but with the start of the new semester looming, it was all that was on her mind. She'd been counting down the days and panicking. She was teaching three classes in the spring semester, and only her Sociology of the Black Family was a new course prep, but she was doing what she normally did and tinkering with all her syllabi, not just the one that needed help. Syllabi trumped everything, which meant that the idea of writing had completely left her brain — not that she'd written much since she submitted that article — because she didn't have time. She couldn't walk into the first day of class without a syllabus, but she could pretend that she'd get another article submitted by spring break.

Her phone rang, and she was almost relieved to have a legitimate reason to take a break from looking at the e-campus course shell or the weekly schedule of readings, trying to divine the exact moment when her students would stop doing the coursework and make her life harder. She rushed from her office to her bedroom, where her cell phone was charging. When she bounced onto her bed, she squealed the moment she saw Alejandro's name on her phone screen. Her finger stilled above the green button to answer the call when she processed the sound she'd just made. "Jesus, get yourself together, girl," she mumbled to herself. "Hey," she answered.

"Hey."

That one word made Deja's stomach clench. She wasn't certain if his voice was always that deep and rumbly or if her brain had morphed it into the voice of her wet dreams because it had been so long since they'd seen each other.

"What are you up to right now?" he asked.

Once again, the world on his end of the line sounded big and noisy and lively, but she'd learned to tune it out and ignore the small frisson of jealousy that it sparked so she could just focus on him. "Just working on my syllabi," she said.

"Working, working, always working," he teased. "Did you rest at all?"

"Not much," she admitted, scooting back onto her bed and lying on her back. "But I did let a boy convince me to have Skype sex a few times."

She could just imagine the blush spreading across his cheeks. "Not nearly enough times," he mumbled, and Deja giggled. "Hey, are you busy tomorrow?" he asked.

"Define busy. I mean, these syllabi won't format themselves."

"I mean," he said, dragging that word out, "do you have any free time tomorrow to pick me up from the airport?"

Deja sat up straight, and her mouth fell open in a gasp. "Wait. What? You're not coming back until Sunday."

"I wasn't supposed to come back until Sunday, but I've

been looking at the forecast, and I'm worried that I'm going to get stuck in Chicago. Again."

Deja nodded absently. "So you changed your ticket? That must have been expensive."

"Not really, one of my sisters-in-law is a travel agent. She found me a ticket, but I need someone to pick me up from the airport. Normally, Mike and I drive back together in his car, but he's not changing his ticket." Alejandro chuckled. "I'm pretty certain that he's trying to get stuck somewhere so he can miss the first day of classes."

Deja licked her lips, too shocked to laugh. "I... Yeah, I can pick you up."

"You sure?" Alejandro asked, his voice brightening. "I can fill up your tank, or—"

"No, that's okay. Not necessary at all. I'm happy to." Her face warmed. Was she putting it on too thick? She thought she might have been, but she'd missed him all break and was finding it hard to contain her excitement at getting to see him earlier than she'd planned and that he'd called her for a ride.

"Okay." She could hear the smile in Alejandro's voice. "Um, I'll send you my itinerary as soon as we get off the phone. Thank you."

"You're welcome. I'm excited to see you."

His sigh was so soft that she almost thought she'd halluci-nated it, but she hadn't. She knew that she hadn't because when he spoke, his voice was just as soft. "I'm really excited to see you, too."

ALEJANDRO BELIEVED in protecting the sanctity of winter break.

He loved being home with his family, running the same

streets where he'd played as a kid and seeing all his friends from school and getting a break from the responsibilities of his job. He always made sure to put his Out of Office message on his email before he left town, it was as much a part of his packing rituals as remembering his travel pillow. He still checked his inbox while he was away, but he was the kind of academic who didn't feel the need to respond to anything less than an urgent message between semesters.

He learned early that the university made everything seem urgent, even when it wasn't, and students notoriously thought their grade complaints were more important than their quiz grades and attendance records throughout the semester, but he didn't have to agree. Even if he needed to change a grade or submit a report to the college, he told everyone that he would be happy to do so once the semester started and he was back on contract. He knew people hated his firm no, but he stood by it each time because sometimes his boundaries were all he had. As soon as the semester started, he made sure to juggle printing off his syllabi and class rosters and beginning to learn his new students' names with handling any old business form the previous semester. If that meant he was on campus for ten hours a day during the first week of the semester, it was worth it if he got to enjoy his time away.

And he did.

Alejandro usually had a long list of people to see while he was home. His family alone could take up his entire vacation if he let it, but his three brothers ate up most of his time, and as usual, kept him up the night before he flew back to Centreville. By the time they headed off to bed or back to their own homes, Alejandro's dad was already puttering around in the kitchen, playing with the new coffee machine they'd gotten them for Christmas. Alejandro had just enough time to shower and change before it was time to go. He carried his bags downstairs, and Angel lugged them into their dad's truck. His mom tried not to cry and shoved a warm foil package into his hands, which he knew would be filled with a couple of small tortillas full of egg and beans. His dad listened to traffic news on the way to the airport, and Alejandro ate his breakfast, the silence comfortable and strong, their hug at the passenger drop-off a final goodbye to home.

He was exhausted by the time he made it onto the plane. As he waited for takeoff, he looked at the to-do list on his phone, a list of things he needed to accomplish before the semester started, so he could hit the ground running as soon as he landed, but exhaustion hit him, and he was fast asleep before they were even at cruising altitude. When he woke up to change planes in Chicago, he wasted nearly his entire layover staring between the schedule of departing flights and the dark gray sky outside, terrified that his flight would be delayed or worse. Relief washed over him as he boarded the plane for the last short flight of the trip, but as soon as he was buckled into his seat, excitement coursed through him knowing that when he landed, Deja would be waiting for him.

ALEJANDRO STUFFED his arms into his coat before he de-planed. The local airport was so small that he could practically see the parking lot as soon as he walked into the terminal. He didn't want to seem too eager rushing toward baggage claim, especially because he knew the ground crew was notoriously slow, so he took a detour to the bathroom. He dug the small bag of toiletries out of his carry-on bag and tried to make himself look presentable. He washed his hands, brushed his teeth, washed his face, put more deodorant under his arms, and then used the small rollerball of cologne on his wrists and neck. He never put in any effort when he met up with Mike, but Mike's laughter didn't make his balls ache, so the extra step was worth it as far as he was concerned.

By the time he made it to baggage claim, his suitcase was on the conveyor belt, and he jogged forward to grab it. He pulled the long handle up and wheeled it forward, only to stop. Deja was standing just a few feet away, smiling shyly at him. He didn't realize just how much he'd missed her until this moment.

His gaze moved up and down her body. She was wearing a thick sweater dress under her winter coat and tall boots. Technically, her knees were the only parts of her legs exposed, but it was more than enough to make his muscles tense with desire. Her knees! He couldn't believe how thirsty he was. When his eyes moved back to her face, she bit down on her bottom lip. He kept his eyes on her face as he walked toward her.

"I parked in the garage," she said when he was close enough that she didn't have to yell. "I wasn't sure if you wanted to meet on the curb, or..." Her voice trailed off, and she looked even more nervous than before. "I texted you," she whispered.

Alejandro's steps faltered, and he dug into his pants pocket. He'd forgotten that he'd turned his phone off before his first flight took off. "Shit, sorry. I forgot to turn it on."

"No, it's okay," she said, shaking her head quickly and smiling at him in relief.

It couldn't have been more than thirty degrees outside, but having Deja smile at him like that made his body hot. In his dreams — because he'd absolutely dreamt about seeing Deja again for the first time more than once while he'd been away — he'd imagined that she would rush into his arms, or he'd sweep her up and kiss the fuck out of her. Instead, they stood awkwardly in front of one another, neither of them certain what to do next.

Finally, though, Deja looked up at him through her

eyelashes with a small smile on her face. "I really want to kiss you," she whispered.

That was all the invitation Alejandro needed.

He dropped his carry-on onto the ground — a vague prayer sounding in his brain that he didn't hear anything smash — and then reached for her. He held her face in his hands and pressed her against the fake column behind her. He stopped when their mouths were just barely touching, enjoying just breathing the same air as her.

"You smell like toothpaste," she said, her breath tickling his mustache.

"I wanted to smell good for you," he freely admitted.

She wrapped her arms around his waist and ground her hips against his, and they both moaned. "Fuck, that's sexy."

He pressed his hips forward, wanting her to feel what she was already doing to him. "This dress is sexy," he whispered back.

"Yeah?" She lifted onto her toes and breathed the question against his mouth and then licked along the curve of his lower lip.

And that was all the restraint Alejandro had. He pulled her face to his and captured her tongue between his lips. Deja moaned into the cavern of his mouth, and he felt that noise in his scalp. This was maybe the best kiss of his life. Was that too soon to say, he wondered? No, it wasn't, he decided immediately. He was thirty-six. He'd kissed a lot of women. He'd even kissed a couple of women at airport arrivals after months apart, but none of those kisses had ever taken him over like this. Every press and retreat of their lips seemed to make his blood rush faster in his veins. It had only been six weeks, but Alejandro felt as if he was pouring years of yearning into kissing Deja, and on some level, he was.

Before this moment, he used to try not to think about

her during winter, spring, and summer breaks. When school was out, he didn't have a reason to run into her, and because he went home regularly, it wasn't like he saw her around town. For over a year, seeing Deja had been like a perk of his job, but he'd always wanted more, and now, he had just that.

He had her body trapped against his and her tongue in his mouth, and classes didn't start for three more days. Time with Deja that had nothing to do with work was the best thing he'd never let himself hope for, and now that he had it, he felt greedy for more.

"Deja," he moaned against her lips, another firm press of his hips into hers.

"Garage," she said, licking his mouth and grinding against him.

Alejandro groaned. Someone was absolutely going to call security on them.

"Let's go to the garage," Deja whispered.

It took him a few seconds — and her hands slipping under his sweater to dig into his back — for him to understand what she was saying.

"Fuck," he breathed.

"Yeah, that's the gist," she giggled at him.

EVEN WHEN SHE WAS YOUNGER, car sex hadn't ever been Deja's thing. She didn't only like sex in a bed, but she did usually prefer to have sex in places where people couldn't see without the need for tint or steam, but as soon as Alejandro had kissed her like a starving man eating his first meal in months, she reconsidered her stance. Besides, she knew she wouldn't make it the hour-long drive home now that she'd felt his skin under her fingertips. Thankfully, Alejandro was on the same page.

They rushed out of the airport terminal to the short-term parking garage.

Alejandro dropped his bags into her trunk, but then his face fell. "Shit," he hissed.

"What's wrong? Did you forget something?"

"No," he mumbled. "I don't have condoms."

Deja hadn't been planning for car sex, of course, but she had stopped by the pharmacy on the way to the airport to get some essentials; cough drops, a few boxes of tissue and hand sanitizer for her office, and condoms, not for her office.

She smiled awkwardly at him. "I have some."

His eyebrows lifted, and he smiled at her. "You do?"

"Women should be prepared."

"I absolutely agree," he laughed, pushing her gently against her car. He gripped her hips, bunching her dress in his fists. "So, you came here prepared to fuck me?"

Every time Alejandro touched her, her body felt as if it was on the verge of overheating, and it was wonderful. He made her feel alive in a way she hadn't in so long. The six weeks apart had been more difficult than she felt comfortable admitting, to anyone, even herself, because they'd just barely begun to date before he left, but now that he was back and touching her, she felt a physical urge to make up for all their time apart. Her heart was racing, her pussy was clenching and damp, and her nipples were tightening just because she was close to him.

Had she come here prepared to fuck him in her car?

"Yes," she breathed. "I guess I did."

He brushed his lips against hers. "Good," he whispered and then kissed her slow and deep.

God, she'd missed him.

They scrambled into the backseat of her small SUV. It was

a tight fit for Alejandro's long legs, but they made it work. He sat in the middle seat as she tore the box of condoms open. He laughed at her eagerness even as he started palming his dick through his pants, revealing just how excited he was as well.

She pulled a foil packet from the box just as Alejandro pulled her onto his lap. She put her hands on his shoulders. She'd missed the feel of him, solid and strong underneath her, above her, inside her. Even though they were both clearly desperate to be together, as soon as they came face-to-face again, they stopped and stared.

"Hi," he whispered.

Her entire body flushed. "Hi."

He placed his palms on her thighs, edging the hem of her dress up her legs, and then he slipped his hands underneath, ghosting up her thighs. She circled her hips as one of his hands moved to grip her ass, and the other pushed between her legs.

"How long have you been wet?" he whispered to her.

"It's an hour's drive up here."

He laughed and pushed his hand into her underwear.

Deja groaned and shivered at how perfect his touch was after so long without it.

He petted her wet lips, stroking into the folds and circling her clit. "Don't move your hands," he directed.

She nodded, and he pushed a finger inside of her. "Fuck," she breathed, and that one word was like a release all on its own. Her head fell back, and she sighed up at the roof of her car.

"I wish we had time for me to get you off like this," he said. "I love the way your pussy feels around my fingers." He pushed another finger inside of her to prove his point.

She moaned and circled her hips, her pussy clenching around his digits, begging him to move them inside of her faster. "What's the rush?" she breathed.

His laughter was a husky burr that made the hair on her arms stand up. "Nothing but my own lust. I don't want to wait any longer to get my dick inside you," he admitted.

Deja found it endearing.

"Get me ready," he groaned to her, pumping his fingers inside her even as he squeezed her ass and encouraged her to settle her clit over the heel of his hand.

She whimpered, so caught up in the feel of him that it took a few seconds — and deep strokes of his fingers — for her to register his words. She looked down at him with bunched eyebrows and panting breaths.

He didn't rush her realization of the condom clutched in her grip, but he did reward her when she finally caught on by pushing one more finger inside her.

"Oh god," she groaned, her fingers already fumbling with the button of his jeans.

He was already semi-hard, but he could get harder. God, could he get harder and thicker and longer, and then he could hit all her favorite spots. He was already hard enough to slip the condom on, but she couldn't resist touching him, just like he couldn't resist her.

Deja set the foil packet aside and then gripped his dick with both hands. Alejandro groaned and pushed his hips up into her hold. Deja's back bowed with a shiver. She started pumping her hands up and down his shaft, stroking him slowly, running her thumb through his wet slit for a bit of lubrication and because his body shuddered each time she did that.

His fingers were still fucking her, and she was dripping into his palm, and now, she understood what he meant.

As much as she wanted them to get each other off with their hands, her pussy was as desperate for him as his dick was for her. Reluctantly, she released him, and his head fell back in a soft sigh. His fingers never stopped moving as she ripped open the condom and rolled it down his shaft.

"Ready?" she moaned, lifting onto her knees and then ducking as the top of her bun brushed the roof.

"For weeks," he said, pulling his hand from between her legs.

Now both hands were squeezing her ass, and the wet grip of the new hand somehow turned Deja on even more. He used his hands to help her position herself over his dick. She rubbed the head of his cock against her clit and then up and down her slit, and they both moaned.

They made eye contact again when the fat head of his dick began to stretch her opening. Alejandro watched her with a heated stare and parted lips as she sank down onto him slow enough to tease them both. They reveled at how amazing it felt to be back together, savoring this moment. Deja swore she could feel every veiny ridge of Alejandro's dick as he entered her, and she settled back into his lap.

"Hi," he breathed again.

Deja laughed as she bent down to kiss him. She slipped her tongue into his mouth, sliding along his. Her right hand moved from his shoulder to his beard. She enjoyed the soft downy feel of his facial hair. She decided that she had to feel it on her pussy before he shaved it. Had. To.

But that would be for later. Right now, he squeezed her ass, and she began to ride him.

She started off slow, with controlled circles of her hips, but that didn't last long. She was too hungry, and he felt the same. He squeezed her ass harder and scraped his teeth over her tongue. She shifted her legs to bring her knees up, and Alejandro moved along with her, resting his thighs under her ass and the backs of his hands against his jeans as he helped her to bounce up and down on top of him.

They were not subtle, and they did not care.

Deja's car was moving with the force of her grinding on top of him, the windows were steaming up, they were both sweating under their winter clothes, and it was a kind of perfection. Soon enough, their hips were meeting each other with loud, wet slaps, and her car filled with their loud, grunting moans.

"Shit. Holy shit," Deja screamed, her knees falling onto the seats and squeezing his hips.

Alejandro didn't stop and let her ride out that orgasm, and she would tell him how grateful she was about that later. He kept pressing his hips up into hers until she felt his dick swell just before he came in the condom with a deep rumbling grunt.

She shivered violently in another shuddering release.

"Kiss me," he moaned desperately.

Deja smiled dreamily, the post-orgasmic haze and foggy windows making the moment feel more special than it probably should have. She covered his mouth with her own and kissed him softly. Somehow, this kiss was the best of them all. The desperate passion of that first kiss in the terminal had made her blood rush, but this gentle familiarity made her heart swell.

"Welcome back," she whispered against his lips, smiling when he cupped the back of her head and pulled her mouth back to his.

SPRING SEMESTER

TWENTY-ONE

LATE JANUARY

As far as Deja was concerned, there were only three weeks in the semester where she got to feel like a human being rather than a walking-talking calendar notification and library help desk; the first week of classes, Thanksgiving break/spring break, and finals week.

Now that winter break was over and it was time to start a new semester, she felt annoyingly optimistic. She hadn't completed all the things she'd planned, but she'd submitted an article — and hadn't been rejected yet — she'd made minor revisions on her book, and Alejandro had fucked her senseless all weekend in between completing their course syllabi and online course shells. If that weekend was anything to go by, Deja thought this might be the best semester of her entire career. She was in such a great mood that she wasn't even complaining that the Faculty Senate had scheduled a meeting right at the beginning of the semester because of "urgent business."

"Hi, please end my suffering," Marie said, sidling up next to Deja.

They both took a second to find their name placards, and

then Deja turned to Marie. "You look great. Classes just started. What's up?"

"I just got invited to the on-campus interview for my job."

"Oh my god," Deja screamed. "That's amazing."

"Is it? I really don't have time to write my job talk, and they're going to observe one of my classes, which might suck because by then, my students might already hate me."

"None of your students hate you," Deja said. "I've literally overheard my students gushing about you and saying I suck in comparison. You'll be fine."

Marie rolled her eyes at Deja's optimism and chewed her lip. "At least I don't have to travel for it," she said eventually.

"There you go, optimistic baby steps. I'm proud of you."

Marie broke into a smile. "Shut up."

"Hard agree," Toni said, sidling up next to them. She plucked her placard from the table. "Why are we telling Deja to shut up?"

It was Deja's turn to roll her eyes. "Marie got the on-campus interview," she told Toni.

"Good. You deserve it. More than deserve it. And you're great in the classroom." She rolled her eyes. "My students won't shut up about you. I think they're giving me hints that they wish I was more like you. Sucks for them. Let's grab our seats, ladies."

She turned away, and Marie and Deja watched her back.

"No one gives compliments quite like her," Marie said, a small blush on her cheeks.

"Thank god," Deja muttered.

They scurried behind Toni into the auditorium. She stopped just in the entrance and looked around before jotting to the right. "Come on," she called over her shoulder.

In the main auditorium, Deja's eyes quickly scanned the

room. She was looking for Alejandro, but she didn't want to seem too obvious about it.

"He's over there," Marie said.

Deja's face warmed, and she ducked her head.

"Yeah, you were super obvious."

Deja turned to her right to see Alejandro standing behind his chair, chatting with Toni, while Mike joined in from his seat. Marie poked her in her side. "Ow. Seriously?"

"Yeah, girl. They can't hold those seats forever."

"Please. Toni will stare down anyone who tries to sit next to her."

"Yeah, but Layla Morgan doesn't feel fear."

And just as Marie said her name, Deja saw Layla step into the auditorium behind them. Deja saw her eyes sweep around the room, a much more obvious version of Deja's perusal. Excitement lit her face as she looked past Deja and Marie and spotted Alejandro.

Deja turned away quickly and headed toward their friends, but not fast enough. Layla brushed past them, making a beeline toward the empty chairs between Alejandro and Toni.

"Told you," Marie muttered, pushing at Deja's back even though they were all but running behind her.

"Is anyone sitting here?" Layla asked Alejandro just as Deja and Marie came to a stop behind her.

She interrupted Toni mid-word, and Alejandro turned toward her with bunched eyebrows. Deja couldn't see Toni's face, but she could just imagine the look her friend was giving Layla, and she shuddered on Layla's behalf. The other woman either didn't see it or didn't care because Layla only had eyes for Alejandro. Deja frowned at the look on Layla's face. She was looking at Alejandro as if they were the only two people in the room.

It wasn't that Deja didn't know that other women were

attracted to him. Oh, she knew. She hadn't been lying to him about that on their first date, but this was the first time that she'd ever seen anyone blatantly hit on him since they'd started dating, and she didn't like that at all, but she had no idea what to do about that feeling and in such a public space. So, she watched, frozen, as Layla waited all too patiently for Alejandro's answer.

But then Alejandro's eyes darted away from Layla's face and landed on Deja. Once they locked eyes, Alejandro's frown lifted into a smile, and his eyes squinted, soft wrinkles appearing at the corners. "Sorry, Layla, Deja and Marie are sitting here."

Marie pressed at Deja's back and pushed her forward. Layla turned toward her with bewilderment written on her face.

"Hey, Layla," Deja said in a bright tone.

Alejandro stepped back to pull the chair next to him back from the table, which made Layla stumble back a few steps. It was the first time they'd seen each other today, and she watched as his already warm eyes heated. She licked her lips, her mouth suddenly dry, knowing what it meant for him to look at her like that; what he might have done to her if they were alone. But they weren't.

"Let's keep it PG, people," Mike mumbled.

Deja dropped her bag onto the table and fell into her seat, the sound of Layla's huffing breath and sharp heel clicks fading as she flounced away.

"Faculty gossip listserv gonna be popping today," Mike said.

"Oh, definitely," Marie added.

"No," Deja said.

"Yes," Toni corrected with a raised and skeptical eyebrow.

"It's okay," Alejandro said, his hand resting on the back of her chair and his thumb lightly massaging her back. "We're not doing anything wrong."

"You don't get to be the judge of that, friend," Mike said. "You registered this thing with HR?"

"N-no," Deja muttered.

Alejandro flattened his hand fully against her back. "Don't freak her out. We have to register a relationship of more than six months. We're not there yet. Chill."

"It's easy to think that," Mike said.

"That's what the HR guidelines say. I read them."

"You did?" Deja gasped.

"Girl, you didn't? Have I taught you nothing?" Toni added with a disappointed shake of her head.

"The point I'm making," Mike interrupted, "is that there's a bit of a loophole. HR recommends that you register any personal relationship over six months, basically to absolve them of any culpability in harassment claims. But they suggest registering relationships sooner, just in case there are any reports of behavior that might violate the University's ethics code."

"That doesn't apply," Alejandro said. His voice was hard as steel, and it shut down the conversation. Mike raised his hands in surrender just as the Faculty Senate president banged on his gavel to start the meeting.

Alejandro turned to Deja with a smile. He squeezed her shoulder before turning in his seat and opening his laptop. Deja's eyes darted around the room until she found Layla. She was sitting next to someone Deja almost recognized from the Business College, talking. The scene didn't strike Deja as worrisome, but she was worried.

Her mind flashed back to her and Alejandro in her office, his hands shoved inside her panties and her tongue deep in his mouth.

And just like that, her new semester bubble burst.

THEY WERE FILING out of the auditorium. This semester, it was Toni who had to rush off to teach. Mike jogged along with her so they could talk about one of their students who'd nearly failed all their classes last semester.

"So, what are you two getting up to now?" Marie asked, tapping at her cell phone.

Alejandro was walking next to Deja, one hand holding the strap of his bag from his shirt, the other hanging at his side, brushing into Deja's every few steps. He wanted to grab her hand in his and hold it firmly, their palms touching, but they were still at work, and he knew she wouldn't allow it. Even though he'd tried to reassure her, Alejandro knew that Deja was freaked out by that encounter with Layla, and that made him want to hold her hand firmly even more, but he resisted.

"No plans yet. Wanna go grab dinner?" Deja asked Marie.

Alejandro had to stop himself from letting his frustration show because even though he liked Marie, he didn't want to go to dinner with her. He wanted to be alone with Deja so they could talk. Well, he wanted to make out with her for a bit, and then they'd talk, but they couldn't do either of those things if Marie came with them.

Marie turned toward them. She was a few steps below them on the staircase, in the crush of faculty trying to get the hell out of the building just in case someone came up with new business they *just* had to cover before next month. It had never happened before, but the possibility of extending that long ass meeting was like an urban legend; everyone knew it was probably fake, but it sounded just real enough to terrify.

"Can't. I need to start working on my job talk," Marie said.

"Oh, yeah. Do you need help?"

"Job talk?" Alejandro asked.

"Marie's interviewing for the tenure track position in Ethnic Studies," Deja said.

Alejandro raised his eyebrows at Marie. "They're making you interview for your own job." It wasn't a question. He knew it happened, and he knew better than most that the chances of her getting the position she'd been doing more than satisfactorily for years were much lower than they should have been. "I'm happy to help, too," he offered, brushing the back of his hand firmly against Deja's.

Marie smiled shyly at them. "I'll remember that," she said. "Maybe when I have a draft. I'll be in touch."

"Sounds good. Let us know how we can help," Deja said.

"Yeah, anything you need from us, we're there," Alejandro said, because he meant it, but also because he liked the way 'us' and 'we' sounded in Deja's bright tone, and he wanted to taste the promise of it right along with her.

"Cool. I'll email when I'm ready," she called, sprinting through a break in the crowd and darting away.

Alejandro wasn't sad to see her go, not in a mean way, at least.

"Well, bye to you, too," Deja muttered at the top of Marie's head as it bobbed away.

Outside, he and Deja turned toward each other, and she smiled before looking away. She was shy. It had been months since she'd been too nervous to meet his gaze. On the one hand, it was adorable, but on the other hand, he hated to think they could be so easily set back.

"Did you walk to campus today?" he asked.

She nodded.

"Want a ride home?"

She finally met his eyes. He watched as she licked her lips and then nodded again, but slowly this time. She sucked her bottom lip into her mouth, and it riveted him like it always did.

He wanted to do the same thing with her lip, to run his tongue along the soft flesh and taste her. And even though they were surrounded by a bunch of their colleagues and Mike's warning was still ringing in his ears, he didn't hide the depths of his desire for her in his eyes. He'd done it for long enough as far as he was concerned.

"Alejandro," she whispered to him. He heard the censure in her voice — he knew he shouldn't be looking at her this way while they were on campus — but he also heard the desire between the syllables of his name.

And fuck if he didn't love that.

"Come on," he said, tilting his head vaguely toward the faculty parking lot.

She took a few steps, and as she passed him, he bent forward to whisper softly into her ear. "I promise not to touch you yet."

She shivered on that last word.

So did he.

IT REALLY DIDN'T TAKE LONG to drive from campus to Deja's apartment complex. On a bad day, like homecoming weekend or graduation, it was probably faster for her to walk than to drive, Alejandro figured as she directed him to her complex. Alejandro was only paying as much attention as it took to turn when and where she said, but the rest of his focus — most of his focus, honestly — was centered on his hand on her thigh.

It was possessive because now that he could finally touch her, he didn't want to stop.

They'd gone over their schedules for the semester and realized that just like last semester, they were going to struggle to see each other as much as they wanted. Deja had early intro classes, and Alejandro had late graduate classes. They had meetings on top of meetings, although there was a bright spot since they were co-chairing that outreach committee together, but he was still waiting on a few people to respond to the Doodle poll, so those meetings weren't on the books yet, and he was worried that by the time they finally set a meeting schedule, something else would have popped up in Deja's schedule, and she'd have to pull out. He'd promised her that he would take on the burden of all the scheduling, so he hadn't shared this fear. He didn't want to her to feel pressured to stay on the committee if she really couldn't make it work, and he really didn't want to put one more stressor on her plate.

The reality was that Alejandro just wanted to take care of Deja as much as she'd let him. But he knew she wouldn't just let him, so he squeezed her thigh with his right hand as he turned left into her apartment complex, reassuring her and himself that he was there. He pulled his car into a parking spot she indicated with one hand and reluctantly let go to shift his car into park and depress the button to turn it off, before grabbing her leg again and squeezing.

He turned to her and smiled. "So..."

A slow smile spread across her mouth in answer. "So," she breathed. "You want to come inside?"

Alejandro had to take a deep breath to collect himself so he could respond appropriately. What he wanted to tell Deja was, "Fuck yes, I want to come inside," because he wanted to see her apartment, see how she lived, and maybe even, if he was lucky, crawl in between her sheets. He'd wanted that before they'd started dating, and it was only stronger now. He could feel the desire to be in every part of Deja's life in his pores, but he didn't want to freak her out. "Yeah, I'd love to," he said with a calm he didn't feel, but he sounded reasonable to his own ears.

Alejandro grabbed Deja's hand for the walk to her apartment. He gripped her waist as she fished her keys from her purse and pushed her door open. They slipped their shoes off at the door, and she locked all the locks behind them.

Her house smelled like apples and cinnamon, but the artificial versions of those scents, like a candle or something. It was warm and inviting, and those were exactly the words that he would have used to describe Deja's tidy apartment.

"Do you want something to drink?" she asked in a shy voice.

Alejandro nodded. "Whatever you have. I'm not picky."

"Okay," she said, taking a couple of steps away before turning to him and gesturing toward her living room. "Make yourself at home."

He had the restraint to wait until she was out of sight before turning into her long living room, bisected by a big burnt orange couch that looked like he would sink right into it when he sat down. On one half of the room, there was a cozy sitting area around a television, and on the other was a wide-open space, with bookshelves around the perimeter and a comfortable chair that matched her couch and a lamp in the corner. A part of Alejandro wanted to know what kind of books she read at home — as opposed to the books in her office — but he was really interested in all the pictures crowded on top of the shelves and hanging on the walls. Who was so important to Deja that she took the time to print out pictures in this day and age and frame them? The answer was clear at once.

"Is this your nephew?" Alejandro called to her.

"Yeah. His name's Jamal. He's the only grandkid, and he's spoiled rotten." Her voice got closer as she spoke, and he turned to see her with two glasses of water in her hands. "But he's, like, the best kid, so it's okay."

"Yeah?"

"Yeah. I mean," she said, her nose wrinkling in the adorable way he loved, "he's got this weird obsession with zombies. We're all hoping he grows out of it, but if he doesn't, it's not a bad hobby. We think. Do you have nieces or nephews? I can't believe I've never asked that before."

"It's okay," he said as she extended a glass of water to him. "I've got two nieces. One of my little brothers, Carlos. He and his wife met in, like, junior high and have been together for forever. Two kids, cute little house down the street from my parents," he said and smiled, shaking his head. "It's a real different kind of life."

"Yeah," Deja said. "That sounds like my sister. My brother-in-law was literally the boy next door. She works at the same company as my dad and lives close enough to walk to my parents' house too. Sometimes, I think I should have followed in her footsteps."

Alejandro nodded. "I think that sometimes, too. Every time I come home, I wonder what my life would be like if I had, but..."

"But?" Alejandro wondered if Deja could hear the desperation in her voice. He understood it, even if she didn't, that need for someone who understood your life to tell you that you'd made the right decision and that you could succeed or to point you in a different direction if you couldn't. He'd felt it, and he'd seen it in other people so many times, but it broke him to hear that tone in her voice and see the hunger for reassurance in her eyes. And even though he knew that Deja wouldn't let him take care of her, he gave her the reassurance she was practically begging for.

"Carlos is a mechanic. He's good at it. He's fucking great at it, and he loves it. He was always a serious kid, and he wanted to be just like papi and have a life just like our parents'. This is what I'm good at. I'm where I'm supposed to be. So are you," he couldn't stop himself from adding.

Alejandro watched as Deja took in his words. He didn't know if they sank in, but he could tell her again, happily, any time she wanted to hear them. He sipped his water, and she did the same. And then she chewed her bottom lip as she thought about what he'd said, and he watched her. They stood in silence for a while until she turned to him with a shaky smile.

"You want to order takeout for dinner?" she asked nervously.

"Fuck, yes," Alejandro breathed.

"THIS IS SO GOOD," Alejandro said, finishing the chicken wing in his hand and tossing it onto the plate between them.

They were sitting on her living room floor, eating wings and onion rings from the best dive bar in Centreville.

"The food in this town might be garbage, but they absolutely get burgers and wings right," Deja said.

He smiled and nodded, dunking another wing in ranch dressing. She preferred blue cheese, but she decided not to hold his dipping sauce against him, he was so perfect in so many other ways. Actually, she thought to herself, Alejandro Mendoza was perfect in every other way, so if he wanted to eat his wings with ranch, at least they'd never fight when they went out for wings.

"So, um..." she said, breaking an onion ring apart between her fingers. "About what Mike said earlier."

He didn't answer for a long stretch of seconds, and she chanced looking up at him. He pointed at his mouth to indicate that he was still chewing. She nodded and popped a piece of the onion ring in her hand into her mouth.

"What about it?" he finally responded.

"Do you...think we should disclose our relationship to HR sooner?" she asked. She was trying for casual, but she didn't think she'd succeeded.

"We can," Alejandro offered carefully. "If we do that, though, it'll mean...you know, that this is real. For us, I mean," he added hastily. "HR doesn't actually give a shit about how serious we are, but I mean...if we disclose, whenever we disclose, I'd hope that meant this is going somewhere."

Deja hadn't thought of it that way, and now she had a new anxiety-inducing piece of information to deal with. Was this relationship with Alejandro going somewhere? She hoped so, but did he? Did he want something more than their casual dating? Or was this it? Was that why he wanted to wait on talking to HR? Did she want to know what he thought? Yes. But also, no.

"We don't have to make any decisions right now," Alejandro said. "And I'm fine to leave it up to you."

Deja shook her head.

"But if it helps..." he said, pulling a wing apart in his hands, "this is a real thing." He said the words so firmly that Deja felt as if her body rocked with each one, as if the force of his certainty knocked into her.

She liked it. She licked her lips and then met his eyes. "You know, I don't usually invite men to my house."

"No?" he asked, smiling in relief. "So, you're saying I'm special?" he asked with a raised eyebrow.

Deja rolled her eyes and popped the rest of her onion ring into her mouth. "You're eating wings with ranch, let's not get cocky, okay?"

"What's wrong with ranch?" he asked with a laugh that Deja felt all over her skin.

She didn't answer his question, and he didn't push. They

ate in companionable silence for a second before he spoke again. "You don't teach tomorrow, right?" he asked.

"Yeah."

"Neither do I."

She tried to bite back her smile. "Yeah. I know. What's your point?"

He shrugged, tossing the chicken bone on the plate between them. "Nothing, just...you know...if you were interested in having a sleepover with the special dude you're dating—"

Deja rolled her eyes and threw a packet of wet wipes at him. "Shut up."

He caught the packet with a deep huff of laughter.

"You really want to spend the night?" she asked.

He looked at her, and it was his turn to roll his eyes. "Of course, I do, but I'm not gonna beg."

"You sure about that?" she asked, her voice dipping with a seedling of arousal; a seed she knew he would water.

His hand froze over the basket of onion rings. She saw his Adam's apple bob, and that made her smile. "Please," he whispered.

She smirked triumphantly. "Thought so."

TWENTY-TWO

FEBRUARY

TUESDAY

Deja's day started off amazingly.

Alejandro had a late graduate course Monday night, but instead of going home after his class, he'd come to her apartment. He'd shown up with dark circles under his eyes, his jacket thrown over the crook of his arm and an overnight bag in his hand.

They hadn't even had sex.

She'd waited nervously in bed while he changed into his pajamas and brushed his teeth. But when he crawled into her bed and wrapped her in his arms, all those nerves had seeped slowly from her body. He was asleep in barely fifteen minutes, and she'd lain awake for a few minutes longer, her cheek pressed against his chest, listening to the soft burr of his slumber. It was perfect.

And then she'd woken up to Alejandro's long body spooning hers, his lips softly kissing over her shoulder and his dick pressing into the curve of her ass. Deja hadn't woken up this well since...well, ever. The feeling of Alejandro in her bed was even better than the first morning after the academic year ended when she woke up knowing that her days were mostly her own for the next three months. Alejandro was better, and that was saying a lot.

"You up?" he whispered into her ear.

She nodded.

"You have time?"

Deja shuddered as he sucked her earlobe into his mouth and pushed his hips forward, pumping lightly into her.

She reached for her cellphone on the bedside table and tipped it up just enough to check the clock. Six in the morning.

"Half an hour," she croaked. That was pushing it. She needed to shower and walk to campus, but if she drove, she could buy them a few minutes. She hadn't double-checked her lecture notes last night because she'd been too busy grading short-answer quizzes and working on her midterm review sheets. She'd given the lecture for her eight o'clock class before, but she had to rush straight from that to her nine-thirty class, and this lecture was entirely new. A small part of her brain was screaming, "Fuck morning sex, bitch, you're already late. That lecture won't edit itself." It was a small but very loud part that she forced herself to ignore because she'd been working on that, not giving into the negative self-talk that told her she wasn't doing enough and never could. She needed to learn not to crumble to the voice that said failure was imminent. She didn't believe it, not really, but that voice was so loud that just ignoring it wasn't really an option. Eventually, she knew she'd have to learn how to replace it with something else, but she wasn't there yet, so ignorance was her temporary friend.

"I'll be quick," Alejandro whispered into her ear, and then his body froze. "That's not what I meant?"

Deja buried her face in her pillow to muffle her laughter.

"I meant I'll get you off quick," Alejandro whined, reaching over her to pull the bedside table drawer open and fish around for a condom. "Deja, stop laughing. You know what I meant."

She turned her head to look at him out of the corner of her right eye. "There are pills for that, you know," she whispered innocently.

Alejandro smiled and shook his head. "Asshole," he muttered to himself while Deja broke into laughter again.

She didn't try to hide it this time.

Alejandro rolled his eyes at her and crawled under the sheets. She heard him muttering against her stomach and thighs as he kissed and licked at her, pushing her legs open and pushing her underwear aside, and then her laughter turned to moans.

His mouth and hands helped her ignore the urgency to do more and be more productive. He grounded her. She'd never had that before. She knew Alejandro was rooting for her, and even better, he was getting her off before her busiest day of the week.

Deja had dated a lot of losers in her life.

Alejandro was no loser.

It took longer than half an hour, and they had to shower together, so she wasn't too late, but letting Alejandro eat her awake and then turn her over and fuck her into her mattress was absolutely worth it. More than worth it.

Great way to start the day.

———————

TWO HOURS LATER, and Deja was having a very bad day.

It started snowing between her first and second classes. She realized only as she was rushing across campus that she'd been in such a rush that she'd forgotten her gloves and scarf. She didn't even have a hat in her bag. By the time she made it to her second class, her ears were so cold they hurt, and her fingers were so cold, it was hard to type. It took her three tries to correctly input her password into the classroom computer.

And then her lecture bombed. It wasn't that she didn't know the material, but something she'd never appreciated as a student was how much a great lecture was the consequence of a sometimes elusive mixture of knowledge, practice, and magic. Deja had the knowledge, but definitely not the practice, and even though she knew she was a good teacher, she always felt like a novice the first time she taught a new class, no matter how well she knew the raw material. Figuring out the perfect combination of visuals and discussion and data to keep students engaged — the magic — didn't come easy to her, and standing in front of her students feeling like a thawing popsicle didn't help.

She was happier than her students when that class was over.

She'd just thawed out only to have to bundle up the best she could and trudge back across campus to Mark Hall, freezing again. Her hands felt like ice blocks by the time she stepped onto the Sociology floor. Her steps faltered for a second as she looked down the East hallway toward her office only to see a line of students already lined up outside her door.

Office hours.

She took a deep breath and began to walk toward her students.

"Hey, Doc," Jerome yelled when she was close.

She put on her work smile and returned his greeting. "Give me five minutes to put my stuff down, okay, y'all," she said to the queue. She could hear her Texas accent fighting to come out and knew she must be damn tired.

She unlocked her office and slipped inside. She took off her winter coat, turned the heater up, and plopped into her office

chair. She signed into her desktop computer and turned grate-
fully to the kettle she kept in her office for just these occasions.
She grabbed a bottle of water from her stash in the bottom left
drawer of her desk, filled her kettle, and turned it on before
turning back to her office door. She took another deep breath
before pulling it open and kicking the doorstop into place.

She leaned out into the hallway. "I hope you all sorted out
an order," she said to the students waiting for her, a mix of Sociology majors and students from her classes. "Whoever's first,
come on in."

For the next two hours, she sat behind her desk, sipping at
her tea, and took a little solace in the fact that she didn't have to
give another lecture today, even as she ignored the calendar
notification about her last meeting of the day.

———

ALEJANDRO HAD BEEN TRYING to tamp down on his
own happy excitement all day.

Technically, there was very little about his afternoon
schedule that would normally inspire any kind of excitement,
just meetings and more meetings, but his last meeting of the
day was with Deja. Other people would be there too, but Deja
was the one that really mattered.

Even though he'd woken up with her in his arms this
morning and it had only been a few hours since they'd seen
each other, he still felt desperate to be near her again. In truth,
that had been the case since he'd arrived back in town from
winter break. It seemed like every day, he felt as if he was
falling deeper into this pit of need for her, and he didn't want to
crawl out.

The only real downside was the few times he saw her
across the Oval or around their building and couldn't touch

her. Sometimes, his fingers would flex with desire, and it would take all his restraint to stop himself, and he was terrified that one day he would fail. She made him feel reckless, and that was the last thing they needed.

If it were up to him, he and Deja would have already gone to HR to register their relationship, so at least he didn't have to stop himself from standing too close to her just in case someone could tell from his body language that they were sleeping together. And maybe once they did that, he could sate his own desire by just holding her hand as they walked across campus together.

But Deja wasn't ready. When they were off-campus, she was all in on their relationship, but it was as if the minute she stepped onto the North Oval, she changed. He didn't want to push her too hard or too fast to make their relationship University-official, because he wasn't even entirely sure that her reticence was about him. So until she was ready, he decided to let her set the pace and be happy that they had an hourlong meeting on the books once a month for the rest of the semester and maybe beyond. Whatever it took to snatch just a few more minutes in her presence.

Alejandro checked his watch as he stepped in line at Go Brews!

"What's up, man?" Mike said behind him, enthusiastic as ever. "You ready for this meeting?"

Alejandro smiled and shrugged. "It's just a meeting."

"Sure," Mike said with a knowing grin.

"Shut up," Alejandro said.

Mike laughed, and Alejandro rolled his eyes.

He spotted Sheila when she stepped into the coffee shop. He waved at her, and she headed straight toward them and stepped into line next to Alejandro.

"You sure you want to teach them that cutting in line is

fair?" he asked, gesturing at the line of students that had formed behind them like magic. This was campus coffee shop rush hour.

Sheila turned to him with a mischievous smile on her face. "We're historians, not philosophers. All we do is teach them life isn't fair."

"That's harsh, Dr. Meyer," a student yelled from somewhere down the line.

Sheila turned and squinted at them. "Shannon, have you done the reading for today?" she called.

"I have," Shannon yelled back, "and you're being a Gilded Age baron right now, FYI."

Mike stifled a puff of laughter, and Alejandro smiled.

Sheila broke into a wide smile at her student. "I like the analogy. Five extra credit points."

"Nice," Shannon yelled back.

She turned to Alejandro with a wink. "Every moment is a teachable moment," she said before turning forward again.

The line moved faster than it normally did at this time. Alejandro, Mike, and Sheila ordered and then stepped aside to wait for their drinks.

Out of the blue, Sheila turned to him and peered at him with focused intent. "Are you seeing anyone?" She asked the question lightly, as if, during eight years in the department, they'd ever talked about his personal life, or as if this was a normal question to ask a colleague.

They'd talked about *her* personal life several times.

Alejandro had always found that it was very common for married faculty to share details of their personal lives without any prompting, and because he was collegial, he listened to them unload about the trials and tribulations of their relationships and children's lives and inadvertently learned more about them than he ever wanted to know. But part of the reason

Alejandro listened was because he didn't want to share. He was shocked at how easy it was for his colleagues to tell him about their lives and never ask about his as if he was their therapist. It was rude, but it made it easier to keep his private life private. And the few times someone asked about his relationship status, he tended toward tightlipped, short responses and waited for the conversation to move along.

But Sheila's question came as a surprise, and Alejandro was unprepared for the overwhelming urge he felt to tell her that he was seeing someone.

"Um," Alejandro muttered, stalling for time. "Why do you ask?"

In the corner of his eye, he saw Mike turn away to hide his laughter.

Sheila shrugged. "No reason. I just realized that I've never asked you that before, and I feel like I know everyone's situation but yours."

Alejandro just nodded, panicking inside at wanting to tell her but knowing that he shouldn't. If Deja wasn't ready to tell HR, she almost certainly didn't want the chair of his department to know.

"Ah, never mind," Sheila said. "That question is probably an HR nightmare. Forget I even said anything."

Alejandro laughed, happy to comply. Mike silently nodded, winking at Alejandro behind Sheila's back.

"Alejandro," the student behind the counter yelled, two cups in her hand. "Oh hey, Profé, what's up?"

Alejandro walked to the counter and smiled at Liliana Juarez. He took the cups of coffee from her. "Lili, where have you been? I thought you were going to be in my 'Revolutions' class this semester."

She shrugged. "I wanted to, but my off-campus job changed my hours this semester, so I had to drop. Maybe next time?"

Alejandro nodded. "I'll make sure I teach it again before you graduate, alright?"

Liliana smiled brightly. "You're the best, Profé, you know that?"

"Say that louder," he teased and tilted his head to Sheila, "Dr. Meyer's my boss."

Sheila laughed, and Liliana waved before moving away to make another drink.

Another student handed Mike a cup, and Alejandro nodded his head at his friend. "We've got a meeting in a bit," he said to Sheila. "Have a good afternoon."

Sheila smiled at him. "Who's the second coffee for?" she asked.

Mike did a bad job of hiding this burst of laughter.

Alejandro thought about lying, but he hated that. Besides, there was a perfectly plausible reason for this. "Um, Deja Evans in Sociology. We're co-chairing that new outreach committee for the Dean. Remember?"

"Oh yes, I know Deja." That was all Sheila said before turning away.

Alejandro and Mike walked out of the coffee shop and through the student union cafeteria. Mike at least had the decency to wait until they were completely outside before he burst out laughing again.

"I hate you," Alejandro muttered.

TWENTY-THREE

Deja closed her office door at exactly two on the dot, and someone knocked before she could even get back to her desk. She exhaled in annoyance, turned, and wrenched the door open again. Her work smile shifted into an actual smile at the sight of Alejandro standing in the hallway, a cup of coffee in each hand.

"Ready?" he asked, entirely too cheerful for this meeting.

She turned around and muttered, "No."

The door closed behind him. "Sounds like you're having a great day."

Deja grabbed her notebook, a pen, and her phone.

"I swear, I haven't had a moment to rest since..." Her voice trailed off as the smile on Alejandro's face widened.

He smiled at her as if they shared a dirty secret because they did, a good and dirty one.

"Since when?" he asked, prodding playfully at her silence. In barely five seconds, his voice had dipped from happy to aroused, deeper and warm, and Deja could feel it across her skin.

"We promised we wouldn't do that here," she whispered. Her mouth was suddenly dry.

"Do what? It's just a question."

Deja turned to her desk, swiping at the sweat on her upper lip. "I need to turn the heater down," she muttered to herself.

Alejandro laughed softly behind her.

She grabbed the water bottle on her desk, sipped, and then walked across the room to turn the heater down. When she turned back to Alejandro, she avoided looking him in the eyes. The last thing she needed was to let him make her horny before a meeting where all eyes would be on them.

"Shouldn't we get to this meeting?" she asked.

He stepped to the side and nodded at her office door. "After you," he said.

"Alejandro," she whispered, walking toward the door.

"Deja," he whispered back as she passed him.

Deja opened the door to Marie's hand, raised as if she was about to knock.

"Well, well, well, what have we here?" Marie sang as her eyes lifted to see Alejandro behind Deja.

"We're just heading up to the meeting," Deja said defensively.

"Mmmmhmm," Toni replied from the hallway.

Deja rolled her eyes and stepped into the hallway. "You two could have gone to the conference room without us. Why are you here?" She closed and locked her door after Alejandro exited.

"Us," Marie whispered to Toni with a smug grin.

Alejandro laughed. Deja let out a frustrated breath.

"We went to the conference room, but Mike was there with Layla Morgan. Hard pass," Toni replied.

"You two left Mike with Layla?" Alejandro asked.

"If he wanted to be saved, he should have said something," Toni said with a shrug.

"Why is she even on this committee again?"

Deja rolled her eyes and turned to Alejandro. He raised his hands in supplication. "She overheard Dean Ward talking to me about it last month and asked to join. I couldn't say no, especially not in front of the Dean. No one asks for more service."

Deja sighed. "What's done is done. Let's just go," she said, a knot of tension forming in her gut.

———

MEETINGS GO SOUTH every day in so many ways, but Deja had assumed that a first meeting just to put all the committee members in the same room for a brainstorming session would be the easiest meeting of her day. Certainly easier than going through a student's essay draft line by line. And while there were still so many things Deja still didn't know about how the university functioned, apparently expecting a smooth meeting was the height of naïveté.

She was surprised into speechlessness. Shocked at first, and then angered.

To be fair, she and Alejandro had handpicked their friends and faculty of color they trusted to be on the committee; Toni, Mike, and Marie, alongside Dr. Keith Tolentino, one of the few full professors of color in the Art department. They were great. But the problems started as soon as the committee veered away from their handpicked members. Layla had spent most of the meeting looking at Alejandro as if she wanted to eat him and wasn't at all worried that the other people in the room would notice. The Dean had asked for one of the Associate Deans, Martin Stampp, to sit in as ex-oficio. He was less of a problem than dead weight, since he'd sat down, introduced himself, and then promptly dozed off for the rest of the meeting. And then there was Caroline Enwright, chair of the Women's Studies department, another of the Dean's appointments.

Deja knew of her by name and had seen her at events around the College. She'd even probably met her at some point, though she didn't remember it. As soon as Caroline had introduced herself, Deja knew she wasn't going to like working with her. It had only gone downhill from there. Caroline was out of touch with student needs, especially the needs of students of color, and she was dismissive of their challenges and downright hostile toward developing programs for their success, which was the entire purpose of this committee. She was also openly condescending to Deja and Marie because they were junior and adjunct faculty. In a nutshell, she was every stereotype of older white women in academia rolled into one thin-lipped, passive-aggressive, elitist form. And in kitten heels to boot.

What should have been a cordial discussion quickly devolved as Caroline talked down to Marie, who just shut down and stopped talking in the first ten minutes. Deja had balled her hands into fists, her body boiling with rage. She wanted to tell Caroline that she should step down from her high horse since Marie, who taught more classes than anyone else in the room, also taught more students of color than them. She was also, as an instructor, overworked and underpaid, and this service assignment was something she'd agreed to because she cared about her students, not because she was looking for yet another line on her CV. But Deja had long since conditioned herself to be deferential to senior faculty as part of her life on the tenure track, so she shut down soon after Marie.

The strain of keeping her mouth shut was too much for Deja to bear. She began to beat herself up internally for not speaking up on her friend's behalf. Deja thought of herself as a principled person, but she sat in that meeting and had to wonder if that was true anymore. Had it ever been?

Meanwhile, Toni and Mike tried to work through Caroline's contrary contributions while Alejandro tried to keep the meeting moving along so they could cover the goals he and Deja had outlined, while Layla hung on his every word but didn't make any meaningful contribution.

It was a mess of a first committee meeting, and Deja wanted nothing more than to back out of this entire endeavor and run for the hills.

———

"OKAY," Alejandro said, a little louder than he meant, cutting Caroline off mid-sentence. "I think that's enough for today. Deja and I," he stressed the words while looking Caroline in the eye, a not-so-subtle reminder that they were the committee's co-chairs, "will go over what we've talked about and send the minutes and points of consideration before our next meeting."

It was only sheer force of will that made his voice sound calm and professional because he felt as if his head was about to explode. This meeting had been a disaster. A big one.

"Have a great evening, everyone," he said through gritted teeth.

Associate Dean Stampp woke up right in that moment, placed both hands on the conference table and stood. "Great work, everyone," he said and turned toward the door.

Caroline darted after him. "Dean Stampp, do you have a second?" she asked in a voice that sounded like nails on a chalkboard to Alejandro.

"I've gotta run to class," Toni said. She grabbed Marie's wrist and squeezed. "I'll call you later, okay?" Marie didn't answer, and it made Alejandro feel terrible.

"Where's your class?" Mike asked Toni.

"Paul," she said.

"I'm going that way; I'll walk you." Toni nodded and headed for the door. Mike turned to look at Alejandro with tired eyes. "I'll call you later."

Alejandro nodded at him and then Keith as they left the room.

In a whirlwind, Marie stood from her chair and grabbed her bag. She mumbled a goodbye to Deja before rushing from the room.

The only people left were him, Deja, and Layla, and Alejandro felt terrible, but he really wanted Layla to just fucking leave.

Instead, she turned to him with a smile. "Alejandro, do you have a second?"

"Actually—" Alejandro started, but Deja cut him off.

"I'll leave you two alone," she said, grabbing her pad of paper and cell phone.

"Deja?" Alejandro called, his face almost hurting with the depth of his frown.

She turned to him and put on her best collegial smile, which only conveyed a fraction of the warmth of her real smile, the smile she'd given him just this morning in her bed. "I've got some grading to do," she said, avoiding his eyes. "I'll email you later."

Alejandro's mouth fell open in shock as he watched her walk swiftly and silently from the room.

"So, Alejandro," Layla whispered in a seductive tone.

He turned to her and had to force himself not to roll his eyes. He knew Layla had a crush on him. He wasn't interested. He didn't care. But he'd never been great at letting people down personally. "What can I help you with, Layla?" he ground out.

She smiled at him and leaned forward, laying her breasts on the table for him to see. He looked away.

"Now that everyone is gone, I just wondered..." She took a deep breath, and Alejandro felt his entire body seize. "This might be forward, but I was wondering if you wanted to get a drink sometime."

"I'm seeing someone," he blurted out. He'd struggled with deciding whether or not to tell Sheila this fact earlier, but not now, not with the memory of Deja's sad smile in his mind. He saw Layla's face crumple, but he didn't sit around to help her through this rejection; it wasn't his job. Besides, he stood with an angry heat in his limbs because Layla had kept him from comforting Deja.

He was mad at her and himself and Caroline and the whole situation. This was not how he'd expected this meeting to go.

TWENTY-FOUR

FRIDAY

One bad day always leads into two bad days. That's at least what Deja had always found to be true. She could never have just one bad day, but a three-day bad day streak was a little much for her to handle.

The only good thing was that it was finally Friday.

She didn't have any classes or meetings, but she was still on campus. She had a list of administrative things to do, and with her sour mood, she knew she wouldn't get them done at home. Nope, if she stayed home, she knew full well that she'd stay in bed and watch *Snapped* all day. It was a tempting thought, but in the end, she'd decided to go to her office and save the murderous women for the weekend.

Normally, Deja took some care with how she looked when she came to campus on weekdays. She liked to look presentable and professional — at the very least she didn't want to dress so casually that she could be mistaken for a student — but today, she didn't care. She showered and threw on a pair of leggings, a t-shirt, a hoodie, and sneakers. She threw her laptop and a thermos of coffee in her backpack and walked to campus. She could have driven and not had to interact with anyone at all, but she needed the walk to campus to clear her head.

She pulled her beanie over her ears, pushed her sunglasses higher on her face, and felt like a burglar sneaking into her office until she firmly shut her door behind her. She didn't want to see or talk to anybody, including Alejandro. Actually, the only person that she wanted to talk to less than Alejandro was Caroline. Or maybe Layla. Everyone. Absolutely everyone she worked with was at the bottom of her list of people she wanted to communicate with today, so she was dodging everyone's text messages and phone calls, including Toni and Alejandro's.

She felt bad about it. She knew it wasn't their fault that the meeting had imploded, and her sour mood was squarely on her own shoulders, but this was what Deja did. When she felt bad or stressed or insecure or anxious, she hid away, cocooning herself in her work and her apartment, and she never asked for help. She knew it was unhealthy, but she didn't know how to break herself of the habit. Toni had, unfortunately, been through this with her before, and she understood. She'd keep texting Deja until Deja was ready to text back. But Alejandro... She didn't know how to explain to Alejandro what she was going through and explain why she needed space even though she didn't blame him, which added another layer of stress. Soon enough, she guessed that he would get sick of reaching out and break up with her, which only sank her deeper into the funk she'd been living in for most of the week because she knew a way to head that off was to talk to him, but...she was terrified that she'd tell him she needed space and he wouldn't understand.

Yeah. *Snapped* marathon imminent, she thought as she opened her laptop and got down to business updating attendance scores, easing herself into the boring work she needed to complete before she could write this week off for good with wine and too much sleep.

———

"COME IN," Toni called through the crack of her office door.

Alejandro pushed it open and stepped inside.

Toni glanced up at him and smiled, almost as if she'd been expecting him. "What can I do for you, Dr. Mendoza?"

Alejandro shoved his hands into his pockets. "Deja," he said simply.

"What about Dr. Evans?"

"Toni," he huffed.

The pen in her hand froze over the essay she was marking up, and she looked at him. "Dr. Ward," she corrected.

Alejandro rolled his eyes. "Deja hasn't been returning my calls or messages."

"Mine, either," she said simply.

"I drove by her apartment, but the lights were off. I thought about going to her classes, but I just... Is she okay? Aren't you worried about her?"

She set the pen in her hand down. "This might shock you, but only if you aren't paying attention. I'm literally always worried about Deja and Marie, and Cristina in Biology, Annette in English, Sun in American Studies, and damn near every other woman of color in the College. Hell, there are some women in the Education and Business colleges I'm worried about as well because, as you know, the university keeps hiring these women of color and then throwing them to the wolves.

They do more service in and out of their departments, on and off-campus. They teach bigger service classes and get some of the worst student evals. They publish far less, and if they don't leave before they go up for tenure — and many, many,

many of them do leave and are trying to leave right now —
they're denied tenure and have to leave anyway. And the ones
that make it through the tenure process are a mess.

They're anxious and have a bunch of health issues they
didn't have when they came here, or their previous conditions
are worse. They're burnt out. And still, they do more service for
little, if any, recognition or support from their departments, the
college, or men of color. And on top of all that, they make much
less than their male colleagues. Far less. Does that sound like
anyone we know?"

"I know this, Toni," Alejandro said.

"I know you know this, and you're one of my favorite men
on this entire campus. That's the only reason I'm going to tell
you where to find Deja."

"You know where she is?"

Toni rolled her eyes. "Of course, I know where she is. Deja
and Marie are creatures of habit. It's easier to keep track of
them and know how to help them whenever they're ready for
help."

"Tell me," Alejandro said.

Toni raised an eyebrow at him, and he shrugged.

"Sorry," he mumbled, like a chastised child.

"You know how this university treats its faculty of color,
but I don't think you realized that it treats us differently than it
treats you. Not until you started dating Deja, at least. And that
was okay. I could always count on you to help faculty of color,
especially Latinx faculty, but I haven't been able to count on
you to notice that there are *no* women of color in your department and bring that up to Sheila when she crows around here
on her diversity kick. I haven't been able to count on you to
point out to Dean Ward that while we're doing better than any
other college in the university hiring faculty of color, that's not
the entire picture. We're doing just as bad in retaining women

of color as everyone else. Meanwhile, we teach most of the students of color, and the burden of retaining and mentoring them falls on us.

So, when you run to Deja and see how anxious and depressed she is, I want you to remember that she's one of the better ones. She doesn't think she is, and certainly, she needs better coping skills, but she's smart as fuck. And her department might suck, but they know there'll be hell to pay if she leaves or doesn't get tenure. The Dean will literally throw a fucking fit. She has so many resources; she's just too afraid to ask for help. So, when you go to her and probably do some real cute shit to help her get back on track, remember that not everyone has you in their corner, so look out for all of us, not just the men."

At some point, while she was talking, Alejandro had sat heavily in the chair on the other side of her desk. More than once, he'd wanted to interject and remind her of people he'd advocated for, but he didn't because it would have been petty, and the more he listened to her, he realized that she wasn't necessarily wrong.

It wasn't that Alejandro ignored the women of color in the faculty. It was simply that, as Toni had noted, there were fewer of them, and every fall, it felt as if one or two had disappeared. And it wasn't that he didn't notice and talk about it with Dean Ward, it was that he didn't talk about the problem in terms of gender. He pushed for a more racially diverse faculty, without noticing how often those new hires were men. And crucially, he never noticed how, when he took on a new service assignment and needed to call on already overworked people, it was more often than not the women that he could count on to rearrange their schedules and say yes.

"I haven't been the best ally to you," he admitted quietly.

Toni smiled. "You've been the best you could. And now

that you know all this, I know you'll be better." She rolled her eyes, "Deja's in her office. She grades and does class prep when she's stressed. She needs hobbies."

"She's just upstairs?" Alejandro asked, jumping up from the chair. The information felt like a bolt of lightning striking his body.

"Sadly," Toni said, turning back to the essay on her desk.

"Thanks," Alejandro said.

Toni looked at him again. "I like you two together," she said with a shrug. "It almost makes me believe in romance again. Almost. But then I remember the world is a hellscape, and Tinder was a sign of the apocalypse. Now, go. Leave me alone. This essay won't grade itself."

DEJA'S EYES were going a bit blurry, and her back was stiff.

She'd been at her desk grading for nearly three hours. It had been a productive time, at least. She'd caught up on the weekly quizzes from her Intro to Sociology course and had updated attendance grades in all her classes. She'd graded all the essays for her Sociology of the Black Family course and was halfway through the essay drafts for her Social Movements class. She looked at the clock on her laptop and decided that she could leave in a couple of hours and finish the rest of the drafts on Monday to hand them back on Tuesday.

It was sad to realize how easily work could distract her from her own emotions. Well, some kinds of work. Not writing or her own research. That kind of work was like a shortcut to triggering her insecurities, and that explained why it was so easy for her to avoid it. Even just thinking about it made her anxious, and she turned back to the stack of essays in front of her when a knock sounded at the door.

She thought about ignoring it and hoping the person on the other side went away. It was a possibility since she wasn't teaching or holding office hours today. Technically, she didn't need to be on campus, so if she didn't answer, there was no proof that she was even around.

"Deja," a voice called from the hallway. "Are you in there?"

The sound of Alejandro's voice made her heart clench like she knew it would, that was why she'd been avoiding his calls. Still, she did seriously consider ignoring him until she heard his soft sigh through the door. Fuck, she definitely did not deserve this man.

She rushed from her desk and pulled the door open just enough to reach out, grab Alejandro's hand, and pull him into her office.

"Deja?" he asked in shock.

"Shhh," she hissed. "I don't... I don't want anyone to know I'm here."

"Including me," he said.

It wasn't a question, and it made her heart hurt. She ducked her head and tried to avoid making eye contact with him, but Alejandro's hands landed on her waist, and he moved her to one of the larger chairs she used when her students didn't need advice on classes or internships and just wanted to vent or shoot the shit. He pulled her onto his lap, and she let him.

She'd missed him.

"Tell me what's going on," he whispered, wrapping his arms around her and pulling her close.

She sank into him immediately. Why had she denied herself this?

"I'm sorry I didn't pick up when you called," she whispered.

"I don't care," he breathed, and she finally turned to look him directly in the eyes.

He smiled. "Okay, I cared. I really fucking cared, but only because I missed you and want to make sure you're okay."

"I really fucking can't stand Caroline."

"Join the club," Alejandro said.

"Or Layla," she whispered, averting her eyes, embarrassed at herself for even feeling jealous.

"Neither do I," Alejandro said. He moved his hand to her chin and gently tipped her head back so they could make eye contact again. "She asked me out after you left."

Deja's body tensed. "And what'd you say?"

"I told her I'm seeing someone," he said matter-of-factly. "What'd you think I'd say?"

"We're not supposed to be telling people until we talk to HR."

"I'm ready when you are," he whispered to her, his eyes dipping to her mouth. She felt his thumb pressing at the curve of her bottom lip.

"Even though I've been avoiding your calls for two days?"

He smiled. "I won't tell HR that if you don't."

She smiled briefly and then frowned. "I should have stuck up for Marie," she admitted quietly.

"What do you mean?"

"Some people treat her like shit because she's an adjunct, and I should have stuck up for her."

"We should have," Alejandro said. "You were the most junior member in the room. It wasn't your job to do that, not alone, at least."

"I know," she said, "but we're friends."

"So are we. Toni's her friend, too. And Mike is just a good guy. Why do you think this is all on you?"

Deja pressed her lips together. That was a great question.

"Is this a thing you do?"

She squinted at him.

"Toni said you're a creature of habit, so I just want to know if taking on the weight of the world is a thing you're prone to do so I can be prepared for the future."

"You talked to Toni about me?"

"Of course. And she lectured me for being a lackluster ally to women of color on campus. I got way more than I bargained for," he said with a smile.

"You sat through one of Toni's lectures? For me?" she asked, shocked, and also warmed by the thought.

"Not to repeat myself, but of course."

"I don't deserve you," she breathed.

"Oh, you definitely do," he whispered, squeezing her soft waist. "But if you need to be reminded of that..." Alejandro's voice trailed off. He bit his bottom lip and smiled up at her through his long eyelashes.

"I missed you."

"Good. I missed you too," he said.

And she accepted that — even though believing that someone could want her as much as she wanted them was hard for her. But how could she deny the truth she could see in his eyes, hear in every word he said, and feel pressing at the curve of her ass?

"How much?" she asked.

"What do you—" His voice gave out before he could finish asking the question because Deja had ground her ass into his lap. "Shit, Deja."

"How much?" she asked again.

"I didn't come here for..." He swallowed thickly as she circled her hips again. His head fell back, and he groaned.

"What'd you come here for?" she whispered and then dipped her head to brush her mouth along his cheek.

"I just wanted to check on you. To let you know that I'm here."

She circled her hips again and moved her mouth up the side of his face to his ear. "I can feel that," she said.

"Fuck," he groaned, his fingers digging into her hips now.

She stood briefly from his lap.

"Wait," he hissed.

"Calm down," she said as she crawled back into his lap, straddling his legs. When she moved her hips now, they both groaned. The thin material of her leggings almost made it feel as if the mound in his pants could touch her in all the ways she wanted. She really had missed him.

"We're not supposed to do this on campus," he moaned even though his big, strong fingers were flexing at her waist, encouraging her to keep moving on top of him.

"I know," she breathed, moving her hands to the nape of his neck before digging her fingers into his hair, "but we missed each other." She moaned those last words, and that seemed to be all the invitation he needed.

Deja just barely swallowed the moan that rose in her throat when he shoved his hand into her leggings and underwear. Of course, she was wet.

"Fuck, Deja," he groaned again, pulling her face to his and kissing her with an urgent, relieved sigh. She tasted amazing.

His fingers stroked over her slit, and she groaned into his mouth.

"Please," she whispered against his lips, and he curled two fingers inside of her without preamble. They both smiled into the kiss as he started fingerfucking her in slow strokes.

"I want to come together," she whispered again.

"What?" Alejandro asked.

Deja answered by moving her hand to his lap and unzipping his pants.

"Oh, fuck," was all he said, and that was all Deja thought needed saying.

The only sounds that mattered were their soft moans and groans as he fingered her, and she stroked his dick in rhythm. They started slowly, but apparently, a couple of days apart was enough to make them near frantic with need for one another. It didn't take long for Deja to start riding Alejandro's hand or to spit into her palm and grip him with both hands, jacking him as she rode him.

It was lewd, and even worse than the last time they'd gotten inappropriate with one another in her office. And this time was even more dangerous since it was the early afternoon. Granted, Deja's floor was near empty on a Friday afternoon, but this was still a gamble. She knew that; she just refused to let herself think about it. She didn't want to think about how pathetically lonely her life had been until he walked her to her office in the fall. She just wanted to feel every inch of Alejandro's body she could get her hands on, and forget everything else in the meantime.

And she did.

Deja's back bowed as her orgasm took her over, and she buried her face in the crook of his neck.

Alejandro moved his free hand to the back of her head and held her there, pressing his own face into her neck. They ended up pressing their mouths tight to one another to muffle their groaning releases.

They didn't have time to be shocked at the mess Alejandro made in Deja's hands and all over their clothes because the sound of a door slamming shut down the hall caught their attention.

Someone else was in their office. Someone might have heard them.

"Fuck," they said at the same time.

TWENTY-FIVE
MARCH

Deja's mother believed chores were the best kind of therapy.

She didn't believe in therapy, but if it existed, she believed that it came in the form of a Luther Vandross playlist on Spotify and enough bleach to burn her nose hairs. Deja had spent years trying to convince her that her definition of therapy was skewed, but when times were hard, she fell right back into that childhood conditioning, cleaning everything she could find. It was even worse when she couldn't sleep, and Deja hadn't been able to sleep much for the past few weeks. Every time she tried to calm her brain and fall asleep, she'd hear someone's office door closing while she held Alejandro's sticky, softening dick in her hands, and she'd be wide awake again.

She'd been up most nights with her headphones in — because she wasn't a terrible neighbor — listening to Luther and Prince and Tina and Aretha, trying to tire herself out enough to sleep for a few hours at a time. She'd also taken to slinking into her office, so she didn't have to see any of her colleagues. And she didn't look anyone in the eye when she ran into them in the hallway. She'd even pretended to be sick to miss a faculty meeting because her brain had conjured a truly ridiculous scenario where someone would pull her aside and out themselves as the person who'd almost certainly heard her and Alejandro's mutual masturbation session.

But she couldn't avoid everything forever, and she needed to sleep. After almost three weeks, she was burnt out — even more burnt out than normal — and she didn't have a concealer opaque enough to hide the dark circles under her eyes anymore. She was up most of last night cleaning before she conked out at three, slept fitfully for about four hours, then got up to clean some more. She was so busy that she didn't immediately hear the alarm on her phone, blaring at her to get in the shower before Alejandro arrived. By the time she heard it, she was behind schedule and had to rush to get ready in time.

She'd just swiped on her best red lipstick when the intercom rent the silence in her apartment. She jumped and smeared some of the lipstick on the tip of her chin. "Shit," she muttered to herself. She grabbed a tissue from the box on her bedside table and dabbed carefully at her chin, trying not to dislodge the foundation underneath. She didn't have time to redo her entire face.

The buzzer blared again, and she jogged toward her front door.

"I'm up," she accidentally screamed into the speaker. "Sorry."

Alejandro's laughter greeted her once she took her finger off the button to speak. "You ready?" he asked. "Or do you need me to come inside?"

Deja shook her head with a smile. She knew what he was insinuating, and if her stomach wasn't tied tight with knots, she might have let him, but she really couldn't do her makeup again, and they had an appointment to keep.

"No, you freak," she laughed. "Give me a minute to grab my bag."

"I'll show you freak..." he mumbled into the intercom.

Deja laughed as she walked to her office to collect her things for work, her steps already so much lighter.

"WAIT HERE," Alejandro said after he put his car in park in the faculty parking lot closest to Mark Hall and the administrative building. He placed his hand on Deja's knee, turning to look at her to cement the point, and waited until she smiled and nodded.

He pushed his own door open and stepped out into the still cool air. It was almost spring, but it had just snowed a few days ago, and there were still icy, dirty chunks of it in the gutters and in between the parked cars. He walked carefully around the back of his car, taking the time to compose himself. Deja was so nervous she'd looked near tears when he'd picked her up this morning. Actually, every time he'd seen her in the past few weeks, it had seemed like some small part of her — some tiny thing he loved — was slowly eroding.

He rounded the car to the passenger side and immediately met Deja's eyes in the side mirror. She smiled at him, and he smiled back, hoping that after today, things would be different.

Alejandro pulled Deja's door open and offered her his hand.

"I can get out of a car on my own," she said, squinting up at him.

"I'll remember that," he said, still holding his hand out to her.

She sighed before finally letting him help her from the car.

They pulled their bags from his backseat, and Alejandro held his hand out to Deja.

Her eyes widened. "We can't," she hissed.

"Yeah. We can."

Being able to hold Deja's hand on campus was the entire reason they were both on campus today even though Deja didn't teach, and Alejandro didn't have to teach his graduate course until this evening. If they hadn't taken this nine o'clock appointment with Human Resources, they'd have had to wait until mid or late April, and while Alejandro hadn't wanted to push Deja, he had.

She'd been so terrified after they'd heard that door slam that her eyes filled with tears, and she'd started shaking in his arms. He'd watched as the fear of being discovered caused her to fall completely apart.

When the hallway was quiet, Alejandro had jumped into action. He'd cleaned them both up with a bottle of water and paper towels from her desk and rushed her to his car and his apartment, and then he held her until she cried herself to sleep, mumbling that her career was over until she passed out.

Toni's voice was a faint echo in his head the entire night. He hadn't doubted her, not necessarily, but he realized that night that she'd been absolutely right. Deja was one of the smartest people he'd ever met — on a campus full of smart people. She was also stronger and more resilient, and if she was this on edge all the time... He couldn't fathom it. So, he'd pushed her to take the earlier meeting with HR. It wouldn't fix all the problems, but it would at least take the fear that they'd be discovered off her plate. Something was better than nothing.

He held out his hand to her because he wanted to remind her that they were in this together and because he just wanted to hold her hand. It could be as simple as that.

She ducked her head to hide her smile and slid her small

hand into his, and they resumed walking toward the administrative building.

"See," he said to her, "this isn't so bad."

"Shut up," Deja laughed.

TWO HOURS later and Deja felt as if she'd stepped into a brand-new world, on a brand-new campus.

"That's it?" she asked Alejandro for the third time since they'd stepped onto the elevator after leaving the HR office.

"That's it."

"But like...how?"

He turned to her with bunched eyebrows. "What do you mean?"

"I thought they would like...interrogate us or something. Ask for documentation? Something more than make us sign a bunch of paperwork."

"Is HR the CIA now?" he asked, laughing.

"Shut up," she said. "That can't be it. Right?"

"Do you want an answer, or am I still shutting up?" he asked playfully.

"Don't make me go right back up there and tell them we've already broken up."

Alejandro burst into laughter. He released her hand to wrap his arm around her shoulders. "That's it. There's nothing else we need to do. As far as the university's concerned, they aren't liable for any mess we make of this relationship. All we have to do is stop getting each other off in your office," he said, whispering that last sentence into her ear.

Deja shivered, in good and bad ways, but for the first time in weeks, she didn't break out in a cold sweat thinking about that door closing.

"No more," she said resolutely. "No kissing on campus, either."

"What?" Alejandro stopped in his tracks and turned her toward him.

Deja started laughing. "No one wants to see us making out in Brews! Chill."

"Okay, I'm not saying we should make out, but I can, like, kiss you hi or goodbye, right?"

"No. Use your words."

"Deja," he started.

"What's up, friends!" Mike called from across the Oval.

They turned to see him walking toward them alongside Toni and Marie.

"Is this a lover's spat?" Toni yelled.

"Jesus. We should get new friends," Alejandro breathed to Deja.

"Very much agree."

"What's up?" Marie said when they were closer. "Did you meet with HR?"

Deja nodded.

"How'd it go?" she asked.

"It's just paperwork," she shrieked.

Alejandro groaned, shaking his head. "Here we go again."

"This is cute," Toni said, gesturing between them. "I expect more of this to ease the pain of student papers."

"We're not dancing monkeys," Alejandro said.

"Sure about that?" Toni asked. "Anyway, come on, we're heading to the Provost's faculty town hall. We're gonna sit in the back and act like undergrads, but we're hitting up Brews! first."

"You two are coming, right?" Mike asked.

"Yeah," Deja said, slipping her right hand into Alejandro's left.

He smiled down at her and squeezed.

"Oye, Profé's got a girlfriend," someone yelled from elsewhere on the Oval.

"Is everybody and their mama out here today?" Deja mumbled, trying to hide her face behind Alejandro's arm.

Mike and Marie laughed and started following Toni toward the Union.

"Mind your business, Tomás," Alejandro yelled at a cluster of students he recognized from the LSU.

They laughed in return.

Deja pushed him to follow their friends. "This is why there's no kissing on campus."

He smiled, "We can discuss it later."

She rolled her eyes at him with a smile. She wasn't exactly back to normal, but in that moment, she felt more like herself than she had in days, especially with him by her side.

TWENTY-SIX

APRIL

Deja really needed a coffee. A big one.

She might have made one at home, except she'd slept at Alejandro's house last night, and while she'd remembered all the essentials — her satin bonnet, toothbrush, makeup, setting spray, and leave-in conditioner to style her hair — she'd forgotten her favorite coffee. That wouldn't have been a problem, except Alejandro — this perfect man she'd been dating for five months and nine days, not that she was keeping exact track — only seemed to have two real flaws; he dunked his wings in ranch and he had the worst taste in coffee.

She wished she had time to run by Brews!, but by the time she realized her mistake, she had ten minutes to get to campus for her office hours and no time to waste. She held onto the faint hope that she'd have time to make a cup of tea before her student arrived. She didn't.

"Hi, Amber," she said as soon as she pulled open the door from the stairwell and saw her student sitting on the ground next to her office door, with a novel in her hand.

Amber looked up. "Hey, Dr. Evans."

"How are you?"

"Alright. I shouldn't crash until two, I worked the overnight shift last night."

Deja didn't have favorites among her students, but if she did, it would have been a tie between Jerome and Amber. "Just one more month," Deja said, pulling her keys from her purse.

"I know. I can't wait." Amber shoved her book into her backpack and stood as Deja unlocked her office door.

"What's the first thing you're going to do after graduation? This'll be your last summer to do as little as possible before graduate school eats all that up."

When Deja turned around, Amber was trying to bite back the smile on her face. Besides Alejandro, the best part of last fall had been writing Amber's letters of recommendation and editing her graduate school applications only for her to get into every program she'd applied to. Amber was one of the students who somehow managed to hold down a nearly full-time job at a local fast food restaurant, while taking a full load of classes, and still excelling in her coursework and holding executive board positions in the BSU and the Asian American Student Union. Of all her advisees, Amber was the only one who preferred email because she just didn't have time to come into Deja's office each week when she needed help. Some semesters, Deja only saw her as they rushed past each other around campus or accidentally at the library checkout desk. But next month, she was graduating with the best GPA in the department, having just accepted an offer to attend one of the best Sociology graduate programs in the country.

"I'm going to sleep," Amber said resolutely. "I'm working right up until two days before I move, but every second I'm not working or packing, I'm just going to sleep."

Deja smiled, "You deserve it."

Amber's face shifted in a way Deja recognized. "Do you think I'll be okay out there?"

The 'out there' could mean so many things. Amber had walked into college a first-generation student with a loving family that supported her emotionally but couldn't help her financially. It was more than some kids had, but the material differences were stark. By the time Deja had arrived and been assigned as her advisor, she'd learned how to function nearly on her own, unsure of who to ask for help with things like applying for scholarships or graduate schools and too nervous to expose all the things she didn't know. So Amber could be asking about the 'out there' off-campus, graduate school, or just generally the world.

Either way, Deja's answer was the same. "You're so much better prepared for the next phase of your life than I ever was. I think you'll be amazing, especially if you learn how to ask for help."

Amber smiled, "I've been working on that."

"Good. Is that all you wanted to talk to me about?"

"You wish? I have an idea for my master's thesis. I want to walk into my new program with good ideas."

Deja groaned and dropped into her chair.

Amber grinned. "You really thought I wouldn't make you advise me right to the end of the road?"

Deja chuckled warmly. "See? Very prepared. I really need coffee, how about you?"

Amber's eyebrows lifted. "I've been up all night. If you're buying..."

Deja jumped from her chair and grabbed her purse from her desk. "Gladly. Come on, you can talk my ear off on the way."

DEJA'S INBOX WAS CLEAR, and her desk was clean. Well, clean-ish. She was now officially ready to receive the influx of blue books and unstapled essays and last-minute requests for an extension. Okay, her desk and inbox were ready for all those things, she was not, but her desk was an important part of the battle. Now that that was done, she grabbed her laptop and purse, locked her door, and headed downstairs.

For whatever reason, the Sociology floor was the quietest. There were rarely students in the hallway unless Deja was holding office hours. Most of her colleagues kept their doors closed, and sometimes it was so quiet up here she could hear a pin drop. Political Science was livelier, especially when Toni's door was open. But Alejandro's floor was always bustling.

Maybe it was because they had the youngest faculty in the building, or because their student outreach was the best in the College. Deja didn't know, but she did know that her department was equal parts annoyed and jealous of History, and she secretly loved it. She also just loved being on this floor. As soon as she pulled the door from the hallway open, she was shocked at how loud it was.

Okay, she loved it, but she couldn't have worked here.

"Hello, Deja," Sheila said as she stepped out of the department's conference room with an iPad in her hand and a smile on her face.

"Hi, Sheila. How are you?"

The woman smiled and rolled her eyes. "Counting down now."

"Yeah, definitely."

"Are you here to see Alejandro?"

For a second, Deja's entire body clenched in fear, but then she remembered that there was nothing to hide. Granted, Sheila didn't need to know all her business, but if she suspected that she and Alejandro were dating, it didn't matter.

"Yep," she said cheerily. "We've got a meeting for that outreach committee we're chairing."

"Oh, right. How's that going?"

Deja's stomach turned in knots. "You know," she said vaguely with a titter of nervous laughter and a head nod.

Sheila watched her intently for a bit. "Caroline Enwright is on that committee, right?"

Deja nodded.

"She can be difficult to work with," Sheila said.

Even just hearing her name made Deja feel queasy; difficult was an understatement. "Hmmmm," she hummed, not exactly sure how to respond. Sheila seemed nice, and Alejandro liked her, but after Deja's review and tenure files left her department, they went to the College-level committee, and she couldn't chance that anyone could hold a grudge and work against her. She couldn't stand Caroline, but she didn't want anyone besides her close friends to know.

Sheila's eyes narrowed, and Deja worried she could see the emotions on Deja's face. She swallowed uncertainly.

"Your department has never been great at mentoring," she said, seemingly out of the blue.

Deja started to protest — even though Sheila was correct — but Sheila stopped her with a nod.

"You don't have to agree. I know. I've been here much longer than you. But I've heard great things about you from Alejandro, and Toni, and the Dean herself. So, if you ever need some...advice, I'm here."

Deja swallowed again. "Th-thanks, Sheila."

Sheila brushed her hand through the air. "Please, this is the least I can do. This building used to hold the Men's Smoking Room."

Deja's eyes widened. "That was real?"

"Yep. They got rid of it sometime in the early eighties.

Sometimes in the summer, I swear I can still smell cigar smoke. Disgusting. So, if I can get as many women in this building to counteract that history, I'll consider that a win." She winked at Deja and then walked briskly away.

Deja watched her go, dumbfounded.

ALEJANDRO MIGHT NOT HAVE SEEN Deja slip by his door except by now he'd become so attuned to just the hint of her that even though he was very focused on the student in front of him, he saw her flit past his cracked door.

"Give me a second," Alejandro said, lifting from his chair.

"No problem."

Alejandro was about to head for the door until Deja appeared fully in the doorway, a hand on her hip. She was beautiful, and she was not looking at him.

"Jerome," she said, in a tone of voice that shockingly made Alejandro wonder if she'd talk to their kids that way.

"Oh, what's up, Doc?" Jerome said with a smile on his face.

"Boy, what are you doing here?"

"Just talking to Doctor Mendoza," Jerome said innocently.

"About?"

"Deja," Alejandro said, but she put a hand up to him as if he wasn't part of this conversation happening in his office.

Jerome smiled sheepishly up at her. "Okay, look, Doc, what had happened was..."

"Boy..." Deja warned.

Jerome's big shoulders jumped with mirth. "So, I think I want to double major in History," he admitted.

Deja turned to Alejandro with a frown. "So you're poaching my best student?" she accused.

"I'm your best student?" Jerome asked, his voice full of pride and mystification.

"He came to me," Alejandro said. "And he said *double* major."

Deja rolled her eyes. "It's always the ones you l..." Her voice trailed off, and Alejandro leaned toward her, his eyes widening in shock.

Deja's eyes widened as well, and she took a step back into the hallway.

"Never mind," she said.

"Deja," Alejandro said.

She ignored him and turned to Jerome. "Office hours. Next week."

"Doc, please, when do I miss your office hours?" Jerome replied with an adorably petulant roll of his eyes, completely oblivious to what had just almost happened.

"Deja."

"See you at the meeting," she said and darted down the hallway.

He wanted to run after her, but that would be very dramatic and very unprofessional. He gave it serious consideration, nonetheless.

"So, y'all dating, huh?" Jerome asked.

Alejandro sighed.

TWENTY-SEVEN

Deja rushed down another flight of stairs to Toni's office. Her door was open, and she peeked inside to see Marie sitting across the desk. She exhaled and slumped into the room without knocking.

"Hello, please help me."

Toni put her hand up. "Marie's just about to share some news."

Deja plopped into the chair next to Marie. "What's up?"

Marie's mouth stretched into a tight smile. "I heard back from the committee."

"Holy shit," Deja breathed. She didn't know what the news was, but she was ready to picket outside of the Ethnic Studies department in a heartbeat.

"And I got it."

Toni's office was quiet, and Deja blinked.

Marie's eyebrows furrowed as she looked back and forth between them. "Hello."

"Can you say that again?" Toni breathed.

Marie frowned. "I got the job. My job. I'll be tenure track starting in the fall."

There was another delayed moment of quiet before Toni and Deja jumped up from their chairs with squeals and pulled Marie up so they could hug her.

"God, I hate hugging," Marie mumbled, but she let them hold her.

"Congratulations, you downer," Deja said.

"You deserve this," Toni added.

Marie's body softened into their holds at those words.

When they pulled away from each other, Marie's eyes were rimmed red. "Let's change the subject."

Deja wanted to tell her no, they still had to celebrate, but Toni stopped her with a surreptitious squeeze of her arm.

"So, what do you need help with this time?" Toni said.

Deja rolled her eyes. "Shut up."

"Oh, it's about Alejandro," Marie said.

"Oh my god, shut up."

"Girl, just tell us what cute shit he did so we can get to this terrible meeting."

"Hey, I'm running the meeting."

"Okay," Toni said. "Do you not know this meeting is about to be terrible?"

Deja rolled her eyes but didn't refute her. "I almost told Alejandro I loved him."

"Y'all ain't did that yet?" Toni shrieked, shaking her head. "Pathetic."

"We've only been dating for a few months."

"Girl, so what? That man is fine, and none of us is getting younger."

"Very, and I don't even like dudes like that," Marie said.

"And he doesn't talk all the damn time," Toni said, grabbing her laptop from her desk.

"Mike doesn't talk that much," Marie countered.

"You only think that because you tune him out. When I tell you that man has never met a thought he didn't want to share..." Toni shooed them out of her office.

Deja squinted at the back of her head while she locked her door.

"So y'all aren't going to help me?" she asked.

Toni turned around with a frown on her face. "With what? You got a fine boyfriend, all those cliquey white women in the English Department are jealous as hell, and your hair looks great today. Some of us have real problems, Deja Evans."

"Yeah," Marie said with a smile on her face as they walked away.

"I truly hate both of you so much," Deja frowned at their retreating backs.

"You can practice saying you love us if that'll help," Marie said over her shoulder.

Deja's mouth fell open in shock as she jogged to catch up with them. "Not even fully on the tenure track, and you're already being an asshole."

Their laughter filled the Political Science hallway.

ALEJANDRO WASN'T RUSHING, but he was rushing.

He'd hoped to get Jerome out of his office early enough to get to the meeting before everyone else and talk to Deja, but when he rushed into the conference room, he deflated. He was the last one there.

"What's up, man?" Mike called. He was sitting next to Toni, who was sitting next to Marie. They were across the table from Layla, Caroline, and Keith. Dean Stampp was sitting in the chair closest to the door, and across the room was Deja, an empty seat next to her.

"There's a seat here," Layla said.

"I'm good," Alejandro replied without looking her way. Mike tried — and failed — to cover his cough of laughter.

Deja didn't look at him as he walked toward her, but he watched her. He set his laptop down on the table and then lowered himself into the seat next to her. Their arms brushed. She still didn't look at him, but he saw the shiver roll through her body.

As soon as his butt hit the seat, Deja looked up at the table. "Okay, let's get started. We sent out the agenda two days ago, and—"

"Actually, I'd like to talk about our mission," Caroline said, interrupting Deja.

Alejandro saw red as half of the table flinched. He opened his mouth to tell Caroline that the time to add something to the agenda was at any point between the last meeting and today, but Deja beat him to it.

"No," she said firmly. A complete sentence.

"Excuse me," Caroline said, with that high-pitched voice and elitist head tilt thing older white women did all over campus.

"Our entire last meeting was devoted to identifying our mission. You should remember since you dominated that conversation, even though Alejandro and I are the co-chairs. We've covered the mission. It's in our shared folders. If you'd like to return to it, please let us know through email, and we'll put it on the agenda for the *next* meeting. This month, we'll be identifying student organizations and offices we can partner with for Welcome Week outreach. I hope everyone came with ideas," she said, smiling at the table as if she hadn't just set Caroline firmly in her place.

They were all silent for a few seconds — except for Caroline's shocked, flapping gums — until Mike broke the ice.

"I talked to the Students of Color Art Collective. They're new and want to focus on recruitment next year, so they're definitely open to whatever we put together," he said, each word full of barely suppressed laughter.

"Uh, yeah," Toni added, "same with the NPHC and NABJ."

Marie coughed, announcing her tentative intention to speak as if she was worried someone — Caroline — would interrupt her. "I talked to the International Students Association, and they want to make sure that we don't forget them since international students usually get here before move-in day and don't have as much support."

"That's a great point," Alejandro said, smiling at Marie and then turning to Deja. He really just wanted any reason to look at her. "We didn't even think of that."

Deja looked at him, finally, with a nod and a small smile. "Yeah," she whispered. "I love that idea."

He felt warm all over at her words. It was probably ridiculous, but he could have sworn that she'd said that sentence for him.

About him.

"Get a room," Mike coughed.

The meeting continued.

———

"OOOOH, CAROLINE HATES YOU," Toni laughed as they walked from Mark Hall to the faculty parking lot.

"She's gonna run and tattle on you to the Dean," Mike laughed.

"Good," Deja said.

They were walking slowly. Their classes and meetings were over, but none of them were in a hurry to get home where they would probably have to keep working for another hour or two.

Marie was the first person to peel away.

"See you guys tomorrow," she called with a wave.

"We're celebrating on Saturday," Deja said.

"Celebrating what?" Mike asked.

"Marie got the job!" Toni yelled at Marie's retreating back.

"Alright. Chill out," Marie said, turning and walking backward.

"Only until Saturday, then we're going all out," Mike said excitedly.

"Who invited you?" Toni asked, drifting away toward her car.

"Me," Mike said, following her.

"Congratulations," Alejandro said to Marie.

Marie smiled wider. "Thanks."

"We're all really happy for you," Deja added.

Marie nodded and waved before turning and walking toward home.

Then it was just her and Alejandro, and the sound of Toni and Mike bickering behind them. "You want to spend the night tonight?" Alejandro bent down to whisper to her.

Deja was already smiling. "I spent the night last night," she whispered back.

"That a problem?"

"No, just making an observation," she replied coyly, leaning into his side as they walked.

He leaned further down, and his lips just kissed her ear. "Whenever you're ready, I'm ready, too."

She didn't know it until he said them, but those were the exact words she'd needed to hear.

"I don't deserve you," she mumbled.

He looked down at her. "Let's discuss that—"

"Over dinner?" she asked.

"In bed," he corrected.

Deja sighed and unlocked her car door before climbing inside with a smile on her face.

MAY

WEDNESDAY

"Last Faculty Senate meeting of the semester," Deja
mumbled to herself in line at Go Brews! "Last. Faculty.
Meeting."

"Next," the cashier called.

Deja rushed forward to order her cup of coffee and one for
Alejandro as well. The coffee shop was packed as usual, and
she had to squeeze through the crowd of students waiting for
their drinks. She pulled out her phone to check her university
inbox while she waited, but for the first time in the longest time,
she didn't have any actually urgent messages. She had a few
new messages from students asking her to read the introductory
paragraphs to their final papers. She starred them, planning to
get through them while she pretended to pay attention in the
Senate meeting, but besides that, there wasn't anything that
required an immediate response.

It was freeing.

"Last Faculty Senate meeting of the year," Alejandro whispered into her ear.

Deja bit her lips to stop from groaning as his lips brushed

the shell of her ear. She turned to him with a smile. "I was just telling myself that."

"Almost free."

She rolled her eyes. "Sure, just Faculty Senate, last departmental meeting, finals week, and then *all that grading*. But yeah —" Deja's words cut off as Alejandro snaked his hand under the thin sweater she was wearing. His fingertips scraped along the skin above the waistband of her skirt. She sucked in a harsh breath and then let it whoosh out of her mouth.

"Almost free," Alejandro repeated.

Deja nodded.

"And once grades are submitted, I'm not letting you—"

Deja's face was hot, and she pushed his hand from her body. "Absolutely not here," she said with a laugh and a warning glare at him.

He shrugged. "Alright, I'll tell you tonight over dinner."

"Are we having dinner together?" she asked playfully because they hadn't spent a single night away from each other in almost a month. It was as if their relationship was settling into something warmer the closer they came to the end of the semester. During the weekdays, tired from teaching, they cooked together and watched television before heading to bed, sometimes too tired to even have sex. They alternated between their apartments, skating around the conversation that both of their leases were ending in a couple of months. That felt like too much, and yet...

Last Saturday afternoon, they'd spent the entire day in Alejandro's living room, each of them in their baggiest sweatpants, with piles of student essays around them — carefully separated — and worked through the massive stacks of grading. They barely spoke, but at the end of the night, they ordered pizza, shared some beers, and then had slow, gentle sex to celebrate that they had no more grading until finals week. Deja had fallen asleep holding the secret fantasy that this could be every night for them if they moved in together.

But it was too soon. Right?

Deja wasn't sure, especially not when Alejandro rolled his eyes at her and spoke as if every day they spent together was a guarantee of another. As if there wasn't anywhere else he wanted to be.

And he did that now. "Of course, we're having dinner together, but Jesus, I don't feel like cooking anymore."

Deja smiled at him. "I'll cook," she volunteered without thinking. "I like to cook. And bake. I'll make dessert, too."

Alejandro's eyebrows lifted, and he shoved his hands into his pockets. "If we weren't in the middle of the Union, I'd kiss you now. You know that, right?"

"I do."

"Deejay," one of the students called from the pickup counter.

Deja sighed at the person mispronouncing her name.

"Her name's Deja," Alejandro called in correction, and then he turned to her. "Did you buy me coffee?"

She rolled her eyes. "Of course, I did."

"WHAT'S UP, DOCS?" Jerome called across the Oval.

Deja and Alejandro were on their way to Founders, walking slowly, enjoying the spring sunshine on their face. They might not get good seats, but it was worth it, especially because they were holding hands. It almost never happened that they had time to just relax and be together, even on weekends, but summer was coming, and he wanted it to be like this.

He had some research trips to Nicaragua and Cuba, and Deja had decided to head home for a couple of weeks to see her family, but besides that, they'd decided to spend as much time as possible just hanging out together around town. And as soon as students left for the summer, they could have more moments like this, walking hand in hand, maybe even making out in front of the burger joint after a couple of drinks with their friends before walking home on a cool summer night. Normally, he couldn't wait to get out of Centreville, but he was looking forward to staying put for a bit.

"Hi, Jerome," Deja said once he was close enough.

"¿Qué pasa, Jerome y Hector?"

"What's up, Profé and Profé's girlfriend," Hector said.

Deja huffed a shocked laugh.

Alejandro rolled his eyes. "Dr. Evans," he corrected.

Hector shrugged, "Profé and Dr. Evans."

"Nice to meet you, Hector. What are you two up to?" Deja asked them.

"We're heading to the library."

"Studying for Profé's hard ass final," Hector said.

"Just study the review sheet," Alejandro said, exasperated.

"The review sheet is hard," Jerome said.

Deja laughed.

"Doc," Jerome said gravely, "your review sheets are worse."

Alejandro turned to her, laughing, and Deja glared at him. "Shut up," she mumbled.

"Oh, hey," Jerome interrupted, "since you don't have any more office hours, I just wanted to let you know I settled on History."

Deja's mouth fell open. "You're changing your major?" She sounded close to tears.

"What? No," Jerome said, "I'm double majoring. I just put the paperwork in."

"Oh," Deja said, turning to Alejandro.

"So now you have to share him," he said.

Deja glared at him and turned back to the boys. "What's your major, Hector?"

"Alright," Alejandro said, waving his hand at the two boys carefully, so he didn't spill his drink as he shooed them away. "Go study." He steered Deja around them and back on their way.

"Hector, the Sociology department is in Mark Hall if you're interested."

"See you two at the final," Alejandro yelled, pulling Deja forward.

The boys' laughter faded, replaced by Deja's giggle. "It's not fun, is it, when someone tries to poach your best student?"

"I didn't poach him, but if you want to make this a competition, I'm sure Sheila would love it."

"I bet she would."

———

"HERE WE GO AGAIN," Marie mumbled as they settled into their seats.

She and Alejandro were on Marie's left, and Toni and Mike were on her right. Alejandro was turned toward the group, his arm casually around the back of Deja's chair, his hand lightly cupping her upper arm. Deja was a bit shocked at the casual affection, and apparently, so was Layla. She and Deja made accidental eye contact across the auditorium. The other woman's face began to turn a bright red, and Deja looked quickly away, focusing on her friends instead.

"I'm giving this committee assignment to someone else next year," Toni said.

"You can't," Mike said.

Toni frowned at him. "The hell I can't."

"We're a team," Mike said. "The five of us."

"We're overworked, underpaid, and on multiple committees together. Chill."

Mike looked as if he was about to say something in return when the Senate President-elect's gavel sounded.

"Let's get started on our last meeting of the year," Sheila called.

The entire auditorium erupted into applause, and a few people hooted.

"Yes, yes, it's not that bad," Sheila laughed.

"Speak for yourself," someone Deja couldn't see called.

Deja laughed as the meeting started. She'd thought maybe Alejandro would take his arm from her chair, but he didn't. She turned to him.

"What?" he whispered.

"Are you going to keep your arm around me the whole time?"

He smiled at her. "I can," he said simply. "I used to think about that, you know?"

"About what?"

"About sitting next to you like this during this long ass meeting." He scooted his chair closer to hers to accentuate the point. Their thighs pressed together.

She licked her lips and moved her left hand to his thigh, just to let it rest there, to feel him underneath her palm for a second before she turned to her computer and started reading essay drafts. Alejandro kept his arm around her shoulder except when he needed to turn the page of the paperback in his other hand.

It was a surprisingly domestic moment between them, even though they were in the middle of the largest university committee on campus. It should have made Deja nervous or self-conscious, but it didn't. She thought of Layla's red face and decided not to look anywhere but at her computer. If she looked and saw that other people had seen them or were watching them, she might push his arm away, and she didn't want to do that, because she didn't care what anyone thought of what they looked like right now.

Besides, if any of the other faculty had an issue with them being together, they could waste their summer break dealing with it on their own time.

SUMMER BREAK

TWENTY-NINE

"Turn it off," Deja mumbled into Alejandro's pillow. She'd been sleeping so well until his alarm started blaring.

They'd both been up until nearly midnight the night before inputting final grades, adding extra credit, and fielding student complaints through email. She'd wanted to sleep in today, but the sun was barely out, and because of his damn alarm, she was awake.

"Turn it off," she groaned.

"It's your phone," he groaned back.

"Oh. Shit."

Deja sat up in bed, groggy. She squinted around his room before turning to the bedside table. She grabbed her phone and glasses at the same time and squinted at her screen. "I thought I turned it off," she said.

"Turn it off now," he said, turning over in bed and wrapping his arms around her waist.

She tapped at her screen and then looked down at him with mussed hair and five o'clock shadow, still struggling to believe this was how her summer would be, with him. She ran her fingers through his hair as he drifted back to sleep. Deja decided to check her email since she was already up.

She sifted through a bunch of emails from the college administration, reminding them that grades were due today and stats about graduation numbers and all the other end-of-the-semester detritus that it took her a year to realize she didn't have to read. She smiled at a few emails from students thanking her for the semester, or asking for summer internship advice, flagging them for reply when she was fully awake and had a cup of coffee in hand.

But then her eyes caught on an email.

"Oh my god," she groaned.

"What?" Alejandro mumbled, probably not because of what she said but because she took her hand from his hair.

She needed both shaking hands to hold her phone steady and open this email and then read it carefully.

"Oh my god," she breathed again.

"What?"

Deja didn't respond; she was too busy reading and re-reading the email just to make sure that it said what she thought it said.

Alejandro sat up next to her and shoved his own glasses onto his face. "What's wrong?"

She turned to him with wide, shocked eyes. "I got an R&R from the *Journal of Comparative Sociology*," she breathed, unable to believe the thing she was saying.

It wasn't a straight-up acceptance — those almost never came from academic journals, especially not for a young scholar like Deja — but *Comparative Sociology* was her tier-one journal, and a revise and resubmit was amazing. The feedback she knew she'd get when she was ready to open their notes would be invaluable, and she spent the entire summer working on her article to resubmit, going into her third-year review with an article under consideration would look really good.

She could hardly fathom it, and her eyes started to water.

"Deja, that's amazing," Alejandro said. "It's okay to cry."

She didn't need his permission, but it felt nice to have it, and even nicer for him to hold her while she did. And the best part was that she got to fall back to sleep in his arms as her happiness transformed into exhaustion.

"WHAT DO you want to do today?" Deja asked as she walked into Alejandro's kitchen.

They'd finally woken up and gotten out of bed at nearly noon. He'd showered while she'd pored over the R&R feedback. He'd finally taken her phone from her hands and pushed her into the bathroom with a promise of brunch.

In the shower, Deja's head was spinning as she tried to think through the revision notes. She wanted to sit back at her laptop and start working on revisions now, but once she was dressed in her favorite skater dress and had her hair in a loose bun on her head, she didn't feel like working anymore. She walked into the kitchen to find Alejandro in a pair of baggy basketball shorts and a t-shirt that clung to every muscle in his back, and her resolve not to do too much too soon hardened.

In fact, as she watched him, she reminded herself of Toni's advice not to overwork herself, to learn to enjoy her breaks when they came, and to let herself rest. It had taken nearly five months to get a response from the journal; she could take the summer to work on her piece before she resubmitted. Her work and her brain would be better for it.

"What are you making?" she asked.

When he turned to her, his eyes dipped to look at her bare

legs. "Right now, just coffee. I wasn't sure what you wanted. Also, I need to go grocery shopping," he laughed.

Deja padded into his kitchen on bare feet. She could feel Alejandro's eyes on her.

He licked his lips and leaned back against the counter. Deja walked up to him and pressed her body against his.

"Are you hungry?"

Deja groaned at the soft rumble of his voice against her chest. She felt it in her body, and it made her nipples hard. "I can wait until lunch," she whispered.

Alejandro's hands moved to the backs of her thighs, and he bent forward to cover her mouth with his own. She opened herself up to him, and he inched his tongue between her lips as his hands pulled her dress up in the back.

She wrapped her arms around his shoulders and deepened their kiss, suckling on his tongue. She spread her legs for his searching hands.

He groaned again. "Deja," he mumbled against her lips.

"What?"

He squeezed her ass with one hand while the other pressed between her legs, his fingers skimming over her bare pussy.

"Why aren't you wearing underwear?"

"What's the point?" she asked, licking at his lips. "Wanna go back to bed?"

"Fuck," he said and lifted her into his arms.

She wrapped her legs around his waist and kissed at his soft stubble as he walked them back to bed. "I hate your coffee anyway," she mumbled.

He smacked her ass with a laugh.

"IS this what summer is going to be like?" Alejandro asked Deja as he threw her onto his bed.

She fell in a sprawl, and he caught a quick glimpse of her pussy as the skirt of her dress bounced.

"Maybe," she said to him, spreading her legs.

He ripped his shirt over his head and pushed his shorts over his hips. His hardening dick bounced, and Deja licked her lips. "Fuck," he hissed.

He was prepared to dive on top of Deja on the bed, but she stopped him, lifting onto her knees.

She put her hand on his abs to keep him standing and grabbed his dick with the other hand.

"Deja," he mumbled.

She looked up at him as her mouth lowered to the head of his dick, and her tongue slipped past her lips and swiped around the crown in a slow taste.

They both groaned.

He cupped the back of her head as she sucked his dick into her hot mouth. Her hands squeezed him at the base and stroked him in circular motions, meeting her lips around his length.

"Fuck. Me," he groaned.

"I will, baby," she said, kissing along his shaft. "We've got all day. All summer."

His hand tightened around her bun as she licked and kissed and stroked him deeper and deeper inside her mouth. His eyes closed, and his back bowed when he touched the back of her throat. If they hadn't been working so hard over the past few weeks reading final exams and essays and the handful of graduate theses, maybe he could have let her keep going, but he couldn't; he wouldn't last.

He pulled her mouth from him with another groan.

Her gaping mouth and his saliva-covered dick sent him over the edge. "On your back."

She smiled at him as she raised up onto her knees. He moved to his bedside table for a condom, his fingers fishing blindly inside the drawer because he refused to take his eyes off her.

She pulled her dress off slowly with a dirty smirk on her face.

He tore the wrapper open and began to roll the condom on.

She grabbed a pillow and moved it to the middle of the bed before slowly settling onto her back, unhurried and hell-bent on teasing him, and then she spread her legs and moved her hand to caress her pussy.

"You're gonna be insufferable all summer," he said with a smile.

"We're going to spend most of July apart," she reminded him. "We have to take advantage of our time together."

"You make some great points," he said and crawled onto the bed. She moaned when he pushed her thighs to the bed and dipped his head between her legs to lick her pussy in a forceful swipe.

He watched her eyes press shut, her back arch, and her hands cup her breasts. She tweaked her nipples as he licked and sucked at her pussy and clit. It couldn't have been more than a day or two since they'd last fucked, but as soon as the taste of her pussy hit his tongue, he realized that he'd missed it.

He couldn't even fathom how he was going to survive a month without her while he was traveling, and the thought of it made him suck her clit in a hard pull, her hips jerking as she squeaked out a moan.

He kissed her mound and then lifted onto his hands and knees to cover her body with his.

She shuddered when the head of his dick hit her opening. "You want to move in with me?" she breathed.

"Yes," he said.

"Good. Please fuck me now," she moaned, wrapping her arms around his neck.

He kissed her and pushed inside of her at the same time. The heady taste of her pussy was on his tongue, and she groaned, licking at his mouth. The tight warmth of her clenched around his dick, locking them together.

He didn't rush, but this wasn't a slow fuck. It was the perfect pounding press of their hips together. Deja's legs locked around his waist and her heels dug into his ass, spurring him on. He could already feel the tightening in his back and the tingling in his balls. He'd come soon. And Deja's shivering pussy let him know she was just as close.

They'd come, maybe nap, and then fuck again. They'd probably just order some food for delivery. It was the first day of summer break, and that always made the world feel as if it was full of possibilities. But it was also the first day of the rest of their lives together, as far as Alejandro was concerned, and Deja was right; they should savor every moment of their time together.

"I think I love you," she moaned, shuddering around his dick as she came.

"Finally," he breathed into her mouth, fucking her harder now, faster, chasing his release. "I love you too," he shouted as he filled the condom between them. "Finally," he breathed again.

EPILOGUE

THREE MONTHS LATER

Fall Semester

It was the first day of classes. Deja was sitting in her office, finishing her syllabus for her first class in an hour.

"What's up, Doc?" a voice called from her open office door.

She looked up to find Jerome at the door and smiled. "Welcome back." He sauntered into her office and plopped down into the chair across her desk. "How was your summer?"

He rolled his eyes with a smile. "Boring. My mom still treats me like I'm a baby."

"You're her baby."

"Okay, but still..." he said. "Anyway, I'm happy to be back."

"You say that now, but I remember your schedule this semester."

His smile turned to a cringe. "Yeah, I might have gotten carried away during registration in the spring."

"That double major is gonna be tough," she said.

"He'll be alright," a voice said from the door.

She turned to see Alejandro leaning against the doorjamb. It had barely been four hours since she'd seen him last, but it felt like forever. She took him in — his new gray three-piece suit and crisp white shirt — and there was something about the sight of his mustard-colored tie that reminded her of this morning. Maybe it was because it matched her dress, or because she'd held onto the knot while riding his lap in his bedroom — their bedroom now. She'd almost made him late.

"What's up, Doc Mendoza?" Jerome said.

"Nothing much. I just came to see Dr. Evans, only to hear her trying to poach you from me. Still."

Deja rolled her eyes and pressed print on the document on her laptop. "I wasn't poaching, I was just letting my advisee know that double majors are difficult, but of course, he can manage."

"*Our* advisee," Alejandro corrected.

"So y'all are still together," Jerome said. "Hector owes me twenty bucks."

Deja's mouth fell open. "Get out," she laughed at Jerome.

Alejandro stepped aside for him to leave, patting him on the back as he passed.

"See you at your office hours, Doc," Jerome called over his shoulder.

Alejandro stepped into her office and took up the seat Jerome had just vacated. He sat regally, straightening his pants before he sat, and as he crossed his legs. He straightened his tie, and Deja could have sworn that his fingers caressed the piece of fabric slowly, as if his brain was taking the same trip down memory lane hers had.

"Behave," she whispered, her eyes darting to her open office door.

He smiled at her. "I can. I will." He licked his lips as if he was tasting her.

She swallowed a groan. "You need to leave, too," she whispered in a shaky voice.

He burst into laughter and stood. He leaned over her desk, and she met his mouth with her own without thinking, not caring, in that moment, who might pass to see their chaste brush of lips.

"I'll tell you what I was just thinking at home tonight," he whispered in a deep, seductive voice.

The frisson of desire that laced through her at his voice, at his words — especially "home" — made her smile so hard her cheeks hurt. She sucked her bottom lip into her mouth, tasting him again. "Please," she whispered back.

He moaned softly. "Yeah, I need to leave now."

It was her turn to laugh as she watched him walk from her office. He turned to wink at her just before walking into the hallway.

Deja didn't know if it was possible to really set the tone of a semester, but if it was, then this was going to be her best semester yet.

HI EVERYONE!

As you may or may not know, I'm a professor. When I first conceived of Deja and the rest of this group, they were amalgamations of friends at various universities who were all struggling with the same things: feelings of loneliness, overwork, mental health issues, etc., but I didn't know what to do with the first draft of the story. I don't love popular depictions of academia and professors. They all seem stuck in some version of the 1960s: everyone's white and upper-middle-class, the professors are all old men in boring gray suits who listen to classical music while they grade in front of the fireplace, and they're always teaching about classic literature or archeology.

That's mad boring. LMAO!

But when I re-read the story, I realized that I liked Deja and Alejandro a lot, and I wanted to write about academia as I've seen it, with people who look like people I know or know exist, people who aren't middle-class and white, and adjuncts who are often erased from representations of academia, even though they do the bulk of the teaching work at most U.S. universities. And if you've made it this far, that's what you got, plus sex and romance (the fictional part). I hope you liked Deja and Alejandro's journey. I hope you'll also take at least three things from this story: check in with yourself, be kind to yourself, and let people help you.

Also, Toni and Mike... amirite??? *wink*

If you liked this story, please consider recommending it to a friend and leaving a review wherever you feel comfortable. And if this is your first story by me, turn the page for a list of my other books, there might be something else there that you like! I hope you're safe and well and washing your hands. <3

OTHER BOOKS BY KATRINA JACKSON

Welcome to Sea Port

From Scratch

Inheritance

Small Town Secrets

Her Christmas Cookie

The Spies Who Loved Her

Pink Slip

Private Eye

Bang & Burn

New Year, New We

His Only Valentine

Erotic Accommodations

Room for Three?

Neighborly

Love At Last

Every New Year

Heist Holidays

Grand Theft N.Y.E.

The Family

Beautiful and Dirty

Standalone stories

Encore

Layover

Office Hours

Milton Keynes UK
Ingram Content Group UK Ltd.
UKHW020809150823
426904UK00018B/943